Path of a Hero

Path of a Hero

C. S. Cooper

For Queenie, who encouraged me to write this series.

CONTENTS

Acknowledgements

I acknowledge Nobuhiro Watsuki, whose manga inspired this story. I also thank the people who read my novel, *Final Flight of the Ranegr*. Since you were so intrigued by *The AXOM Saga*, and requested paperback copies, here you go. Then, there are my parents and family, who encouraged me to publish it.

The Story So Far

Seeds of great change have been planted in the world in the last few years alone.

Until a few months ago, Nathan Grant lived a regular life in the dormitories of Warrawul Boarding School in Wollongong, Australia.

What he thought was a nightmare, in which a mechanical snake killed him, turned out to be a chilling reality. An Alchemic Warrior named Astrid Rachelle saved his life by implanting an Alchemic talisman, known as a Kakugane, into his chest. According to her, his town was infested with homunculi: malicious man-eating beasts that disguise themselves as trustworthy people. Immortal and immune to conventional weaponry, they could only be destroyed by an Arms Alchemy: a human soul, manifested in physical form by an activated Kakugane.

Having realised that his sister Ariadne and his friends were at risk of being hunted, Nathan decided to harness his new powers under Astrid's tutelage. Upon activating the Kakugane in his chest, he summoned a lance into existence, with which he helped Astrid destroy the homunculi in their town.

As they investigated, the duo learned that a rogue Alchemist, codenamed Papillon for the butterfly mask he wore, was creating the beasts. They determined that Papillon was a reclusive student at Nathan's school, named

Koushaku Chouno. When they confronted him, they learned that he suffered from a terminal disease and would soon die. But if he were to turn himself into a homunculus, he would be cured and live forever.

Nathan attempted to stop Papillon from succeeding in his final experiment, but failed. He reluctantly killed Papillon, ending his rampage of carnage. And yet, despite Astrid's best efforts to keep secret the existence of homunculi and the Arms Alchemy, she couldn't stop Nathan's best friend Klein finding out. Rumours started to spread across Wollongong of the Starlight Lancer, defending the people from the beasts in the shadows.

The Lee Clan and the agents of the Demon Weapon Meister Academy weren't the only ones anxiously watching these events unfold ...

1 | An end-of-year sermon

The bell rang, heralding a stampede of black-leather-clad feet from the classrooms. In unison, the blue-uniformed female parade trotted through the halls toward the cafeteria, modestly simmering with polite conversation and pockmarked with the sounds of clattering rosary beads. The students came to a stop in front of the chairs lining the long, hardwood tables. When Mother-Superior gave her silent consent, the students sat before their place settings.

Every pair of hands clasped above the table, and Mother-Superior led the congregation in grace: "We give thanks for the Earth that upholds us, for the food that nourishes us, to the Lord on high, whom we serve in our lives ahead. In His name …"

"Amen!" replied the congregation.

Now, in most movies depicting a Catholic all-girl school, the eating hall would be deathly silent save for the soft slurps of water and tings of metal spoons on the floors of soup bowls. Luckily, this particular school was far more lax, and even the nuns running the place seemed the better for it. A wide array of conversations across the tables accompanied the meal, some of it concerning the latest One-Direction album and various students' plans for the upcoming school holidays.

One particular conversation centred on a girl with dark

brown hair at the end of one of the tables. A long scar crawled across the bridge of her nose, but none of her friends seemed to mind. She grinned warmly as the blonde opposite her raised a glass.

"Though her time here has been short, I'd like to thank Miss Dubois for being with us this term," said the girl.

"Sank you, Vicky," murmured the dark-haired girl with a pronounced French accent.

"We really wish you could stay longer, Marie," said another girl.

Marie smiled gauchely and mumbled, "Me, also. Eet az been wonderfool!"

"I hope you'll remember us when you go back to France," said another girl tearfully.

"Of courseh, I wille," said Marie, clasping the girl's hands. "I friended you all on facebookeh, so we stey in toucheh."

The conversation continued onto reminiscing about the exchange student's experiences and considering her future plans, which she eagerly engaged in with a smile. They continued chatting until mealtime was done, at which point Mother-Superior rung a bell and diverted the student body out of the hall.

Afternoon classes droned on, far less interesting than the conversations in which Marie engaged. Then the last bell of the day rung, and the classrooms emptied. A half-hour later, the school poured into the church and took their seats.

Marie sat amid her friends, Vicky to her side. Her eyes wandered about the church, taking it its details for the last time: heavy hard wood trusses and braces supporting an arched roof, reeking of incense, oils, and holy water; pews packed to the brim with students, far more than half bored of the rituals of church; stained glass windows lacking hinges; three doors to the building, each with different locks.

Won't be a problem, thought Marie, without a French

accent.

Her eyes fixated upon the tabernacle, her lips upturned ever so slightly.

"You alright?" asked Vicky in a low whisper.

"Oui, oui," replied Marie.

When the congregation was settled, the priest proclaimed: "E nomine de patris et filii et spiritus sancti. Amen."

And the congregation followed suit.

The service went from prayer to ritual after ritual. The priest engaged in a well-practiced dance of humming prayers in song, splashes of holy water, and kneeling before the effigy of the crucified Christ hanging above the tabernacle. Then he stepped up to the pulpit and addressed the crowd.

"A year has come to an end," he said. "A successful year for all of you, I hope. Every new year is a rebirth, a chance for change. But for some of you, this year marks a true milestone. I refer of course to all the year twelve students who have completed their HSC[1] examinations. *Some* of you," – he added with a smirk of faux disapproval – "might already be planning your schoolies[2] trips; others, applying for university or TAFE[3]; others, going abroad. For you, Newton's Apple Academy has been your cocoon, preparing you to emerge into the adult world as butterflies, with wings that will carry you to your bright futures.

"As you fly, I hope you will always remember the Lord's teachings: feed the hungry and care for the weakest among you. Treat your fellow human beings with decency,

---

[1] Higher School Certificate, the final examinations in Australian high schools. Scores from these examinations are used to determine university admissions.

[2] Schoolies is a slang for a holiday, most often taken to tourist spots in Australia, by students after graduating high school. It is similar to American 'Spring Break' and often receives the same criticism for drunkenness and lewd behaviour.

[3] Technical And Further Education, an institution of further education in Australia. In some ways, it is similar to college in America.

even when they do not do the same for you. True, we can never go as far as our friend here," – he indicated the statue of Jesus – "Trust me, mercy and forgiveness of that level is truly divine."

That earned him a few chuckles from the congregation.

"But we can learn to forgive those who wrong us, and in so doing, move forward with our lives and leave the bad behind. Because, as Jesus knew, holding onto the bad can make us do bad to others – the source of cruelty isn't Satan, my friends. It is our own suffering that we over time take out on others. Mercy not only sets our enemies free, but also ourselves.

"So as you eagerly race home to your parents, and your Playstations and Facebook and iPhones, enjoy yourselves. As you excitedly race to university for a degree in engineering, or science, or maybe even religious studies – no pressure! – remember the greatest teaching of our Lord, to have mercy and to forgive."

The congregation was silent a moment, with every eye downturned in prayer. Then the synthesised sound of an organ echoed through the church as the priest and his helpers moved to open the tabernacle. Marie's arm hairs stood erect as two items, draped in fine cloth, emerged from within the sanctum. The first was a gold-painted bowl of communion wafers, the second a hexagonal talisman with the Roman numeral for seventy engraved on its metallic surface. The priest ate a communion wafer, and then placed his forehead to the talisman. His alter servers did the same, before moving to the front of the congregation.

One by one, the pews emptied as the students lined up for communion. They each sampled of the Body of Christ before placing their foreheads to the grey metal talisman. Then Marie's turn came, and as she sampled the bland piece of soluble cardboard, she willed her heart to slow. Her forehead came down on the talisman, and only for a slightest second sensed what no one else felt: the deep power swirling within. A maelstrom nobody else could see flowed from the talisman, brushing against her soul and making her shudder. It took all her mental effort to control her body and remain nonchalant, though she couldn't help a certain giddiness creeping through her soul.

The priest gave the final benediction and the service was done. The girls flowed out of the church in droves. Marie made for the dormitories with her friends. They picked up their packed suitcases and headed for the school entrance where a flurry of parents waited to collect them. Hugs were thrown about as parents urged their daughters to divulge all their experiences over the school year. Buses ranked a bit further down the street, for those girls whose parents were absent. Marie and Vicky were among them.

"So you'll be going back to France tonight?" asked Vicky, threading her fingers through Marie's.

"Oui," said Marie. "Would be goode to spende more time 'ere, zough."

"You shouldn't stay too far away from your family," said Vicky.

"I'll certainlie chat on Facebookeh," said Marie, her eyes stinging. She gave her friend a hug, and hopped onto the bus headed for the Brisbane airport. Around her were girls from other classes, with whom she wasn't as close. The tiniest part of her heart ached that she couldn't spend more time with her friends there, especially Victoria. But she had to remind herself that she wasn't the kind of normal person who could have friends like that.

It was a nice vacation, she thought.

The bus came to a halt outside the airport, and the passengers grabbed their bags from the hold like hungry ants nabbing bits of food. Marie was the last to collect her bags, and she made for the International Terminal. When she was satisfied she was out of sight, she turned a corner and entered the car park. Her suitcase still in her hand, she stopped beside a column of pipes in the corner of the car park.

At that moment, her French accent vanished, and an Australian accent replaced it.

"I've confirmed it," she said. "Kakugane Serial Number Seventy."

"Three months to confirm? You should have finished it sooner, Astrid," said the cloaked man, hidden behind the pipes.

"The nut-jobs thought it was a sacred object," replied the girl whose name was not Marie Dubois. "I couldn't just steal it and then vanish. My name and face would be all over the Brisbane news."

"Get it done tonight, Warrior Rachelle," snapped the cloaked man.

"Yes, Commander," said Astrid. She opened her mouth to speak more, but her voice caught in her throat.

"Something more?" asked the shadow.

I'm sure I felt something different about that Kakugane, she mused. *But it might just be nothing. Maybe I was just glad to be done with this mission.*

"Nothing," said Astrid. "I will recover the Kakugane tonight and report back to you."

A rush of air blew gently over Astrid's face, and the shadow was gone.

* * *

The Moon flooded the campus with pale light. Only a few security guards remained awake, while the nuns and priest were asleep. Those guards were much too enthralled in their phones to notice the shadow creeping across the school grounds. It reached the church, but darted around the front entrance and moved to the north-facing side.

Astrid reached the side entrance, beyond which laid the priest's office. She took a gadget from her pocket and inserted it into the door lock. It let out a few soft squeaks as its motors worked the lock's tumblers, until the door gave way with a satisfying clack. The air within blasted her with a stronger odour of holy water, yet she pushed past it and entered the church.

The main hall felt almost spooky in the middle of the night. The faint moonlight trickling through the technicolour stained glass windows, and the smells of incense made for a scene out of a Bram Stoker novel.

Astrid moved to the tabernacle, her heart thumping wildly as she threw off the ornate covering and opened God's room. There was the Kakugane, giving off the same aura that had thrilled her every Friday and Sunday for the last three months. When she took it in her hand, her heart fluttered and she smiled.

"Finally," she murmured.

A flash of light whizzed past her, and she swivelled to see flashlights outside the church. The sounds of whispering security guards reached her ears as she noted a tripped switch linked to the tabernacle's hinges.

Astrid, you moron!

She sprinted to the south exit, busting it open with her shoulder, and leapt over the fence. No longer caring for discretion, she raced through the bushes and fled from the alerted guards yelling after her. She was too fast for them, and they lost her trail.

Still, she ran for several streets until she reached a park some distance from the school. When she was satisfied with her safety, she collapsed onto a swing in the middle of the park to catch her breath. She took her phone from her pocket, and called her contact.

"Kakugane Seventy is secure," she reported. "There was a tripwire on the tabernacle, so security was alerted, but they didn't see my face and I left no prints."

"Understood, Warrior Rachelle," said the man.

"Returning to base … E.T.A. –"

"Check that, Astrid," the man interjected. "We have another mission for you."

"I just spent three months undercover," Astrid complained. "I had leave booked –"

"Cancel it," the man said flatly. "There's been a

homunculus outbreak, and you're the only one available to clean it up."

Astrid's body went rigid at the mention of 'homunculus outbreak.' She huffed heavily, as the prospect of a nice vacation melted in the fires of a vision of man-eating monsters.

With a sigh, she growled, "Location?"

"Wollongong, New South Wales," replied the voice.

"Estimated numbers?" asked Astrid.

"At least ten confirmed hostiles," said the voice.

"I'll be there in two hours," said Astrid.

"Bravo!" exclaimed the voice, and the call ended.

Astrid raised her head to the sky and sighed. Her body still trembled, though she wasn't sure if it was leftover adrenaline from her near capture, or anticipation of killing more monsters.

Slaughtering those bastards is plenty fun for a vacation, she thought, bloodlust filling her. She looked down at the stolen Kakugane in her hands, and took her own from her pocket.

"I guess you'll be with me a while longer," she said.

* * *

The security guards scanned the campus for the thief, but came up empty. The priest and nuns were mortified that their school's heirloom had been stolen. Some tearfully made their statements to sleepy police while others prayed.

A figure stood on the church steeple, brushing her blonde hair out of her face and smiling at the rabble going on below.

"Is this enough, Mother?" she murmured.

"Yes, Victoria," said a woman's voice. "Everything is going according to plan."

2 | Regret

Nathan Grant had spent the last period of the day in the boy's toilet. He wasn't wagging class, though. He'd had a free period, but instead of studying in the library like he should have, he preferred to hide.

He hunched over a sink, glaring at himself in the mirror. A flash of blood and screams flew through his consciousness, and the voice of Koushaku Chouno pierced his mental eardrums: *Don't apologise to me!*

He straightened up, and ran his hand over his sternum. His fingers slipped between the buttons of his shirt, and felt the abrasive texture of the skin over his heart. That metal talisman thumped with tremendous force.

I'm surprised nobody notices, he thought. *If Astrid were here, I'd be able to ask her about it.*

He checked the date indicator on his watch and realised with dismay how many months had passed since she left. All he received as goodbye was pancakes and a fist-bump.

Then she checks out of her hotel and vanishes, he inwardly growled. *Now I have to deal with nightmares about Chouno and people pestering me about it. At least, if she were here …*

The digital chime of three ascending tones heralded the end of the day. Nathan tidied up his dishevelled uniform, and sucked back the last of his tears.

Don't worry about Chouno anymore, he ordered himself.

He's dead, and you gotta live. Astrid gave you that life. Ain't that enough?

Nathan strutted out of the bathroom, his gait not as determined or confident as he thought. He trudged through the crowd that parted reverently in response to his presence, and grabbed his bag from his locker. He glanced at the students around him, some of whom eyed him with fear, others with excited grins. He rolled his eyes and walked out of the school, down the path to the dormitories.

He walked, his eyes downturned, such that he didn't notice the girl three quarters his height race up from behind and leap onto his shoulders.

"Nathan," screeched Ariadne as her brother struggled to regain his balance.

"You seem to be in a good mood," said Nathan. "Was school fun?"

"Oh yeah! We started astronomy in science today," said Ariadne.

"Sounds like fun," droned Nathan. "You'll get to learn about planets and stars."

"And speaking of 'stars,'" Ariadne began, her eyes fixated on him.

"No," said Nathan flatly.

"Oh, come on! Tell me!" she snapped.

"I just did," replied Nathan. "I'm *not* the Starlight Lancer."

Ariadne scoffed, "Oh, you so are! Just tell me so I can tell everyone my big brother's superhero."

"Yeah, and the cops can come and axe my arse," retorted Nathan.

Ariadne pursed her lips in a scowl, like a child denied hot chocolate after dinner. Nathan was quite content to ignore her pouting all the way back to the dormitories. When he saw the building, he directed his eyes down as quickly as he could, to avoid seeing the newly painted wall where Chouno's dorm room used to be.

Much to Nathan's relief, Ariadne had homework, and her dorm was on a different floor, on the other side of the building. This freed Nathan for other things, like moping alone. He changed out of his uniform and went to the roof, bought a coke from the vending machine, and sat on the seats set out near the ledge.

Streaking clouds hung overhead, growing denser toward the horizon that was still blue despite the late hour. Unfortunately, afternoon means the winds picked up in speed and carried chilling air. It was one of the drawbacks of the roof lookout, but he could bear that if it gave him a moment's peace.

He heard footsteps behind him, and knew it was Klein. Still in his uniform, tie-less and dishevelled, he dropped down next to his friend.

"Hey, Nathan, are you the Starlight Lancer?" he asked with half-hearted sarcasm. His friend just burped in reply. "Sorry mate, gotta do it."

"Why? You already know," replied Nathan.

"Yeah, but if I keep asking, people won't suspect me as much," replied Klein. "They don't suspect me, then they won't ask me about it, and it'll help keep the secret."

Nathan shot him a surprised glance. "You've clearly thought a lot about this."

"Surprised at how much I care about my friend?" asked Klein.

"Nope, just surprised that you can actually think," replied Nathan. Klein retorted with a head-slap that knocked the coke can out of Nathan's hand. The drink spilled all over his shoes. "Thanks," spat Nathan testily.

Klein offered to buy him another, but Nathan declined. There was a moment, during which Klein checked to see if no one was eavesdropping. Then he leaned in and whispered, "Had any problems with ... you know?"

"Nope," replied Nathan.

"Have you ... umm ... activated it at all?" asked Klein.

"Not once," said Nathan. "I haven't had a reason to.

No kids going missing anymore, and no teachers turning into snakes and eating Ariadne."

The phrase was like a lightning bolt to his repressed memory centres. His whole body trembled with the vision of a giant snake devouring his sister right then and there. The timing could not have been worse, as a pair of Asian-looking students emerged onto the roof. Within Nathan's ear-reach, the couple mentioned the name 'Ol' Chambo.'

"Nobody found any trace of him," said the male student. "His car was still there, his keys were in his office."

Nathan's jaw tightened.

"He just vanished?" asked the female student.

Stop it, Nathan roared internally.

"An awful lot like Asuna," said the boy. "Remember her? She was really nice wasn't she? Gone, just like Ol' Chambo."

"His poor wife must be traumatised," said the girl.

The metal armrest crumpled with a deafening creak. The students jumped three feet into the air. Their shocked eyes searched for the horrible sound, and landed on Nathan. The boy looked over his shoulder, ignoring his worried friend, and glared at the two students.

"What?" he barked. "I have weird sounding farts. Sod off!"

The students promptly vanished, and Nathan's gaze turned back to his bloody hand. He heaved through his teeth as the wounds quickly healed, and nervously eyed the scrunched up armrest where his hand had gripped it.

Klein only watched, his lips pursed with worry as his friend healed like Wolverine. A part of his mind, not concerned with his super-powered friend's sanity, congratulated him on maintaining his own. Of course, he had to remind himself that it was easy, considering he was only a spectator to a heart replaced with a magic talisman. Nathan endured the experience. However, the remainder of his mind dedicated itself to wishing himself in Nathan's position.

"Ya know what kind of amazing things I could do with that thing?" he growled softly, his eyes fixed on Nathan's chest. "Forget man-eating monsters, you should use your abilities just saving people with regular problems!"

"Yeah, I could save cats from trees, deal with hostage crises, I could even go and fight ISIS ... and get a tonne of people killed in the process," retorted Nathan.

"Save a tonne too," replied Klein. "Maybe you could volunteer for the fire fighters or SES. You wouldn't even need to use that spear."

"Forget it," Nathan said flatly.

"Why?" snapped Klein. "What? Afraid people might discover you're actually capable of doing some good? Or maybe Hollywood might make really crappy movies about you?"

"I said, *forget it*," Nathan blurted.

Klein fumed, "Jesus Christ, Nathan! Do I need to quote Churchill?"

"No!" roared Nathan. Every eye on the ground below turned upward, though none could see the faces of the people arguing. The bellow echoed a little longer, until there was silence, and people resumed going about their business.

Completely unfazed, Klein pressed, "Churchill, right? He said, 'With great power comes great responsibility.'"

"That's Spiderman, you dumb shit!" snapped Nathan.

"No, Churchill said it first," said Klein, his finger pointed at his friend. "Then Confucius said it before him. And then Jesus said it too."

"What, so Jesus was negative-second?" growled Nathan, clearly frustrated with the conversation.

"Shut up! It was like the Sixth Commandment or something!" cried Klein, determined to keep the conversation going. "You got skills, and you gotta do something good with 'em."

"I tried," blurted Nathan. "Didn't Astrid tell you? I flat

out said I wanted to help her beat all those monsters. But all that did was get her into shit with that embryo. Then I tried to find Chouno and get him to give me the antidote, but I screwed up and ended up getting the dorms blown up. I put Ariadne at risk! I should have just bailed out when Astrid told me to go home. But, no, I had to be cool!"

"But you got her the antidote, you retard!" snapped Klein. "And even she said you did really good. And even that newspaper said you did good by that Chouno dude in the end. You couldn't've done anything for him, anyway."

"I could've taken him prisoner and then looked for a way to undo his transformation," said Nathan, his eyes reddening. "I could've done something, anything other than kill him. Oh, and by the way, the Sixth Commandment said 'Don't kill.'"

Klein's brow tightened up so much he almost burst a blood vessel. Then he sighed and said, "I really shoulnd't enjoy this, but I will."

Nathan turned to his friend, only to have his glance met with a fist. He flew to the ground in a daze, while Klein cradled a very sore set of knuckles. Already, Nathan's bruised cheek and cut lip started to heal, but his dizziness kept him off his feet.

Klein glared down at him and said, "Bullshit! That arsehole, Chouno, he'd killed so many people, and would've killed more. Don't give me that crap, 'Oh, sanctity of life!' Sanctity's gotta be earned, and people should only get saved if they deserve it. He forfeited his when he started killing. Sure, he had AIDS or whatever. Doesn't excuse what he did, and you did the right thing by taking him out."

By then, Nathan had regained his senses, and returned Klein's glare.

"I keep trying to remember if I'd seen him before I met Astrid," he mumbled. "I think, if I'd met him before all that, maybe I could've prevented the whole thing."

Klein shook his head furiously. "Nathan, Astrid's supposed to be just one out of an agency. A freaking *agency!* If there's enough creeps like Chouno out there that they need an agency for them, then the same kinda stuff is going on everywhere. You gonna get depressed about all those other arseholes? Why not *do* something about them? Bring the *next* one to justice."

"I tried calling Astrid to let me join, but she must've changed her number," said Nathan.

"Well then, I guess all you can do is wait for another homer to show up," replied Klein, as he offered his hand. He hefted Nathan to his feet and said, "Until then, do something useful with your powers." He eyed the strangled metal railing. "Besides wrecking school property."

Nathan sighed, his mind hardly there on account of the punch and his mounting fatigue. He shook his head acquiescently and said, "Fine, I'll go and bend steel rods for the poor."

Klein shook his head with dismay.

"You shithead," he murmured under his voice. He threw his arms around his friend, who welcomed the comfort. Nathan held onto him for a while. Just as Klein started to feel weird about the prolonged contact, a strange odour tickled at his nostrils.

He asked nervously, "Nathan, did you –"

"Payback for the punch," replied Nathan and gripped tighter. Klein tried to push his friend away, but was caught in a vice-grip. He struggled as the rancid odour of Nathan's flatulence flooded his nasal cavity and made him gag. He only managed to escape thanks to Nathan's evil laughter. As Klein fled, Nathan bellowed, "Breathe it in, my friend! Breathe!"

* * *

Nathan woke the following day in a better mood. He ate breakfast with his friends, while eyeing his sister seated a few tables away amid her own friends. Unfortunately, Nathan hadn't bothered to learn their names.

"Some brother you are," said Paul as he slurped his coffee.

"Come on, I've been busy," replied Nathan.

"Busy being a superhero, eh?" jibed Jessie through a mouth of rice-bubbles. Nathan didn't dignify the joke with a response. He returned his gaze to his food.

"Oh, hang on a tick," said Klein with an interested whistle. "Check out the hunk that's sitting near her."

That set Nathan's ears ablaze, and his eyes shot across the room to the boy that sat a few seats away from his baby sister. Klein's label was right on the money, because the guy was smoking hot – from a completely objective point of view.

And that made Nathan really nervous.

In an instant, he rose from the table, his cereal forgotten, and marched over to Ariadne's table. She saw him approach and almost choked on her mouthful.

"Nathan! Good morning," she said gauchely. "Everything alright?"

"Sure, everything's fine," said Nathan, his glare fixed on the Chinese male model seated at his baby sister's table. "Just wanted to meet your friends."

Ariadne's brow furrowed, "You've already met them."

"I forgot their names," said Nathan, his eyes boring holes into the boy's face.

Ariadne introduced her girlfriends, clearly not for the first time, though it was also clear that Nathan wasn't listening. His brain only listened for when she was finished, after which he asked, "So what's with this Year Ten dude sitting with a bunch of Year Seven girls."

Annoyed, Ariadne pursed her lips. "Nathan, I just told you. This is Tao Wu. He's captain of the fencing club."

"So?" asked Nathan.

"I joined the fencing club last month," Ariadne said very slowly. "Don't you remember when I told you?"

Nathan folded his arms, his gaze darting between the boy and his sister. His suspicious brain still had the upper hand as his eyes narrowed on the boy, but other dissenting voices arose to remind him of his sister's announcement a month passed. Slowly, he calmed down, and held his hand out to the boy.

"Nice to meet you, Wu," he said.

"Oh, please call me Tao," said the boy, accepting the handshake. "Sorry about yesterday."

Nathan frowned, "Yesterday?"

"Yes, my sister and I were up on the roof at the vending machines," said Tao, prompting Nathan's jaw to drop. "I assume we did something to bother you. So, sorry."

Nathan waved his hand to quickly dispel the thought.

"Never mind about that, I was being an idiot," he said. "So you're captain of Ariadne's club, eh?"

"Yes, and my sister here is the manager," said Tao, indicating the Chinese girl sitting next to him. She had his eyes and mouth.

Nathan leaned down to his sister and whispered, "What're they? Clones?"

Ariadne rolled her eyes, "They're twins."

"Hi, I'm Shu," said the girl with a wave of her hand.

"You're into fencing too?" asked Nathan, now a tad more interested in the pair.

"Nope, I just like managing things," replied Shu. "I'm thinking of doing business management at university."

Nathan raised his eyebrows and said, "That sounds like a good idea." He turned to Ariadne, "You should look up to her. She'll make a good role model for you."

"Better than you?" asked Ariadne snidely. Nathan gave her a faux warning with his pointed finger, to which she responded with a poke of her tongue. He took his leave and went back to the table.

"No danger of Bruce Lee swooping in on your baby sister?" jibed Paul.

"Nah," said Klein, interrupting Nathan. He eyed Shu and said, "Looks like he's already got a girlfriend."

"That's not a girlfriend," said Nathan. "It's his twin sister."

Klein's eyes bugged out in amazement. He made a bewildered expression that made his friends curious. They asked him what he was thinking and he said, "If those two ain't a couple, then why're they holding hands under the table?" Jessie, Paul, and Nathan tried to nonchalantly edge their gazes to confirm Klein's observations. Their eyebrows shot up when they saw the twins' hands clasped together. Paul's keen eyes even caught Shu's thumb brush against Tao's knee. Klein finished a mouthful of food and said, "Either they're just mega-super-close, or we got some Luke-Leia-in-Empire up in this business."

Nathan scoffed and shrugged Klein's silliness away. The friends finished their food, grabbed their bags and made for school. They stored their bags in the lockers, grabbed their books for first period, and then went to homeroom. Klein and Paul were in different houses[4] from Jessie and Nathan, and thus their homerooms were elsewhere. Jessie and Nathan sat quietly beside each other in their homeroom, in the middle of the music block, and waited for their teacher to finish all the usual announcements.

However, there was one unusual announcement that caught every bored ear in the room.

"On a positive note, we have a new student joining Guwarra[5] House," said the teacher excitedly. She opened the door to admit the new arrival, and Nathan and Jessie's jaws dropped. The girl, dressed in the yellow blazer and skirt combination of Warrawul boarding school, marched into the room. She wrote her name on the board, the same name he knew her by, and then turned to face the class.

---

[4]   In some Australian schools, students are divided into houses. These are often used to determine teams for sporting events.

[5]   Dharwal: "Wind."

The scar across the bridge of her nose crinkled in the most gorgeous way possible as she beamed.

"I'm Astrid Rachelle," she said with a chipper tone. "I'm really glad to be here."

3 | A not-so-new student

The homeroom teacher beamed and said, "Anyone have any questions for Astrid?"

Most of class eyed the girl with bored expressions. A few guys failed to supress lascivious grins. There were, however, plenty of friendly people, who raised their hands.

"What's with the scar?" asked one girl.

"Oh, this was an accident when I was really little," said Astrid, gingerly stroking the mark on her face. "I got hold of a knife and accidentally fell on it. Lucky, it didn't get my eyes."

"I reckon it makes ya look cool," said one of the guys, shooting a wink her way. Astrid chuckled gauchely and thanked him for the complement. The boy continued, "What kinda music ya like?"

"Oooh, that's a hard one," said Astrid as she stroked her chin. "I suppose Britney Spears is fun … Bruno Mars too … Oh, I know! Guy Sebastian!" That earned her quite a few hoots from the class. Astrid's grin widened and she exclaimed, "Oh, isn't he such an amazing singer?"

"And a cutie too," said another girl.

Nathan watched, his jaw ajar and drool pooling on his desk, as Astrid engaged the class in chats. Jessie managed to relocate his own jaw and asked his friend, "Hey, ain't that the girl with the slipped disc?" His face went pale with pent-up excitement when Nathan nodded. He grabbed his phone, texted someone, and then launched to his feet. The class looked at him frightened as he roared, "Is Nathan the Starlight Lancer?"

Horrified, Nathan tried to drag Jessie back to his seat. But he couldn't silence his friend before sounds of a commotion trickled through the door. The footsteps grew louder until the door opened, and in burst Ariadne and Paul, Klein reluctantly in tow.

"It really is Astrid," screamed Ariadne and she tackled the new girl. "Hey, Astrid! Tell us really, is my big brother a superhero?" Her eyes glimmered excitedly, while Astrid's returned a surprised gaze that tried to look confused but came off as miffed. The teacher stifled amazed laughter at the sight, though was a tad bewildered at the intrusion. She tried to bring the class back to order, but as more students became aware of the new girl and her connection to Nathan, the classroom grew fuller and the rabble more unruly.

A loud clack burst from the front of the classroom as Astrid struck the whiteboard with a sprayed palm. The whole room fell silent, save for Astrid's nervous panting.

"Listen!" she shouted, a sliver of her true personality seeping through the cracks in her mask. "Yes, I know Nathan. We did paintball together. I thought his school looked nice and decided to transfer." Her expression softened and she gave an incredulous smile. "But I seriously know nothing about this starlight thing you've got going here. I don't know what you're talking about, really!" She made her way through the crowd to Nathan and asked, "What've you been telling them?"

Nathan threw his hands up defensively.

"Just that we're friends, nothing more! I swear!" he said, his voice a little shaky.

Oh my God! I'm a much better liar than I thought. Sure, it helps that I'm not lying here, he thought despite his nerves.

He pointed at the curious mob and said, "Remember

that night I took you back home after your slipped disc? There was some weird thing in the newspapers about a guy jousting a cannibal and they all thought it was me."

"Jousting?" exclaimed Astrid. She glanced over at the group of students and said, "Why do you think he can joust? The guy can't even land a paintball on me."

A force gripped Nathan – the same that once took hold whenever he and Astrid needed to improvise. He leapt to his feet and said, "Hey now, I got you real good last match."

"Oh please, Grant!" retorted Astrid. "You mistook me for a guy and tried to get a crotch-shot!"

"Proves I can get you with a paintball," replied Nathan.

Klein interjected, "Yeah, I bet it's the only way you'll ever get a girl, Nathan."

That comment set the class alight with laughter, in which even the teacher joined. Playful taunts went Nathan's way, omens that the superhero issue had gone to the backs of everyone's minds. Most guys started begrudging Nathan for his luck in scoring such a hot girl, while most girls grimaced at the sight of this nice lady with such a geek. Eventually, other homeroom teachers appeared to herd their students back to their rooms.

When the bell clanged, the classroom emptied. Astrid leaned over to Nathan and said, "Let's chat later." Then the other girls whisked her away, leaving the boy bewildered.

She's back, he mused. *Is she on holiday or something? Or did we miss a few homunculi?*

The Kakugane in his chest hummed at that last worrisome thought.

* * *

Classes proceeded at an excruciatingly boring pace, mostly due to Nathan's nerves. His brain would not stop concocting theories for Astrid's presence, and each new idea was more paranoid than the last. More than once, he saw Chouno or the frog homunculus out the corner of his eye, but it was always just his jittery imagination. It didn't help that Astrid seemed to share no other classes with him, except for English.

That used to be Ol' Chambo's class. Although the new guy running the class – who was also the new dormitory manager – was plenty nice, it was still Nathan's most bothersome subject. Over the last month, he'd done little more than daydream in that subject, which he knew his parents weren't going to like, but he didn't care. Any topic, from the movies currently out to the contents of his last bowel movement, was better than looking to the front of the class and imagining a giant mechanical snake coming at him.

Today, however, was different, because Astrid was there. He waltzed into the classroom and saw her. He immediately charged over, took a seat next to her, and shot daggers at the girl he'd beaten to the spot. Then he turned to her and whispered, "What's going on then?"

"I don't know what you mean, Nathan," said Astrid. "Right now, we're in school." She enunciated the last word, and Nathan decided to back down despite the adrenaline still pumping through his head. That distracted him quite a bit during class, so that he couldn't daydream, and didn't want to look at the teacher either. Thankfully, nobody had superhuman hearing, and thus didn't know how hard Nathan's heart was thudding against his ribcage – except Astrid.

She pushed a small sliver of paper onto his desk, which read, "Calm down or your Arms Alchemy might spontaneously activate."

Nathan gritted his teeth irately. He grabbed a pen and scrawled a response: "Bite me! You run off for two months then suddenly show up, all happy and girly? What's going on?"

Astrid surreptitiously penned her response calmly: "Reason one: I violated regulations, sacrificed a precious resource, and created a rogue element. That being you. I've got to supervise you now. Also Klein, obviously. And now anyone else you might've been bragging to."

Nathan pursed his lips to stifle a furious scoff. He glared at Astrid out the corner of his eye, even more ticked off that she still looked like she was taking notes diligently. She even had an interested smile to go with it.

She's not careful, I really will tell everyone who I am, he grumbled internally.

He wrote his response, a little more delicately than before: "I haven't told anyone. Klein neither. Maybe if you hadn't showed up like this, we wouldn't have any problems."

Astrid's response came as if she'd rehearsed it: "Don't blame me, Nathan. This was my superior's idea."

Nathan rolled his eyes, and moved to write another retort. But he paused, and recalled his fight with Klein the day before.

"Astrid's supposed to be one of an agency," Klein had said.

Well then, I can't blame her if she's been ordered to, he concluded. *But I can still get pissed for her disappearing.*

He passed her his response: "Still not forgiving you for buggering off. What's reason two?"

Astrid had barely put her pen to the paper before it was ripped away. There it was in the teacher's hand, a snide grin on his face.

"Now then, what've we got here?" he exclaimed. He glanced at the pair and said, "Writin' love letters ain't allowed in my class. You've gotta share 'em."

Panic filled Nathan, and he glanced at Astrid, whose expression was as perplexing as it was infuriating. A red hue rode on her cheeks that crowned her gauche smile. Her shoulders reached up to touch her ears as she made a show of embarrassment.

What the Hell is going on here, Nathan cried inwardly. The teacher straightened out the paper and started reading.

"First one's handwriting's pretty girly, so I'll assume it's yours, Nathan," he said with a poke of his tongue. "It reads:

"'Oh, my dear, last night was the most incredible night of my life.'

"'Mine too, my love. When do you want to *meet* again?'

"'Soon, please! Let's go to the beach at night, and swim in the waves!'"

The whole class chortled and wooed at the love letter, throwing balls of paper at the two lovers. Astrid covered her face shyly, while Nathan just stood dumbstruck and perplexed. The teacher finished his dramatic reading before tearing up the letter and pocketing the shreds.

"Listen, you two," he said. "Nice that you're so in love, but two things. One: keep the lovey-dovey crap outta class. And two: make sure you got a just-in-case."

"Yes, Mister Costable," chirped Astrid, her face still very red.

"Oi, Grant, you got that?" snapped the teacher when Nathan didn't respond.

Nathan snapped out of his near-comatose state and murmured, "Umm … I didn't hear what you said."

The teacher pursed his lips, clearly annoyed at having to repeat himself. He pointed a finger at the boy and sternly said, "Behave yourself in class, mate. We gonna have a problem with this?"

But what's going on? That's not what the notes said. We weren't arranging any beach thing at all! And last night? What the Hell! Is he stoned or something?

His internal screaming dribbled out of his lips in the form of inane babble. The loud chimes of the bell snapped the boy out of his confusion. With an annoyed scoff, the teacher said, "Well, end of class. All of you, chapters four and six tomorrow. I want to know what you think about Huxley's crematorium scene." Then he turned to Nathan and Astrid and said, "I want to see *you* back at the dormitories."

* * *

Nathan's brain was a jumbled confused mess, so much that Astrid had to drag him by the hand from school. This only fanned the flames of rumours that they were a couple – a view Astrid was not all that keen on encouraging. It took all her effort to maintain a happy-but-embarrassed façade as she walked hand-in-hand with the babbling idiot beside her through a parade of wolf-whistles and salacious squeals.

Fortunately, Nathan wasn't so far gone that he couldn't recognise when they were alone in one of the halls. He stopped Astrid's advance and turned her to face him. Finally, he saw the real Astrid that lay beneath the disguise. Her eyes radiated irritation, the full brunt of which hit him hard.

"What the Hell is wrong with you?" snapped Astrid. "How hard can it be to keep quiet?"

"Keep quiet?" retorted Nathan. "I still haven't been given a straight answer about what's going on. What're you doing here? And what's with all the nice, cutie act?"

"I'm fitting in," exclaimed Astrid. "Didn't I say I'm here to supervise you? How can I do that if I don't make myself look like real student?"

Nathan shook his head and threw his arms up. "Well then, you won't have to do that now that Costable's found out."

Astrid's eyes narrowed. She looked about her surroundings as if searching for something to remedy her confusion. Finally she said, "What do you mean, Costable's found out?"

Nathan gripped his head in frustration.

"Duh! He saw our notes," he snapped. "Now he's gonna demand to know what they mean."

Astrid willed her breathing to slow, and she very calmly said, "Nathan, he saw the notes, then he read them as something different."

"So?" asked Nathan.

"That means … he is …" her voice trailed off as she waited for him to finish her sentence.

Nathan wondered if this idiot really was Astrid. His irritation reached a critical peak and he just guessed.

"Dyslexic?" he asked.

Astrid boxed his ears, and then dragged him down the hall. They reached the manager's office and knocked. Mister Costable met them, having exchanged his suit and tie for a tee shirt and shorts. He let them in, locked the door, and turned to Nathan.

Astrid sighed away the rest of her chagrin and said, "Nathan Grant, let me introduce Commander Tristan Costable of the Alchemic Regiment."

Nathan shook the man's hand, but it was clear he hadn't heard a thing. Then the man walked over to the desk drawer, took a locked case from the bottom-most draw, and placed it on the table. A press of his thumb to a screen on the side released the locks, and revealed a hexagonal talisman with the Roman numeral fifty etched into its surface.

"Hey, you've got a Kakugane," murmured Nathan. Then he exclaimed, "Oh! You're an Alchemic Warrior."

The man's eyes widened nervously and he murmured, "Probably not too loud, mate." He picked up the Kakugane and twiddled it in his hands. "But, yeah, I am. Commander Costable, Alchemic Regiment, Australia Division. Codename: Captain Bravo. You can call me Bravo for short."

Astrid spoke up, "This is my superior."

"Oh right! So this was all his idea for you to show up and freak me out?" said Nathan, his nerves quieted enough to at least smile. That earned a chuckle from the man, who returned his talisman to its hiding place and plonked down on his desk chair.

"To be honest, it wasn't really to freak you out," said Bravo. "We're not here to prank you. We're actually here on serious business." He motioned for Astrid to explain.

"Nathan, there's some problems with you," she said. "A Kakugane is meant to respond to your instincts for survival and amplify them. There's an old-wives tale that, if you embedded it in another person's body, as close to the mid-thorax as possible, you could, *theoretically*, prevent that person from dying."

Nathan cocked his head. "Like what you did for me?"

"After you died so gallantly," said Bravo, a smirk riding on his lips.

"After he acted like an idiot," replied Astrid irately. "But you'd only tried to help me. I honestly didn't think it'd work, but I thought you'd be worth saving ... A decision I sometimes regret."

Nathan could have burst into tears at the sentiment.

"But it *did* work," Astrid continued. "Now that's where the problem is."

"Problem?" murmured Nathan as he covered his chest protectively.

"Grant, how much has Astrid told you about our organisation?" said Bravo.

"You hunt homunculi and rogue Alchemists," said Nathan. "I also recall something about Alison Hannigan."

"Who?" snapped Astrid.

"He's talking about someone who plays a witch in a TV show," Bravo interjected. "There *are* Witches, but we don't deal with them, fortunately. Yes, you're right, that's what we do. There are some other things beside that, one of which is tracking all the Kakugane in existence. The raw materials were so rare that only a hundred of these buggers could ever be made. So obviously they're precious. Problem is, only sixty-two are accounted for. The Regiment has been searching for the rest for the last five-hundred years."

"And you still haven't found them all?" exclaimed Nathan.

"Hey, mate! We're a shadow organisation and we've got a freakin' shoestring budget," replied Bravo. "That allows us to search about half a per cent of the world, and it's a big-arse world."

"The point is," interjected Astrid. "Our top priority is keeping track of these Kakugane. And you know really well how dangerous these things are. If thirty-eight of these are missing, that's thirty-eight potentially world-ending events right there."

"Like something out of a Tom Clancy novel," said Bravo.

"I was going to say a Ben Affleck movie," added Nathan, his face turning pale at the thought of crazy people from ISIS getting their hands on an Arms Alchemy.

"Now usually, when we find a Kakugane, we steal it and lock it away in our vaults," said Astrid. "But this is a really unique situation here."

Nathan's glance darted between the two, whose gazes fixated upon him and his chest. His heart started to race, and they could hear it.

"You're gonna take this back?" he asked breathlessly.

Astrid looked to Bravo, who pursed his lips thoughtfully. Finally he said, "Not yet." That didn't ease Nathan's nerves, and his palm edged toward his chest. Bravo held out his hand reassuringly and urged, "Listen, Grant, you've got nothing to fear from either me or Astrid. We're fully aware that that Kakugane is keeping you alive, and we're not going to take it from you."

Nathan's nerves would not quiet. "So what then?"

"I can offer you a choice," said Bravo, his hands still raised calmly. "Your first option is that we can surgically remove the talisman from your chest. Since, without that thing, your heart would give out, we're talking about a heart transplant here. We get that Kakugane back, and you can go back to your ordinary life."

Nathan's eyes widened at the prospect. His mind went over the last few months and all the interrogatories from his friends and classmates over his identity. He pondered the energy he'd expended trying to keep his Arms

Alchemy from erupting from his chest like a baby alien, and his lips tugged upwards at the idea that he could leave all that behind.

No more fanboys and fangirls asking if I've got a secret double life. No more double life! No more monsters trying to eat my sister …

His smile suddenly vanished as the image of that snake slipped into his mind. That same image that had horrified him at least once a day for months felt different at that moment. As he massaged the flesh where that snake had struck, he went over the rest of that traumatic moment. What stood out, in particular, was the first time he had placed his hands to his heart and roared those two words that gave him power. With that power he saved his sister and, later, Astrid. His eyes darted slightly toward Astrid's stomach, hidden by her uniform and yet, he could tell, still baring the mark of the homunculus embryo she'd taken for him.

He couldn't help but wonder, *What if I could actually use this power to do something good, like Klein said?*

He turned to Bravo and asked, "Any other options?"

With an intrigued hum, Bravo said, "We can train you to be an Alchemic Warrior, just like Astrid."

"So I can fight more homunculi and protect my friends and family," Nathan concluded.

"Yep," said Bravo. "With that, I'd warn you. The pay's shoddy, the work's awful, and you could probably never retire."

"And I'd have to keep trying to hide my secret identity," said Nathan.

"Which you haven't done a good job of keeping," said Astrid.

Bravo glared at her facetiously. "Don't be so cocky, Spartan Valkyrie. As I understand your report, it was *your* fault that this other kid found out."

"Only because my judgement was dulled by the embryo I took for him," retorted Astrid indignantly. Bravo only shot her a grin that infuriated her. "Commander, could you be serious? I don't like that you have so much in common with this idiot."

"Idiot who got the antidote in the end," added Nathan with a grin.

"Okay, no one is denying the operation here was a major cockup," said Bravo. "Let's move forward. Grant," he looked fixedly at the boy, "What's your choice? Walk away, or be one of us?"

Nathan huffed, rubbing his chest as he pondered the life-changing decision before him. He met Bravo's gaze, and then looked to Astrid. The look in those orbs on her scarred face filled him with resolve. For the first time in a long while, he felt determined.

"There's no choice there," he said with a confident grin. "Walk away? I'd never see this beauty again!" He nodded in Astrid's direction, though she merely responded with a roll of her eyes.

"Be serious, you idiot," she snapped.

"I am," said Nathan. He rose to his feet and said, "Bravo, I will be an Alchemic Warrior."

Bravo similarly stood, towering over the boy. "You sure? You'll be stuck with the job forever."

"I've got a sister and friends to protect," retorted Nathan, stretching his spine in vain attempt to match Bravo's height. "Train me and I'll be the best Alchemic Warrior in history!" He then added with a wink Astrid's way, "Plus, how can I pass up a chance to prank her forever?"

The girl's face drained of blood. She threw her hands up defensively and cried, "Oh, no! No! No! No! Go with the heart transplant!"

"Too late," said Nathan, his grin widening. "Already made my decision."

"Unmake it!" snapped Astrid.

"Impossible!" cried Nathan.

Bravo shoved his hand into the space between them

and said, "Well, that settles it. Put it there!" Nathan grasped Bravo's hand and shook it hard. "Welcome to the Alchemic Regiment, Starlight Lancer."

4 | Training on the Mountain

The sun's rays pierced the canopy of gum trees and struck the dry leaves that carpeted the dirt path. A red-bellied black snake slithered through the masses and took refuge under a wooden plank as a trio of hikers strode over it. Twigs cracked under their feet that carried them toward the top of the escarpment.

The two leading hikers, barely panting, turned to see the third lumbering up the path a fair way behind them. One of them chuckled, the other one sighed wearily.

"Nathan, pick up the pace, mate!" said Bravo.

"Yeah, Bravo, I heard you," Nathan panted. He reached the pair and slumped onto his knees. "I've been slacking off on gym the last few months," he moaned. "Seriously, why does this count as training?"

"Need to build up your stamina," said Bravo with a grin.

"Every Alchemic Warrior goes through this," said Astrid.

"Why couldn't you have told me this *before* I joined up?" Nathan exclaimed.

"Oh, I'm sorry, I should have spent some time explaining the whole thing to you while you lay there with your heart ripped out," retorted Astrid. Nathan tried to reply, but his burning lungs kept his responses limited to hefty pants and gasps. "Seriously?" Astrid exclaimed. "You were able to carry me down Mount Ousley. You ran for almost sixteen hours straight! You're just being lazy now!"

Now Nathan mustered a retort, "Your life ain't in danger now. Maybe if you got another homunculus infection, I'd suck it all up."

"That can be arranged," snapped Astrid. "Just follow me around and eventually I'll have to dive in to save you again."

Bravo laughed so hysterically it broke through their bickering. When he sobered, he mumbled, "Nathan, you must be a real charmer. I've never seen Astrid act like this before."

"Act like what?" snapped Astrid.

"Like you're an old married couple," said Bravo in between chuckles.

That put an overly excited grin on Nathan's face and a furious expression on Astrid's. Her fingers brushed absentmindedly against the Kakugane in her pocket as her vengeful nature started to take hold. Her rational mind reminded her of her rank relative to Bravo, and she stayed her hand.

"We should keep going," she snapped before pushing ahead of the group.

Nathan climbed to his feet and stared after the girl. Beside him, Bravo just shook his head, his grin still present on his face. He slapped Nathan on the shoulder and pushed him along the path.

They finally pushed through the branches at the end of the path, and emerged onto a decrepit car park. The asphalt was riddled with cracks through which blades of grass peaked and colonies of ants worked. Nathan took a moment to lament the rundown state of the building nearby, which housed a once-bustling café. Now, it stood in a state of disrepair and neglect.

"Mum and Dad used to bring me here when I was a kid," he mumbled through his panting. "The café served the nicest pancakes and ice cream."

Astrid's stern demeanour broke slightly, and she shot him a smirk. "I hope the one's *I* shouted you were as good."

Slightly taken aback by her expression, he said, "*Your* pancakes were like Episode Seven … They were good, but nothing compares to nostalgia."

The joke went completely over Astrid's head, only to be caught by Bravo, who burst into another fit of laughter.

"Astrid didn't tell me you were this funny, Nathan," he exclaimed.

Astrid turned and demanded an explanation from the Commander, while Nathan strutted toward the edge of the car park, near the old café, where there was a lookout. From there, his eyes scanned the cityscape of Wollongong, mashed between the slopes of Mount Keira and the southeast coast of the Pacific. The city carpeted the lands stretching north, toward Bulli, Thirroul, and Stanwall Park beyond. To the south, Nathan eyed the industrial areas of Port Kembla, the metropolis of rusting metal and smokestacks that was the steelworks where his grandfather used to work. The sight reinvigorated him as he thought, *This is my town, and I will defend it.*

He swivelled to see Bravo and Astrid gazing at him.

"So, what's next in training?" he said resolutely.

"Astrid!" exclaimed Bravo with a jovial tone, his eyes never leaving Nathan.

At that, the Spartan Valkyrie wordlessly raised her Kakugane. A flash of blue light enveloped her, forming the four articulated limbs of her Valkyrie Skirt. Nathan didn't get a chance to admire the new design embodying the blades, as they immediately lunged for him. His heart skipped a few beats before he leapt out of the way. Astrid swiped at him again, the front arms of her terrifying Arms Alchemy whizzing to-and-fro like a pair of scissors while the rear arms propelled her forward. Nathan dove to the ground, hairs on the back of his head giving way to the passage of her blades just shy of his skin.

Astrid stopped her advance and swivelled to glare at him, her scar glistening in the sunlight as the eyes above it radiated murderous intent. A slack-jawed Nathan returned a bewildered, terrified stare. He turned to Bravo who applauded him and said, "Good reaction times, Nathan!"

"What the Hell is going on?" the boy screamed.

"I wanted to see how you fared sparing with Astrid," said Bravo. "That way, I can decide how to train you."

"*This* is sparring?" exclaimed Nathan.

"You had it easy with Papillon," said Astrid. "A real humanoid homunculus is far stronger and way worse than him. And that embryo hampered me. Now, the *real* training starts."

Nathan stared back at her, and then at Bravo. His grin, cocky even by Nathan's standards, transmitted his confidence toward the boy, almost infecting him. The Kakugane in Nathan's chest started to hum with excitement as he leapt to his feet.

Let's see if you're on to something, Klein, he thought.

His hand to his chest, he bellowed, "Arms Alchemy! Sunlight's Heart!"

His heart ignited in a blinding flash of golden light, which then rapidly condensed into the lance that was his namesake. Its gold and silver hull shimmered in the sunlight, and when he took it in his hand, it pulsated with his combat instincts. His eyes lit up with excitement, and to Astrid he said, "I forgot how cool this thing is."

"It's not super power, Nathan," said Astrid, though she wasn't much better than Bravo at hiding her admiration. "Remember, this is a burden, and you have to bear it properly."

Nathan twirled the lance in his hand and assumed a battle-ready stance. "Bring it!"

Astrid's hind-legs launched her toward him, her forelegs bringing a double blow. Nathan deflected the blade to his left and twirled to parry the right blow. Astrid's hind-legs ripped through the ground beneath her to swipe up toward Nathan's shoulders. Her opponent stood sideways-on to avoid the dual uppercut before lunging with the butt of his lance. Astrid cocked her head aside to dodge the blow, and then brought her hind-legs back down on his shoulders, their blunt edges striking with enough force throw the boy to the ground. Her forelegs flipped her over him, while her hind-legs locked under his armpits and used the momentum to hurl him. Nathan flew head-over-heels screaming, until he struck the asphalt hard and rolled down the cobblestone stairs toward the old lookout.

His head spinning, Nathan looked up with just enough sense to see his lance within reach and Astrid advancing quickly. She leapt into the air, somersaulting as she turned her Valkyrie Skirt into a buzz saw determined to deprive his arms of a body. He grabbed the red sash, glimmering with his fighting spirit, and yanked the spear to him in time to block Astrid's ballistic attack. At that moment, their eyes met, and he saw the Rambo-esque sneer she'd worn the night they met.

Even when she's trying to kill me, she's still cool, he marvelled.

He pushed back against her. Then she came at him, her mechanical arms throwing blow after blow as she drove him back. He walked backwards, parrying and dodging every blow, while Astrid's smirk grew into a confident grin. Then Nathan's back met something he knew was the railing of the old lookout.

At that moment, Astrid's four blades charged as one toward his neck.

"Enough!" yelled Bravo.

The blades came to an inertia-less stop, barely touching Nathan's jugular. Despite her clear victory, Astrid's grin was gone at the sight of that gold and silver lance, its blade inches from her own neck. She locked eyes with Nathan, and recalled a moment from long ago when she had seen in him the kind of confidence and determination that made her save his life. Her body trembled at the sight, and her lips upturned into an excited grin Nathan had never seen her wear.

They quietly pulled their blades away, and Nathan promptly ruined the moment by screaming, "Oh my God, that was so cool!"

That made Astrid plant her face in her palm.

"Could you be less of a child?" she exclaimed. "I wasn't playing around just then, you know? I could have really hurt you."

"But you didn't," replied Nathan, thrusting his spear into the air. "We were both totally in control, just like something out of a Jet Li movie."

Descending the stairs, Bravo butt in, "We'll talk the best *wuxia*[6] movie some other time, Grant. But that wasn't bad for a spar."

"Cheers, Bravo," said Nathan.

Bravo took a position facing the duo. Nathan's arm hairs started to quiver at the energy that emanated from the man simply by standing there. Astrid inhaled sharply at the sensation. Then, his forearms angled outward, Bravo said, "Both of you, come at me."

"Commander, your Arms Alchemy?" mumbled Astrid.

"I'll do without," said Bravo confidently.

When Nathan glanced nervously at Astrid and saw her take a fighting stance, he knew it wasn't a joke. He took a similar stance, his lance at the ready.

"Let's go!" snapped Astrid. She took off first, Nathan lagging hesitantly. She brought her blades to bear on the Commander. Bravo nimbly dodged the swipes from the four arms, taking a moment to duck Nathan's charge as the boy sailed over him. He then swatted Astrid's blades aside with his palms, before giving a swift blow to Astrid's forehead and knocking her back. He swivelled as Nathan charged again. With the subtlest touch of his fingers, Bravo deflected the lance, kneed Nathan in the stomach to

---

6   The genre of films depicting Chinese Martial Arts.

halt his charge, and then diverted the shaft over his head with his forearm to block Astrid's next barrage. He delivered another punch to Astrid's face, before backhanding Nathan.

Of course, his blows were too soft to harm them, but strong enough to daze them.

Bravo hardly paid Astrid mind, his gaze fixed on Nathan, as he said, "Good! You've got drive befitting an Alchemic Warrior. Your weapon responds to your intention, as it should."

The praise went a little too far to Nathan's head. Grinning, he bellowed, "Damn straight it does!"

With that, he charged again, only to receive a swift palm to the chest that sent him flying. Bravo came at him before he'd even hit the ground, his fingers outstretched like a knife.

"Bisection! Bravo Chop!" he roared.

His hand hit metal. There stood Astrid, between Bravo and Nathan, one of her blades held up to parry the barehanded blow. Her eyes were riddled with horror at what may have been in her superior's head. Bravo looked fixedly at her and smiled, before he relaxed his body and stepped back. Astrid's knees knocked as she stepped back toward the railing for support. Nathan stood up and first saw Astrid's dazed expression. Then he noted the blade with which she'd parried the blow. A rather large dent marred the blunt edge where Bravo's strike landed. Both Nathan's spear and his jaw hit the ground at the sight. The boy fell to his knees when he saw Bravo's pristine, bruise-less hand.

"What the Hell?" he mumbled.

"I have trained my body into my weapon," said Bravo, his more calm, aloof demeanour resurfacing. "That's because my Arms Alchemy isn't exactly what you'd call offensive." He edged toward them, his eyes narrowing at Astrid's still fearful expression. Then he pulled Nathan to his feet. As he herded the boy back to the car park, he said,

"You work well on your feet. You're able to adapt and improvise, though your technique does need *a lot* of polish." The comment made Nathan whimper sheepishly. Bravo patted him on the back and said, "We can fix that though. I'll get you trained!"

"The Hell you will!" snapped a voice that filled Bravo with panic. Both Nathan and Astrid shuddered at the terror and grief that flooded from Bravo. All eyes turned to the abandoned café building, upon the roof of which stood a tall, muscular man of apparent Indian descent, his grin sporting pronounced canines and a long-held grudge. His colourless eyes stared down his nose, focused entirely on Bravo.

Bravo huffed away as much of his repressed fury as he could and said, "Janjira! Four years I've been hunting you, and you just show up."

"I'm here to settle the score, Captain Bravo," spat Janjira.

Nathan eyed Bravo, and heard Astrid's blades rattle. They both had the same look in their eyes: disgust. He turned his gaze back to the man, certain that there was something about him. A scent started to tickle at his nostrils, the air carrying odours that he couldn't put his finger on.

I know this feeling somewhere, he thought.

Faint memories surfaced in his mind of Ol' Chambo, the frog, and Burrumering, and the scent was indeed similar, but still off. He gasped as the realisation set in.

"Astrid, this is one of *them*," he mumbled.

"A humanoid homunculus," she confirmed.

Bravo held up his hand, "Stay back. This is mine."

"I think not, Bravo!" yelled Janjira. He licked his lips ravenously. "Unlike four years ago, I've finally got the power to match you." The man reached into his pocket and procured a Kakugane. He chuckled at the looks of shock on his enemies' faces and yelled, "*Shastree kimayaa!*[7] *Brahmastra!*[8]"

The Kakugane exploded in a cloud of green light and smoke, which coalesced around the man's right forearm. Seeds of metal grew into pistons and thick plates of armour welded to the man's skin, until a gauntlet took shape. Janjira burst forward, carried by flames that erupted from the gauntlet's elbow. He aimed a meteoric punch for Bravo's head.

A flash of golden light entered his field of view, and Nathan stood before him. The boy swiped his lance, deflecting Janjira's punch into the ground. He then brought his lance about to strike the homunculus' head.

I got this one, he thought triumphantly as his red sash glimmered.

The back of a heavy, hand-shaped object the size of a car suddenly struck him. The wind knocked out of him along with his senses, Nathan hit the ground hard. Janjira's gauntlet returned to its normal size with a series of whirrs and clicks. He let out a frustrated growl as flames burst from his elbow again. This time, Nathan was his target.

Astrid leapt through the air and landed between them, her four blades locked tightly into the metal carapace of Janjira's gauntlet. She braced herself against the asphalt and parried the rocket-powered blow. She then pushed back and her four blades launched a fierce counterattack against the homunculus. Janjira blocked and deflected her blows as she twirled and danced about him, until he saw an opening and swiped. Astrid arched backwards to dodge the blow, just as Nathan – having regained his senses once again – flew over her with his lance aimed at Janjira's head.

Janjira avoided the brunt of Nathan's attack, sustaining only a gash to his shoulder that oozed grey dust. He back-

---

[7]   Marathi for "Arms Alchemy."
[8]   Brahmastra is a mythical weapon featured in the Hindu epic, Mahabharata, capable of destroying worlds.

flipped out of the way of the two warriors, but retaliated quickly. His gauntlet once again expanded to an incredible size and weight, and he brought the palm down flat upon them. Nathan braced himself to parry the attack, but Astrid quickly kicked him out of the way and parried it herself. He flew clear of the hand's radius, rolled to a stop on the asphalt and saw Astrid straining under the weight of the massive hand.

Janjira swiped his hand out of the way and kicked an overwhelmed Astrid in the head. The girl flew across the car park, defeated. Then Janjira turned to Bravo, his eyes almost lidless with excitement, his dislocated jaw bearing rows of sharp teeth that reminded Nathan of Chouno's transformation. But the boy was far too fatigued to get up, much less move to stop the homunculus' advance.

"Just like four years ago, Bravo!" said Janjira. "Couldn't stop me from taking out your comrades then, and you won't stop me now."

"I can't stop people from dying," said Bravo. "Least of all, Alchemic Warriors. Death comes for us all in the end."

"Oooh, that's cold, isn't it?" intoned Janjira. "Looks like your death will come today."

"Not today," Bravo growled. With that, he reached into his jacket pocket and took out the Kakugane Fifty. "Arms Alchemy! Silver Skin!"

White light enveloped the man, clothing him in a long metal jacket that concealed even his face. With what little energy Nathan had left, he marvelled, *Consummate coolness!*

Unfazed, Janjira bellowed, "Your glorified iron-man costume won't save you now!" The gauntlet hand extended its fingers, and began to spin rapidly like a drill. The elbow rocket reactivated, and Janjira flew at the man, cackling hysterically as he went. When he hit Bravo's chest, the asphalt behind the man's feet was ripped up from the hard rock foundations below and thrown several metres, but Bravo did not move an inch. The creases in his jacket glistened, as if they'd hardened into something tougher than diamond. Janjira's gauntlet continued to grind against the impregnable armour until it started to smoke, and the homunculus' face went from cocky to concerned to very nervous.

Bravo's gloved hand suddenly clamped down on the spinning gauntlet, and the machine stopped with the deafening sounds of stripping gears. With the slightest twist of his forearm, Bravo shattered the gauntlet. Janjira fell backward, his eyes alight with alarm.

Time stood still as Nathan watched the man single-handedly disable what his and Astrid's blades couldn't even dent. His body shook at the sheer magnitude of power that Bravo radiated, and marvelled that his substitute English teacher had hidden such strength for months. His marvel turned to horror when time resumed.

With a throaty roar, Bravo launched an unrelenting assault on Janjira's body. His fists struck the homunculus' body with tremendous force. Bones cracked and black dust gushed under the merciless attacks, until Bravo paused. Janjira crumpled to the ground, an unrecognisable mass of homunculus matter. What used to be his mouth flapped feebly, "You got serious anger issues, Bravo!"

Bravo grabbed the homunculus' head. "This isn't anger, you baby-eating son of a bitch." Then he hefted the creature over his head and slammed it back into the asphalt. Janjira fell still.

The metal jacket vanished from Bravo's body and he pocketed his Kakugane. Then he reached down and picked up Janjira's inert talisman. He sighed as he studied it, while Nathan studied his face. He saw the faintest redness to the man's eyes, and thought, *He looks so sad.*

Bravo pocketed the recovered talisman and helped his comrades to their feet. Astrid rubbed the side of her head, which sported an awful cut that bruised at the edges. She deactivated her Arms Alchemy and held the Kakugane to her chest to accelerate her healing. Nathan did the same, even though his injuries were far less severe. He finally pulled his gaze away from Bravo's expression when Astrid said, "You missed his vitals."

"Meant to," said Bravo, his voice barely above a whisper. "He needs to be interrogated."

"Why?" asked Nathan. "I thought he was just an old grudge come to settle the score."

"If it were just that, he'd be road kill by now," said Bravo. "This guy is part of a troupe the Regiment's been hunting for a long time. Can't give up this lead, can we?" Bravo bent down and lifted the mass that was Janjira. He thrust the broken man against a tree and growled, "Start talking, scumbag."

Janjira gurgled and spat a mass of black blood onto the ground. Despite his injuries, he maintained his vicious grin.

"What'll we talk about, eh?" he chortled.

"Where's the head of your organisation?" asked Bravo.

"What organisation?" mumbled Janjira. Bravo kneed him in the stomach, forcing more black matter out his gullet. He coughed and spluttered, and finally ground out, "Oh, you mean our *league?*"

"Yes, the League of Extraordinary Gentlemen," snapped Bravo.

"What, like the Alan Moore comic?" asked Nathan.

"He ripped it off us," snapped Janjira. "Oh, and by the way, since we got ladies in our league, it's now the League of Extraordinary *Elects!* The L.X.E!"

Bravo stepped back from the tree, rolling his eyes. "They were always a bunch of try-hards." His hands on his hips, he glared at Janjira, "You've obviously got an outpost here. Where, and how many?"

"Everywhere and millions," Janjira blurted, his grin growing wider.

"So just a few dip-shits living in a sewer," Bravo translated, having completely lost patience with the man's bluster.

"Hardly!" snapped Janjira, his eyes piercing into Bravo's stare. He reached upwards to his neck, where

Nathan could see a helix tattoo glimmering just beneath the skin. Janjira went on, "Doctor Butterfly has completed his work, and soon, *he* will rise."

Butterfly, the word leapt out at Nathan and Astrid.

"You mean Papillon?" snapped Astrid. Fear gripped Nathan's heart.

Bravo's face had grown far darker, and he intoned, "No ... Doctor Butterfly is leader of their team – the second-most hunted man in the history of the Regiment." He crossed the distance between him and Janjira, and gripped the man's jaw. "Who's going to rise?" He bellowed the question fervently, though at his core he desperately wanted to avoid the answer.

Janjira thrust his sharp fingernail through the tattoo, and let out a strangled gurgle like his heart had been ripped from his chest. His entire body wriggled in agony as his extremities started to evaporate.

Bravo didn't let up his entreaties, shaking what little remained of the homunculus' body and roaring, "Who is *he?*"

With his last smothered breath, Janjira belched two syllables: "Victor."

The beast's remains evaporated and wafted away in the light breeze. Nathan could almost hear the man's voice continue on the winds like an eerie send off to the hereafter, and it sent chills down his spine. He turned to Astrid, whose face radiated confusion. Then he looked at Bravo, and saw a man who had just met the Devil.

"We gotta go," he snapped. He swivelled and almost sprinted back down the path they'd trodden. Nathan and Astrid struggled to keep up with their superior, who pressed down the slope like a man possessed.

"Bravo! What's going on?" he yelled.

"Who's this Victor?" asked Astrid.

"I'll explain when we get back," snapped Bravo.

Nathan couldn't accept the answer, and raced forward. He grabbed Bravo by the shoulders, in an effort to stop him. He suddenly found himself pressed against a tree, held there only by Bravo's outstretched finger. The man's eyes overflowed with fury, frustration, and indignation.

"Starlight Lancer," he intoned slowly. "Usually, I'm pretty lax. But remember: I am your superior. And remember your place, *under my command*. Is that understood?"

Out the corner of Nathan's eye, he saw Astrid pale-faced, and knew that even she hadn't seen Bravo like this before. He grabbed the reins of the wild beast fuelling his nerves, and willed himself to calm down. He finally murmured, "Understood, Commander."

"Good," said Bravo. "Now, fall in line."

With that, the man strutted down the mountain path. He didn't wait for his subordinates, and before long disappeared behind the brush. Astrid approached Nathan, her nose scar knitted with her own nerves, and placed a hand on his shoulder.

"I'm sorry," said Astrid. "Usually, he's not like this. In fact, most of the time, he's more aloof than you. For the longest time, I couldn't figure out why he was a Commander." She gazed down the path after Bravo. "I've never seen him so angry," she muttered.

"That's not anger," said Nathan. "I think he was about to cry."

5 | History Lesson

Bravo said nothing on the drive back to the dorms, aside from a brisk, "I need to make a few calls."

That put quite the damper on Nathan's spirits, which would have otherwise been elated by the spar with Astrid and their commander, not to mention his first encounter with a real humanoid homunculus. When they reached the dormitory, Bravo left the car without a word, leaving his subordinates speechless.

"Come on," said Astrid upon noting Nathan's head hanging in disappointment. "We should get homework done before dinner."

Even though Nathan was discouraged by Bravo's sudden change in demeanour, his mood remained high enough to recall something Astrid said to him months ago. Curious, he leaned over and said, "Hey, Astrid, remember the day after we first met, you said homunculi couldn't use Kakugane. What was with Janjira then?"

Astrid glanced at him a moment with a blank face. Clearly, she was caught up in her own musings, and stammered a bit before collecting her thoughts.

"Basically, animal and plant types are only as a smart as the creatures used to culture the cells. Remember Burrumering? He was an eagle, making him a good hunter and an extreme loyalist. That toad you fought ... well, I guess you can figure what kind of person he was. It all depends on the animal used to make the culture."

Nathan palmed his hand, "Oh, I get it. So if it's a human, then they'll be able to use tools and stuff, right? And Kakugane is like a tool."

Astrid shot him a bewildered look. When he inquired, she said, "I'm just surprised you caught on so quick."

"I have my moments," he said with a grin.

A short creature suddenly leapt onto Nathan's shoulders and yelled, "Were you and Triddy having a moment, Nathan?"

Bewildered at the sudden weight on his shoulders, Nathan stumbled as he tried to blow Ariadne's hair out of his face. Astrid just stood to the side, at first a little shocked at the girl's appearance. As she watched the siblings roughhouse, a smile started to form on her lips, which did not go unnoticed by the three boys approaching.

"I agree, it is fun watching Nathan get beat-up by his little sister," said Paul.

Jessie's smile was less evident behind his concerned eyes as he said, "But she ruined Nathan's moment with Astrid."

That drew Astrid's grimacing face his way, but Klein cut in before she could retort. "Nah, ya need someone to keep ya a gentleman. That's all Ariadne's doing."

Recalling an incident involving a mechanical toad, something overcame Astrid, and it widened her grin and made her jibe, "Considering the magazines you read, I'd say you'd need a little sister more than Nathan."

The group erupted into a chorus of gasps, chuckles, and announcements of "Burn!" Behind her chuckles, Astrid marvelled, *Wow! I'm actually making jokes with these people.*

Nathan finally caught a hold of Ariadne and managed to settle her.

"Ari, you're in high school now. It's time to lose the little kid thing," he chided.

"Oh, please, Nathan!" exclaimed Ariadne and Astrid

simultaneously. Ariadne beamed as Astrid's cheeks turned beet-red. Now the scarred girl was the target, and the little sister threw her arms around her and screamed, "It's like we're sisters now!"

Nathan, glad for the respite from the overly clingy girl, sauntered down the hall with his friends toward the common room. Just as they fell down on one of the couches, the TV became available and Jessie proposed, "Smash Brothers?"

Klein was Shulk, Paul was Marth, Jessie was Pikachu, and Nathan was Cloud. They started their three-stock free-for-all game, which quickly devolved into a cacophony of cartoony sound effects, light flashes, and digital particle streams pockmarked by the strangled screams of the various characters being blasted off-screen in a painfully colourful screen-side explosion. The play continued for six minutes until it was just Pikachu and Cloud left on the screen. Cloud's buster sword glimmered, while Pikachu's cheeks made like mini lightning storms. Both combatants, and their digital counterparts, eyed each other off, with particular attention paid to the one remaining stock each, and the over-two-hundred-per-cent damage they both sported. Invisible attacks flew between the combatants as their hearts raced with every beat of the background music bellowing *audi famam*.

Cloud burst forward, ready to slash. The blow flew through Pikachu, who flashed with a familiar glimmer that made Nathan's heart stop. Then came the horrible chant from the yellow electric mouse: "Pika!" The lightning hit. Nobody even saw Cloud leave the screen before it exploded, and the TV bellowed, "Game!"

Jessie proceeded to dance in front of the TV, as was the right of the victor to gloat to his heart's content upon such a nail-biting victory. Cheers erupted from the crowd behind the couch, and Jessie drank it all in. Nathan looked over his shoulder to see Astrid giving Ariadne a piggyback, which she was clearly enjoying far more than she wanted to let on. The grin Nathan shot Astrid made the girl blush even more. He stood up from the couch, handed his controller to someone else, and approached the two girls.

"Ariadne was just telling me the fencing club has a meet in a few weeks," said Astrid.

"You two're coming!" said Ariadne matter-of-factly. Nathan just grinned and tussled his sister's hair. The girl yelped at her messy hair and hopped off Astrid's back to straighten it out.

The games went on for another few matches, changing players every time. The only one still standing was Jessie, still as Pikachu. Bravo entered the room just as a match ended, Jessie ever the victorious. The elated boy saw the manager approach and said, "Hey, Mister Costable! You any good at Smash?"

Bravo's bad mood seemed gone, as evidenced by his usual carefree smile. But when the invitation to play the game went his way, he backed away.

"Oh no, you don't want to play me, Mister Nelson," he said, chuckling nervously.

"Afraid you'll lose?" taunted Jessie, earning him a few hoots from the excited crowd.

Nathan eyed Bravo, recalling the ferociousness with which the man fought. He leaned down to Astrid and whispered, "Should Jessie be pushing his luck?"

Astrid smiled with piqued interest, "Probably not."

The crowd started chanting Bravo's name, until the man gave in and murmured, "Your funeral, mate."

He took one of the controllers, and selected his character. The whole crowd chuckled.

"Seriously, you're going with Kirby?" exclaimed Jessie.

"Kirby's the bomb!" replied Bravo. Jessie just scoffed. Bravo grinned cockily and said, "Ya know what? How's about we make this interesting? Let's do three-on-one! I'll even take a high handicap."

Nathan's heart raced, so much that he almost confessed his identity as the Starlight Lancer and Bravo's true nature, if only to stop Jessie from being horribly embarrassed. But he kept his mouth shut as the teams and handicaps were assigned.

The fight was over in less than two minutes. Every jaw was on the floor as Bravo stood from the couch and dropped his controller as if it was a microphone and he was a rock star.

"Oh, and what time was it again?" he asked, sardonically checking his watch. "That's right, time to dance!" He proceeded to jig around in front of the TV to the amazed applause of the crowd and even the players. Even Jessie clapped, his lips upturned into an incredulous grin. He approached Bravo and exclaimed, "Master! Please accept me as your disciple!"

"Ah, dear boy, the Bravo Techniques are not for the faint of heart," Bravo proclaimed. He started to sober, and with a huff he turned to Astrid and Nathan. "You two, I'd like to have a chat in my office."

"Uh-Oh! The love-birds're gonna get busted!" jibed Klein. Over the din of laughter, which overshadowed Astrid's desire to dismember the boy with her bare hands, Bravo's voice rumbled, "Oi! Stevens! You in my office too!"

Klein made a show of sheepishness as he followed the dorm manager and his friends, a chorus of jeers and chuckles playing him off. Once he was out of sight, the nervous looks on the three student's faces changed to expressions of anticipation, with a considerable amount of worry mixed into Astrid and Nathan's gazes.

Once inside Bravo's office, the door locked behind them and he beckoned them to sit.

"First off," Bravo began, his eyes focused on Nathan. "I'm sorry about my behaviour before, Warrior Grant. Janjira's taunts really rattled me, but I shouldn't have taken it out on you."

Nathan waved it off, "No problem, mate."

"What's more important is why it rattled you?" said

Astrid. She shot an annoyed look at Klein and grumbled, "Also, why is this idiot listening in?"

"Like it or not, Warrior Rachelle, Stevens is involved," said Bravo. He regarded Klein, "You might be an asset for us."

"Oi, if you're gonna recruit me into this Arms Alchemy thing, I'm out," said Klein defensively. "I'm not up for a hunk of metal in my chest, thanks. I've just been tryin' to support Nathan here."

"Wasn't planning on that, Stevens," said Bravo. "You can be an asset by doing just that."

"Your pep-talks've been real helpful in keeping me in check," said Nathan with a grateful smile. "You're like the Pepper Potts to my Tony Stark."

At that, all the blood drained from Klein's face as Bravo and even Astrid started to snicker. Klein shuffled his chair away from Nathan slightly, fanning those snickers into genuine laughs. Bravo sobered first and went on, "All joking aside, I will keep you informed of what is going on, Stevens. So you'll need to sit in our meetings. If things go pear-shaped, you'll have to get everyone as far away as possible. Understand?"

Klein gazed fixedly at Bravo and said, "Got it."

Bravo clapped his hands together and bellowed, "Right! Now that's out of the way, to the important stuff." He looked to Astrid. "Rachelle, you've never heard of Victor Powers, have you?"

"Can't say I have, Commander," said Astrid.

"You might've," said Bravo. He turned to Nathan. "Remember a few days ago when I said only sixty-two Kakugane are accounted for? Well, the truth is, we haven't been searching for them for hundreds of years. In fact, until about 1940, the Regiment had all hundred of them. And we'd come real close to wiping out the homunculus race once and for all. The one leading the charge was Victor, the greatest Alchemic Warrior in history. You know Stallone and Schwarzenegger? They got their personas from this guy.

"But something happened. We're not sure what. Either the enemy obtained some of his DNA, grew a homunculus embryo out of it, and infected him ... Or he infected himself, out of a lust for even more power. The Regiment isn't sure why but he became a monster unlike anything they'd ever seen. He murdered his wife and daughter, slaughtered his comrades, and started feeding on both human and homunculus alike. In the chaos, a few surviving homunculi stole half the Kakugane and went into hiding, leaving the Regiment to deal with Victor.

"They were able to beat him, obviously. Only, it took a nuclear bomb going off in his face. You know Operation Crossroads?"

"Oh yeah," said Klein. "They blew up a tropical island in, like, 1945?"

"'46," said Bravo. "That was where the Regiment managed to beat Victor, or so they thought."

"So, you think Janjira was working with Victor?" asked Nathan.

"Janjira?" asked Klein.

"A humanoid homunculus we just took out at Mount Kiera Lookout," said Astrid. She turned to Bravo, "Commander, how do you know he wasn't just pulling your leg?"

"I doubt that," returned Bravo. "Janjira was a relatively young homunculus, not to mention a total moron. There's no way he would've known about Victor unless someone told him."

"And we're sure this Doctor Butterfly he mentioned isn't Chouno?" asked Nathan, his knuckles white with concern.

"Relax, Nathan," said Bravo. "Doctor Butterfly has been on our radar for way longer than you've been alive. I've contacted the Regiment and called for reinforcements. Too bad, though, they don't share my concern."

"They don't believe you?" asked Astrid.

"General Rodrigo does, but not the rest of those geezers," said Bravo. "Rodrigo said he'd look outside the organisation while we investigate the L.X.E. presence here in Wollongong."

"Outside?" exclaimed Astrid. "Who's he going to ask?"

Bravo pursed his lips, as if a bad taste filled his mouth, and he murmured, "The Scot."

Astrid shot up and roared, "The Scot! You're joking!"

"Whoa, Astrid, don't burst a blood vessel," cried Nathan.

"Who's the Scot?" asked Klein.

Astrid huffed irately, "He's a wizard I wish I'd never met."

"A wizard?" asked Nathan. "As in Harry Potter?"

"No, think more obnoxious," said Bravo. "He's really not pleasant to be around."

Klein and Nathan exchanged glances and mumbled, "Harry Potter's pretty obnoxious."

"If we have to accept help from that shithead, I'd rather we go it alone," said Astrid.

"I second that," murmured Bravo. "But if his history is anything to go on, he'll probably tell Rodrigo to go to Hell and that'll be it."

Astrid sat down, her arms crossed tightly and a scowl marring her face. Her face scar crinkled as more unpleasant thoughts bubbled into her consciousness, but she managed to shoo them away enough to ask, "So, let's assume the best case scenario: we're on our own. What should we do, Commander?"

"First thing's first," said Bravo, taking Janjira's Kakugane from his pocket and handing it to her. "I don't have enough space in the case for this one, so you're on guard duty tonight. It's possible one of Janjira's comrades might try to take it back. If they do, kill clearance is granted, but try to capture them if you can." He turned to Klein. "If, at any time, Astrid gives you the signal, get as many kids out of the way as you can. Got it?"

"Got it, Captain Bravo," said Klein with an over-serious, wrong-handed salute.

"That leaves you, Grant," said Bravo. "Having seen you fight, I know you're not ready for the L.X.E. But that's gonna change. Starting tonight, I'll train you."

Nathan palmed his fist excitedly. "Sounds great, Master Bravo."

"Don't get cocky, Grant," said Bravo with a grin. "You're gonna start in extra hard mode, so prepare yourself."

Klein and Nathan left, a big excited grin on the latter's face, while Astrid lingered a moment longer.

"Commander, let me help with Nathan's training," she said, a dash of concern to her voice that Bravo very quickly picked up on.

"No, I need you here to guard the fort," he said as he took his Kakugane from the case.

"I can look after the Kakugane at the same time," Astrid insisted.

Bravo promptly silenced her and said, "I saw you fighting too, today. When you were sparring with Nathan, I could see you were pulling every single punch. And when you fought Janjira, you were more worried about Nathan than you were the fight. He was more worried about you too. You both need to learn to focus on the fight, and not be concerned with each other."

Astrid rolled her eyes irately. "We're *not* a couple."

"That doesn't matter," said Bravo. "You're still more concerned with him than you are the mission at hand. That's what made you take that embryo, and what made you give up that Kakugane now in his chest. You can't be afraid to lose someone you care about." He patted her on the shoulder and said, "Rediscover your warrior spirit, Rachelle. Be resolved to do everything necessary to complete the mission, understood?"

She huffed, the words draining warmth from her body and replacing it with a familiar yet unpalatable kind of conviction. It left a sour taste in her mouth that lingered long after she left Bravo's office.

Hours later, as she watched Nathan and Bravo race to finish their dinner, it bothered her.

You can't be afraid to lose someone you care about, she thought. *But, isn't that why we're Alchemic Warriors? To protect the ones we care about?*

She eyed Nathan, and knew that was certainly his motivation. Her thoughts started drifting toward her own motivations, but they edged into darker, murkier regions of her mental landscape and quickly scurried back upon her sudden shuddering.

Bravo and Nathan bussed their plates and left the dorm, much to everyone's curiosity. When asked what he was doing with Bravo, Nathan simply replied, "Special Training!"

Astrid slurped her tea pensively, hardly aware that Nathan and Bravo had left. A hand plonked on the top of her head, and she saw Ariadne, a big grin on her face as she petted her.

"Watcha thinkin' about?" asked the beaming girl. "You had a really bothered look about you?"

"Nothing," said Astrid as she swatted the hand away.

"Oh, right, you're sad that Nathan's going off with Bravo and you're left alone," Ariadne concluded.

As the younger girl plopped onto the seat next to Astrid, Jessie and Paul sat opposite her and asked, "So, you know what's this trainin' Bravo's doing for Nathan?"

Astrid stammered nervously, her earlier ponderings stymieing her improvisational skills.

"Oh, I know," exclaimed Ariadne. "He's doing fighting training so that he can protect you! Right, Astrid?"

"I suppose that's it," she murmured, a red hue on her face that was more irritation than shyness. She would have rather said, "It's more all of you he's training for," but she kept her mouth shut.

Questions turned into conversations, the contents of

which she'd luckily grown accustomed to over the last few days. The jibes at her and Nathan's relationship had subsided, as the boarders had clearly grown bored of the teasing. Instead the students moved on to finding common ground with her. A rather large part of her mind welcomed the idea excitedly, as if voraciously consuming something it had silently desired for as long as she could remember. Another part of her mind growled, with increasing softness, that she should resist getting too close to these kids.

That, the mounting concern she felt for Captain Bravo, and the words he'd given her before, made for a nervous cocktail that eventually drove her to distraction.

"Oi, Astrid," said Klein from across the table.

Astrid snapped to attention, and noticed everyone staring at her. She cleared her throat, "Sorry, I must've zoned out."

"You looked like you were real pissed at something," murmured Paul as he adjusted his glasses.

Crap!

She shrugged off the sudden flood of panic that hit her and blurted, "You know, I'm just tired. I've had a bit of a long day, and I've also got homework."

She managed to dart out of Ariadne's grip just in time to bid everyone good night, and then scurried to her dorm room. She didn't do her homework, and hardly slept. Instead, she spent the whole night pondering Bravo's words, as she gazed at Janjira's Kakugane, the serial number fifty-two hardly visible beneath centuries of overuse.

More than once during the night, she wondered if she was looking in a mirror.

6 | Busted!

There's an area of Port Kembla, near Tom Thumb's Lagoon, where one can see the freighters chug their way into port. Just a bit south of there is the grain terminal. Most dads who worked at the steelworks would bring their kids to the seldom-travelled roads in that area, for their first driving lessons.

That's during the day. At night, the place is completely deserted, making it the perfect place for training.

Nathan hopped out of the car and breathed deeply. He quickly coughed and gagged at the cocktail of coke oven fumes and oil stench wafting from the lagoon.

"Get that into ya!" exclaimed Bravo. "When I was a kid in Clermont, my dad'd sometimes take me to the coal fields up where he worked. Man, did it smell good there!"

"Dude, do you have any sense of smell?" exclaimed Nathan.

Bravo just chuckled and gave him a stiff pat on the back. He locked the car and herded Nathan into the middle of the dark area. The boy took in his surroundings, finding them more foreboding than the Chouno Estate – even after the cannibalistic carnage.

Luckily, there was a full moon out, shedding an eerie white glow across the landscape. A soft wind blew through from the east, and pushed a cleaner sea-smelling draught through the buildings. This did some good for Nathan's psyche, but not so much for his internal thermostat, and he shivered in the cold. He gazed up at Bravo, compared to whom he felt like a worn-out plastic tricycle next to a roaring monster truck. The man wore a light pair of pants and a black tee-shirt, while Nathan was huddled up in jeans and a jumper, and was still cold!

Nathan quickly reminded himself, *Remember what you saw today. This guy is an Alchemic Warrior, with years of training. Even Astrid looks up to the guy. And he's gonna teach you how to fight like him and be a hero.*

He huffed resolutely: *Prepare yourself, Starlight Lancer.*

Bravo caught his stiff exhale and mumbled, "Psyching yourself up?"

"Yep!" replied Nathan. He turned and faced Bravo. "I'm ready, Captain Bravo."

"Bravo!" exclaimed the man, cracking his knuckles excitedly. He stopped Nathan, whose hand edged toward his chest, and said, "No weapons yet. Come at me with your fists."

Nathan grinned excitedly. "Okay, Bravo! You asked for it!"

Hang on a sec, thought a tiny, feeble voice in his mind too soft for his cocky brain to hear. He burst into a sprint toward Bravo, clenched his fist, and thrust forward.

Bang!

The boy fell to his knees, fighting back tears as he cradled a hand that had gone numb. Bravo simply stood there in a Superman-pose, his fists on his hips and a toothy grin on his face, and proclaimed, "One of the thirteen Bravo techniques! Bravo Ab-Wall! Once I have begun this move, not even a freight train can move me!" He offered Nathan a hand, which the boy took feebly. In the next instant, Nathan flew over Bravo's shoulder. The man roared, "Two of the thirteen Bravo techniques! Bravo Suplex!"

The man wasted no time. Before Nathan hit the ground, Bravo threw a barrage of punches at him, some of which his fear- and pain-addled brain found the presence to deflect. Most of them hit the mark, and he fell on his back, one big bruise all over his body.

That's how it feels, at least, cried his mind.

His metal heart clattered as his wounds healed, yet he couldn't find the strength to stand.

Bravo cracked his neck, his grin unwavering as he pronounced, "That's it for the warm-up!"

"Bollocks, that was a warm-up!" snapped Nathan. "You tryin' to bully me outta bein' an Alchemic Warrior?"

"You think that was bad?" exclaimed Bravo as he stretched his hamstrings and quads.

Nathan's mind recalled the fight with Papillon: not even a complete homunculus, and yet he burst through a hard wood cricket bat with a single finger. Since Nathan still had feeling in his toes and his wounds were healing, he knew the attack could have been much worse. His mind then went to the fight with Janjira that day. He eyed Bravo, who nonchalantly nibbled a banana, and he remembered the ferocity with which he had, barehanded, turned an Arms Alchemy to dust.

And he'd been holding back even then.

The real homunculus would be even worse, he concluded. *So would he in a real fight.*

He leapt to his feet, still a little shaky from Bravo's insanely-named 'warm-up.' He threw off his jacket and unzipped the seams on his trousers, turning them into shorts. He did a few stretches, and then faced Bravo.

"On second thoughts," said Nathan. The tone of his voice piqued Bravo's interest, and the man's ears pricked. "I felt worse after I fought Papillon. If I'm gonna be an Alchemic Warrior, I need to beat something way stronger than him. So don't hold back, Bravo. Come at me as if I were really Victor."

Bravo's eyebrows shot up the length of his forehead. He then started laughing so hard he almost choked on the last mouthful of banana. When he sobered, he cried,

"Good on ya, Grant! That's what a true warrior says ... Come to think of it, Rachelle said the same thing when I started training her."

Nathan's heart fluttered at the comment, as if overjoyed that he and Astrid were at least somewhat similar. That part of his brain responsible for his tummy fetish instantly concocted a number of fantasies of the girl admitting her undying love for him, purely for the sake of their desire to beat all homunculi. It took quite a bit of wrangling on the part of his rational mind to put those delusions away.

"All enthusiasm aside," said Bravo, patting him on the shoulder. "If I came at you, full-power, you'd be dead before you reached orbit, *around the Moon*." Instantly, all the fantasies and daydreams whirling around Nathan's cocky mind vanished. He just stood there, awestruck at the man. Bravo drew his Kakugane and said, "We'll start you at easy mode, and move as I say."

Nathan inhaled deeply, and shook his body to psych himself up. Then he placed his hand to his chest.

"Ready, Bravo," he bellowed.

"Good on ya!" replied Bravo.

The area echoed with their unified roar: "Arms Alchemy!"

* * *

Nathan pressed an icepack to his head, although that was only one part of the bruise that covered his entire body.

"Bollocks, that's easy mode," he grumbled.

Astrid leaned back in the chair next to his bed and yawned. Her watch read eleven-thirty in the evening. It was quite the surprise to find herself so tired, when she'd pulled all nighters hundreds of times. Once, she went three days without sleep and had no problem whatsoever. Now, she found it hard just to keep her eyes open and focused on the twitching mass complaining on the bed in front of her.

"Look at it this way," she mumbled. "You asked Bravo not to hold back. Aren't you glad he did?"

Nathan removed the icepack and glared at her. "You suggesting I should take it easy?"

"Wouldn't be the worst idea," said Astrid. "You're gonna need sleep so you can keep up your school grades. Healing with the Kakugane takes a lot of energy too."

Nathan mulled Astrid's suggestion with pursed lips.

Might not be a bad idea. You've been at it with Bravo for a week, and it's takin' your all just to heal. And that's with **two** *Kakugane.*

He looked at Kakugane fifty-two, pressed against his chest to complement his healing factor. Instantly, he was reminded of where it came from, and he grit his teeth.

"No," he said defiantly. "I couldn't even hold my own against Janjira. And he's supposed to be the weakest of this L.X.E. mob. I need to train more."

With a wince, Astrid said, "Nathan, it's been a week, and we haven't had any leads yet. And Bravo and I are here to deal with them if they come around. The world won't end if you take a break."

"No!" he barked, before collapsing back on the bed with a growl. "I need to be stronger, so that Ariadne won't be in danger. And so you won't have to take any risks for me."

Astrid's nose scar drooped as she gave a rare smile. She placed a hand on his forehead and said, "I really don't mind." Nathan looked back at her, his eyebrows raised as to her meaning. She saw his unspoken question, and her heart sank into her gut. She pulled back and stammered, "I don't mean like that. It's just that you're my subordinate, and being the experienced warrior, I'm supposed to look after the trainees."

Nathan pursed his lips mischievously. With a wink, he said, "Whatever you say."

Astrid almost strangled him right then and there.

Outside the dorm room, Klein ignored the sock on

Nathan's doorknob and strained his ear to eavesdrop. Anyone passing by at such a late hour would veer away him, viewing him as some perve trying to listen in on his friends' intimate moments.

It was the perfect cover.

He cringed every time one of Nathan's moans of pain seeped through the wooden doors. He wondered just what Bravo was putting him through, and for what purpose. Sure, he needed to be able to fight homunculi. Klein could understand that perfectly, having been punched by that butterfly undies man. And that was a failed homunculus. So Klein could only imagine what a real one would be like.

To be honest, I don't want to imagine it, he thought with a shudder. All aside, he found this absolutely ridiculous. *On top of all this crap, he's gotta make sure he does okay in school so his parents won't show up wingin'! Forget 'Starlight,' he'll be a white dwarf before long!*

Klein took a moment to congratulate himself on remembering astronomy class. All of Paul's tutoring had paid off, and it only cost him his cigarette budget for two months.

Pah! What's a nicotine addiction when you can avoid a lecture from your parents about schoolwork that won't matter a decade from now?

Then an idea struck him. He scrambled away from Nathan's room with a grin and hopped down to Paul's dorm room. Jessie, who often hung out in that room, was listening to music on the bed and running a pencil over a sketchpad, while Paul had claimed a monopoly on the desk.

"How's Nathan?" asked Jessie, pausing his iPod.

"Tired and hurt," replied Klein.

"You know what he's been doing with Bravo all this time?" Jessie asked.

"Training for something, I assume," replied Klein, his eyes directed at Paul.

"To be the Starlight Lancer, right?" jibed Jessie.

"Maybe," droned Klein.

Jessie's eyes narrowed and he leaned forward suspiciously. "You know more about this than you're letting on, don't you?"

"No shit, Sherlock," blurted Klein. "Of course, I know about Nathan, and I know who Astrid really is. And I know their relationship." He clamped his mouth shut to restrain the torrent of frustration-driven honesty bursting forth. Paul stopped writing, while Jessie's jaw hung open with excitement. Klein settled himself and added, "But look at my face. Do you really want to know?"

Paul swivelled on his chair to study his friend's face. There were bags under Klein's eyes, burdened by worry and stress. They had both noticed Klein's distress over the last few days. The only one who seemed more bothered was Nathan.

The atmosphere at the school was indeed tense. The teachers shushed it when it came up in class, but even they were concerned about missing students. Everyone in the school knew it had something to do with this rumoured Starlight Lancer. Nathan's constant denial just made the students more stressed at a lack of answers.

With that in mind, plus Nathan's dream of the Catholic schoolgirl, and Astrid's joining Warrawul, Jessie and Paul both concluded the same thing.

"It's probably best we don't know," said Paul.

"If Nathan wants to let us in on it, fine, but we shouldn't stress him any more than he is," said Jessie.

"We've got our studies to focus on too," Paul added. "That said, if he needs our support, he'll get it."

Klein sighed with relief, and grinned as he said, "Actually, that's why I'm here. Paul, how much would it cost me to get you to forge Nathan's handwriting?"

* * *

A red whiteboard marker flew through the air and struck Nathan's head. He shot up pale faced and horrified, and held up his dukes for a fight.

"Come and get me, Bravo!" he bellowed.

When his consciousness caught up with his muscle memory, he shook his head and realised he was in the middle of math class. The whole class started chuckling.

Three weeks of training, he thought in a dismayed daze.

"Did you have a nice nap, Mister Grant?" snapped the math teacher.

"Sorry, Miss Hayden," drone Nathan. "It won't happen again." His response was well practiced.

The teacher grabbed another marker and went back to writing the equations on the board. She finished, prescribed the textbook exercise for the class, and watched as they set to work.

Nathan let his weary gaze scan the room. A table over, Astrid kept her head down, focused on the assigned problems. Behind him, Klein daydreamed while Paul hastily scrawled. Next to him, Jessie doodled in the margins of his grid book. Quiet chatter simmered in the air over his head.

This is nice, he thought. *This is their school life I'm training to protect.*

His eyes turned to his blank page.

If so, then why, oh, bloody Hell, why do I just want to throw in the towel? I just want a decent night's sleep!

On cue, his brain had a vision of his mother and father towering over him. In his hand, he felt a sphere of stitched leather. Behind him, a man in a butterfly mask sneered, "Don't apologise to me, you hypocrite!"

"Nathan Grant!" called out the teacher, shocking the boy out of his waking nightmare. "Could you bring me your homework from last night, please?"

You haven't done it, his brain mused as he flipped his grid book to the previous night's page. He hardly noticed the page's contents as he handed it to the teacher. He was already prepared to receive the routine scolding for not doing homework. But it never came.

"Well, you might not be good in class, but at least you still come through with homework," said the teacher.

Wait, what?

"Thanks, Miss Hayden," said his mouth, though his brain was completely befuddled. He trudged back to his seat, his eyes regaining enough focus to look at his page, which he found full of working for all the problems in the previous night's exercise.

That looks like my handwriting too, he thought amazed. *I might be sleep-learning!*

The same thing happened in chemistry class. The teacher called him forward to see his lab report, and his workbook pages had the experimental method, results, and conclusions ready to present. English, Physics, and even French were the same.

The discovery helped improve his mood. When he went for his training session with Bravo that night, his good mood helped him get a few decent hits on his superior officer, though the spear couldn't even dent that metal jacket. It didn't bother him. He kept a smile on his face all through classes the next day, and the next.

One night, it started raining just half way through their training. Before Bravo was even warmed up – which usually happened long after Nathan had been pummelled – he decided to cancel the session. As the rain intensified on their way home, they realised it was the right call.

They scurried from the car to the safety of the dorm, and yet the rain still soaked them. Nathan bade Bravo good night and made for his room. He couldn't help but curse the weather for stealing his precious training time. Bravo kept telling him he was on easy mode, and yet he could still barely hit the guy. He could not stop thinking he'd fail against the L.X.E., and it put a real damper on his mood.

At least I've got time now to do my homework and remember it, he thought.

With a huff, he went into his dorm room, and found

Klein trying to jam something into his schoolbag.

"What're you doing?" he asked.

Klein looked like a spooked rabbit about to be mauled by a wolf. He dropped the bag in shock and started babbling. Nathan grabbed the bag, finding the notebooks for all his subjects hanging out haphazardly. He eyed his friend as he opened the French book, and found all the drills the teacher had set that day, already written and self-marked in his own handwriting.

"What the Hell?" he yelled. "I know for a fact I ain't done this work yet." He glared at Klein. "How the Hell did this happen?"

With a resigned sigh, Klein dropped his arms and shook his head. "Listen, Nathan, you weren't supposed to know about this."

Suddenly, the last few weeks started making sense.

"What? *You've* been doing my homework for me?" he exclaimed, a tad impressed amid his anger. "I didn't think you were that good!"

Klein raised his hands to silence his friend and whispered, "Just keep it down. I ain't been doing your homework."

"I have," came Paul's voice from behind him. Nathan swivelled to see him and Jessie, looks of concern on their faces.

"We wanted make it look like you were keeping up with school," said Jessie.

Nathan winced with confusion. "Why?"

"Keep the teachers off ya back so ya can focus on your trainin'," said Klein. "That's more important than some bullshit school assignment you'll forget in two years, right?"

"So ... What? I think I'm goin' good in school until I get bitch-slapped in the half-yearlies?[9]" asked Nathan. "Who's dumbass idea was this?"

---

[9]   It is common in Australian schools to have major examinations in the middle of the year.

Jessie and Paul pointed at Klein, who put his hands on his hips and irately muttered, "Cheers, gents! Really!"

"How did you even come up with such a crazy idea, anyway?" yelled Nathan.

"He gets me to do his stuff all the time," said Paul with a grimace. "Pays me too."

Nathan's eyes flashed white with fury, which he directed at Klein. He was so angry he couldn't find the words. All his mind could come up with was, "How much did it cost to royally stuff me up?"

Klein was silent.

"Nathan, calm down," begged Jessie.

"How much, Stevens?" Nathan roared.

"I did it for free!" snapped Paul, raising his voice above a calm octave for the first time since any of them had met him.

At that, Nathan fell dead silent. His anger left him as if a bucket of cold water had snuffed out the flames, leaving him feeling numb with shock. He looked at Paul, then to Jessie, then finally to Klein. They all had looks of concern on their faces, which at first soothed Nathan's nerves, but then irritated him.

"This is *my* fight, guys!" he growled. "You shouldn't be involved in this. You can't be."

"We're not," said Jessie. "You're going out doing God-knows-what. All we're doing is your homework. And when the exams come around, we'll help you cram for it."

Paul adjusted his glasses and, resuming his usual demeanour, said, "I was planning to just switch the papers out."

"What, so you can all get knicked?" asked Nathan.

"So we can support you, like Bravo asked," interjected Klein.

"Why is that so damn important, Klein?" spat Nathan. By now he was so far gone with irritation that he didn't care what he spilled. "Why are you so bloody determined to be my Alfred? What? You want to have the glory of being a superhero's sidekick without having to risk dying?"

Murderous rage flashed across Klein's face, and he punched Nathan squarely on the cheek. He flew backward, into a bewildered Jessie's arms. He and Paul struggled to restrain their friend. Fortunately for them, Nathan's sleep debt, constant spars with Bravo, and Klein's blow dampened his strength.

Klein didn't back down, and he thrust a finger at his friend.

"You didn't knock that ball, you bloody whinge-bag!" he yelled.

Paul and Jessie's brows furrowed with confusion, while Nathan gasped. It was as if Klein had uttered the Devil's name, and the blood drained from his face. Every single nightmare he'd had of that infernal cricket ball screeched in his mind and sapped away his energy.

Klein didn't let up. "You just ducked. I hit it. Me! *I* was the one who almost —" he silenced himself. He let out a huff, in order to blow away as much of his anger as he could. He slumped against the desk, and spoke in as low a whisper as his frazzled nerves would allow. "You got into this mess because of your bloody messiah complex. One you wouldn't've had if I hadn't been a crap batsman."

Nathan rolled his eyes irately. "We were in kindie, man."

Klein burst into laughter. "Seriously! You'll tell me that, but you still act like you're responsible for the friggin' Holocaust? Chouno was right. You *are* a hypocrite."

Jessie raised a hand, "Umm … what's this about a ball?"

Nathan sighed reluctantly and said, "When Klein and I were little, we played with a pro-cricket ball. I bowl, he knocks, I duck, and Ariadne gets six stitches above the hairline." He sniffed away his tears. "She almost died."

"Jesus Christ!" exclaimed Paul as Jessie covered his mouth in horror.

"And now this arsehole won't climb down off his cross

and do something with his life," growled Klein.

"Excuse me," snapped Nathan indignantly. "I *have* been doing something."

"Which you won't tell us about," interjected Jessie, his head spinning from the vision of a dead Ariadne.

Nathan shot them a pleading glance and said, "Guys, seriously. The less you know, the better. Klein only found out by accident."

Jessie started to protest, but Paul silenced him with a pat on the shoulder. He looked fixedly at Nathan.

"Is there something we should be prepared for? As in, an attack?" he asked.

Nathan pondered a moment, though his head ached from weeks of sleepless nights. He eyed Klein, and thought about how he'd had saved him from Papillon. His mind went to Bravo, who had been preparing him for battle with the L.X.E., and to Astrid, who was ready to fight by his side. He thought about the battles he'd already fought, against Chouno and his homunculi, and even against Janjira. He thought about Ariadne, and the fact that he'd saved her with his Sunlight's Heart.

As long as the Starlight Lancer is here, they'll definitely be all right, he thought.

He returned Paul's glance and said, "So long as I'm here, you'll have nothing to worry about."

The boys grinned. Paul straightened and said, "Well then, I'll consider that payment for continuing to forge your homework."

Nathan fumed, his brain screaming at him to refuse. He turned to Klein, who snapped, "Stop tryin' to do stuff on ya own."

Nathan's brow furrowed irately. Strangely, the voice telling him to refuse started to sound a lot like Astrid, and he recalled his fellow warrior, prone on a field of grass with a parasite burrowing through her body. Back then, he'd ignored her orders to leave, and pushed his help on her.

I guess I know how she feels now, he thought. *Then again, if I hadn't, she'd not be here, makin' friends with everyone. Hell! I'd probably not be here either.*

"Fine," he said with a sigh. He pointed straight at Paul. "But! I don't wanna suddenly get top marks in everything. Last thing I want is my parents runnin' around sayin' I got dux[10]. Got it?"

* * *

As the boys left Nathan's room, they didn't notice the shadowy figure down the hall, eavesdropping on their conversation. Her nose scar twitched, her brow knitted with discomfort.

Astrid mused, *Is this why I found him so interesting? The support system?*

She touched the Kakugane in her pocket.

Maybe ... that's what I should be fighting for.

---

[10]   The top academic achiever in a school.

7 | Diversion

Bravo pulled into the grain terminal, and engaged the park brake. He let out a huff, which condensed as steam in the cold air. He murmured sternly, "Did you tell them anything more?"

Nathan shook his head. He was still sore from a restless night's sleep and a nerve-racking day in which he knowingly offered forged homework to his teachers. He ran his hands through his hair and sighed.

"I didn't ask them to do this, I swear," he said.

"That's fine, I believe you," said Bravo. "But make sure no one else finds out, otherwise the school will get involved. That's the last thing we need at the moment." His furrowed brow relaxed and he patted Nathan's shoulder. "But all things considered, that's one good bunch of mates you got there," he said with a grin. "Not many Alchemic Warriors have that under their belt when they start."

"I think I know why," mumbled Nathan as he blocked out images of homunculi attacking his friends and sister.

As if reading his mind, Bravo said, "Make that your power, Nathan. Fight to keep those images as they are now."

"Terrifying?" asked Nathan.

"Imagination," corrected Bravo. That made Nathan chuckle. He pondered the idea a little longer, and his mind went back to one of the lessons Astrid had given him a long time ago. He'd activated his spear without a verbal command simply by the thought of his sister being eaten.

Fighting to avoid something is okay, I guess, he concluded, though a part of him found the idea unsatisfying.

Without another word, they exited the car and walked into the middle of the field. The air still reeked of an oil and salt cocktail, but Nathan hardly noticed it as he faced Bravo.

The older man activated his Arms Alchemy, cloaking him in that impenetrable silver armour. He assumed a fighting stance and bellowed, "Ready, Nathan?"

Something jumped out at Nathan about Bravo's Silver Skin, which distracted him momentarily from the training. Being honest with himself, the guy reminded him a little of *Ironman.* That thought sent his mind a few weeks back: he was seated on his bed, watching a bootleg of *Doctor Strange.* He remembered the actor's poses as he performed his time-screwing magic spells, which had given him an idea he had theretofore forgotten.

He breathed deeply, and leaned forward like a runner at the start-line. With his hands, he made a triangle in front of his chest, and focused his mind.

Astrid's voice echoed in his mind, *It's your soul! It will respond to your will!*

Well, then this should work, he thought. Then he began an internal chant: *My heart is a bullet!*

His internal voice grew louder and louder, until it hit a zenith and he roared, "Arms Alchemy!" His chest flashed like a solar flare, and his lance materialised from within the bright inferno. It shot outward, just like a bullet. Nathan caught the handle just in time to join it on its ballistic quest for Bravo's chest. In the next instant, Nathan flew face-first into the asphalt, which crumbled under the force of the impact. He spat out a mouthful of granite and dust, and coughed and spluttered in sheer surprise.

Bravo was even more surprised at the break in the

glove of his Silver Skin, which healed itself not before he saw the smallest cut on the skin of his palm. His high-standing collar hid his grin of admiration as he stared back at the boy.

"That was amazing, Grant," he exclaimed. "How did you come up with that idea?"

Nathan shrugged, "I remembered Astrid telling me that the spear is my soul and it'll do what I want it to. And to be honest, I just thought it'd be cool if I could shoot the spear out like a gun."

"It's definitely cool, mate," Bravo chuckled. "But make sure you catch it before it gets away. The way you are, if that spear is destroyed, you'd kark it."

"Got it!" said Nathan. He assumed a battle-ready stance.

"Hang on a tick," said Bravo, his hand raised. "I've been wanting to mention something to you. Notice how you're holding the spear right now? You've got it gripped pretty tightly."

Nathan glanced at his white knuckles clamped around the lance's handle. "I suppose you're right. I guess it helps me keep focused, otherwise I'd just swing it around and end up dropping it."

"It actually makes it hard for you to use the weapon," said Bravo. "Your fighting ends up being rigid and easy to read."

"Well, I've got to make sure I hold onto my weapon, right?" asked Nathan sardonically.

Bravo gave a confused scoff. "Mate, did you forget what you just said? That spear is your soul, and it'll do what you want it to. So, if you want it to stay in your hands, it will." Nathan raised an eyebrow as his gaze darted between Bravo and the spear. Bravo said, "Try focusing on keeping the spear in your hand, and then open your hand."

Nathan held the spear out and opened his hand. Sure enough, the spear clanged to the ground. At Bravo's instruction, he tried again, and again. Frustration started to build.

Stop! Don't get pissed when you know you can do it.

He held the lance out again.

You are my soul. Respond to my will!

He opened his fingers, and the shaft of the lance remained in place. It was as if his hands were magnetic. He glanced at Bravo with wide, excited eyes. The lance started to drop as his lost his focus, and he clumsily caught it. Bravo encouraged him to try again, and he managed to keep it in his hands even longer.

"Right, now try controlling its movement," said Bravo. "While the lance is in contact with your body, you can move it as if it were *part* of your body."

Nathan looked back at the lance, just barely in contact with his palm. His focus kept it in place, and he tried to direct it to rotate in his palm. At first, it only twitched like a broken compass unsure of the direction of north. He took another breath and tried again. Slowly, but surely, the spear started to gyrate. He angled his palm away from his body as the spear made a full circle under his mental command. He gasped with amazement as it continued to spin, until he closed his hand and held it tightly.

"Good on ya, Starlight Lancer!" exclaimed Bravo, offering his fist for Nathan to bump. He slapped the delighted boy on the back and said, "You'll be an Alchemic Warrior yet!"

"You'll be dead yet!" screeched a boisterous voice.

The burly creature appeared with such suddenness, with sharp claws vectoring for Nathan's throat. A cloud of metal plates hardened into a shield between him and the beast. Nathan looked to Bravo, his hand outstretched and the sleeve of his Silver Skin gone. With a growl, Bravo swiped his hand and threw the creature back before summoning the shield back into his jacket.

The green-skinned man hit the ground with a thud, his sheer weight leaving footprints in the concrete beneath him. His bulging blood vessels pulsated with frustration.

His eyes were dull red orbs deeply inset in a skull seemingly made of jagged rock, and they shot a death glare at the silver-clad man. His leathery skin made crinkling noises as he clenched his fists.

Nathan stood bewildered, in awe of the monstrosity. It didn't take long before he noticed the glyph on the creature's forehead. It was the same on Janjira's neck.

"That's the glyph of the L.X.E.," he exclaimed.

"Got that right," bellowed another voice, this one far more strident. Behind them stood a lanky, muscular being with a toothy grin that looked much too big for his face. His glyph was on his chest.

A third appeared. This one was clad in a long black leather coat with a red pentagram embossed into it. Two long horns protruded from his forehead and snaked a helical path down the back of his head, and they quivered when he grinned. His glyph sat right on his Adam's Apple, and it jumped up and down as he laughed.

"Yajuj, Majuj, do you not remember the plan?" he grumbled as if upset, though it was clear he was enjoying the moment a lot more than was appropriate.

"Sneak up on 'em, right?" exclaimed the burly one.

"Yeah, at the same time, you dumbass Yajuj!" exclaimed the other. "Ya bugger'd it up for us!"

Nathan whispered, "Bravo, these guy's're homunculi, aren't they?"

"Yep," said Bravo. Nathan glanced upward, expecting to see the same horror that Janjira instilled. Instead, he saw amusement.

Bravo pointed at the burly monster and said, "So, you're Yajuj." To the lanky one, he said, "You must be Majuj." Then he turned to the horned leather-man and, with a chuckle, he added, "Well then, Clarence, what're you? Satan?"

The leather-man's brow furrowed slightly, but his horns gave away his distress. He growled, "I am Shaitan! And I come to carry out the will of Doctor Butterfly!"

Nathan was so shocked at Bravo's cockiness that he almost choked on his words as he said, "You know these guys too?"

"Know 'em? Me mates and me used to laugh about these idiots," exclaimed Bravo. He pointed at Shaitan. "This guy's real name is Clarence, who *was* a low-end bank robber. That was until they put a price on his capture, and he turned himself in hoping he'd get the reward. I guess he finally got the money, considering those fake horns." Nathan started to chuckle. Bravo moved onto Majuj, "This idiot's real name is Percy, and he got busted tryin' to knock over an ATM at gun point. Only his gun was his freakin' finger in his pocket!"

"Are you serious?" exclaimed Nathan. He pointed at Yajuj. "What about him?"

"This shithead," said Bravo, barely able to stifle his laughter. "Successfully robbed a petrol station, but he didn't like his mug-shot on the news, so he tweeted a better picture to the cops, and they tracked his mobile."

"Are you kidding?" Nathan cried, tears of merriment trickling from his eyes.

"Wanna know what his name is?" asked Bravo. "Meredith!"

They both fell into a paroxysm of laughter. Yajuj's blood pressure went sky high, and steam started billowing from his ears. Majuj's teeth started to crack as he clenched his jaw with fury. Shaitan's horns wiggled about his head. He finally snapped, "Kill them!"

They charged, and butt heads as Nathan and Bravo leapt out of the way and landed outside their circle. The warriors continued to chuckle at their enemies.

"So, how much did you have to beg the L.X.E. to take you on?" asked Bravo.

"Not very extraordinary, are they?" intoned Nathan.

"Ah, on the contrary, Starlight Lancer," said Bravo. "They are indeed *extra ordinary.*"

This just made the beasts madder. They exchanged

glances and nodded, and then began to roar. Their bodies bulged and started to grow in height, until they were at least a foot taller than before. Nathan was slightly fazed by their sudden growth spurt, but he continued to giggle at their backstories.

Bravo turned to him and said, "You feel confident to take them on?"

"Sure," said Nathan.

"We'll need to interrogate 'em, so no killing," said Bravo.

"Got it, Captain," said Nathan. "It'll be a fun training session, eh?"

"Training?" exclaimed Shaitan, his voice deeper and more beastly. "You're fighting the Devil himself!"

"In the awesome words of Batman, you're not the Devil," said Nathan with a grin. He stepped forward, twirled his spear, and yelled, "You're Clarence!"

The creatures charged him. Nathan twirled his spear and swatted Yajuj aside with the handle. He then leapt upward, using the dazed stocky creature as a leg-up, and brought the face of his spear's blade down on Shaitan's head. The moulded plastic crumpled under the force of his blow, and sent Shaitan tumbling right into range of Bravo's fist.

Bravo delivered a swift blow on Shaitan's downturned head, and sent him face-first into the asphalt. He then dodged Majuj's swipes and punches. Concern took hold when he noticed the man's blows coming a little too close to their mark for his comfort.

Oh, right, Percy had taken karate, he thought disinterestedly.

He blocked the man's blows with one hand, and when the right moment came, he caught Majuj's right wrist and wrenched it aside. Majuj instinctively threw a punch with his left, which Bravo caught. He then yanked the much taller creature down with all his might, and pushed his head upwards into Majuj's face. Every tooth in the homunculus' mouth flowed out like wet sand as he toppled to the ground.

Bravo glanced over and saw Nathan battling with Yajuj. His eyes widened with surprise and pride as Nathan deftly swatted away the homunculus' blows with a twirl of his spear. Yajuj came with his left, which Nathan deflected into the ground. He used his angular momentum to come about with the spear and slash at Yajuj's face. The creature howled as grey muck flowed from a gash down his cheek, and Nathan yelled with excitement.

Probably shouldn't've done that, he thought as Yajuj's right fist hit him squarely in the face. He flew backwards, tumbling head over heels on the concrete. When he came to a stop, he looked up and saw the burly homunculus coming at him. He scrambled to his feet, but felt dizzy and he fell on his knees.

Before Yajuj could land the blow he had lined up, a pair of silver-clad legs wrapped around his neck and jerked him to the ground. Bravo delivered a swift punch to the creature's scalp, knocking it out.

A savage howl reached Bravo's ears. He looked up and saw Shaitan, galloping toward him like an enraged bull – albeit with plastic horns. Bravo wasted no time. He leapt into the air, swivelled, swiped his left foot against Shaitan's face, pressed his right knee against the homunculus' neck, and drove his head into the ground.

The homunculus hit the asphalt with a crash that echoed through the site. Bravo stepped back to admire his work: Shaitan's head wedged in a crater, his body twitching like a fish a hair's breadth from the pearly gates. Each of Shaitan's spasms provoked another chortle from the silver-clad man, who eyed Yajuj and Majuj, still unconscious metres away.

Nathan collected himself and moved toward Bravo, his lance used like a crutch. Sweaty and sore, he felt far less jovial than the man next to him, who hadn't even broken a sweat. He said, "I guess my training still has a ways to go before I'm out of easy mode."

"What're ya talkin' about, Grant?" exclaimed Bravo. "You did great!"

"Doesn't feel like it," droned the boy. "They don't even have Kakugane on them, and that one still sloshed me."

Bravo patted him on the back, "Trust me, they almost had me a few times. You did bravo!"

Nathan managed a chuckle. "Thanks." His mind moved to an earlier point. "By the way, why don't they have Kakugane? Are they animal or plant types?"

Bravo kneeled down and yanked Shaitan's head out of the crater. He quickly glanced over the homunculus' features, before blurting, "Nah, these're humanoid ones. But you're right, it's a dumbass move to come after us unarmed."

"You'd think they wouldn't do that," intoned Nathan as he deactivated his lance. "If the L.X.E. really wanted to make a move, they'd come with weapons, I'd think."

Bravo snorted, "Yep. In fact, they've only pulled this kind of stunt is …" He was silent a moment. Nathan couldn't see his face, and when the silence became awkward, he paced around so the man's expression was in view. His face was ashen, as if he'd just been shown the deepest part of the infinite inferno.

Before Nathan could ask what his problem was, Bravo was in motion.

"The car, Grant! Now!" he roared, sprinting toward where they'd parked.

Nathan lingered, his gaze darting toward their motionless victims.

"What about interrogating them?" he exclaimed.

Bravo was already starting the car as he yelled, "No time! Move!"

Nathan had to leap through the driver-side window as Bravo swerved the car toward the exit.

"What the Hell, Bravo?" exclaimed the bewildered boy. "What's your problem?"

"The dormitories!" snapped Bravo, his face a waterfall of cold sweat. "The L.X.E. are at the dormitories!"

8 | The Valkyrie Awakens

Ariadne edged her shaking hand toward the deck of cards. To the side lay the discard pile, topped with multiple 'Skips' and 'Attacks,' interlaced with the ghastly red 'Nope' cards. To her left sat her friend Nina, glaring almost malevolently at the deck for which she nervously reached.

Please not a kitten! Please not a kitten! Please not a kitten!

She snatched a card away.

"Whew!" she cried as beads of cold sweat finally dropped from her forehead.

"So, what did you get?" asked Nina as she brushed her blonde hair out of her face.

"Not supposed to tell, right?" retorted Ariadne. She tried not to look dejectedly at the face card she'd picked up.

Nina played a 'See-the-future' and snickered at the top three cards. She took the top card confidently. Next was Astrid, and she eyed Nina with pursed lips. The younger girl nonchalantly diverted her eyes and hummed an innocent tune. Astrid eyed the green 'Defuse' card in her hand – the only one left in the game – and glanced at the dwindling pile.

Still a low chance, she thought. *Risk it!*

She grabbed a card and looked at it.

"Merde!" she snapped, dropping the newly-drawn

'Exploding Kitten' card. She dropped her 'Defuse' on the discard pile and put the offending card at the bottom of the deck. "That way it's as far away as possible!" she exclaimed.

Shu's eyes gleamed evilly, and she played a 'Shuffle' card. Astrid sighed with dismay as the deck was shuffled in the Chinese girl's deft hands. With a grin, Shu drew a card from the newly-shuffled deck, and screamed, "Oh, come on!" She showed the 'Exploding Kitten' card – the very same Astrid had just drawn!

The table erupted into laughter as Shu, red-faced with amusement and frustration, dropped her hand on the discard pile.

"I bloody hate this game!" she cried with a grin.

"At least it's not Cards Against Humanity," said Astrid.

"Hey, that game's awesome," said Nina with a gleam in her eyes.

Astrid shot her a horrified glance. "Seriously? It's gross!"

"That's what makes it awesome," insisted Nina.

"Nathan and his friends play it all the time," said Ariadne dejectedly. "They never let me play."

"Maybe because it's not a game for nice ladies, Ariadne," said Astrid.

"That's right," said Shu. "Take it from your seniors. You shouldn't get involved with dirty games."

Nina shot evils at the other girls and said, "Are you gonna keep calling me dirty, or are you gonna play?"

Though she was out of the nerve-racking game, Shu remained to watch the outcome. Ariadne got lucky with the next few draws, as did Nina. With no more 'Defuse' cards and the deck dwindling, the table got even tenser. Astrid had to fight hard to keep the two Kakugane in her pocket from spontaneously activating.

She silently marvelled, *Why do I even play this game?*

With no usable action cards in her hand, she used her face cards to engage in a round of favours, none of which came to fruition. All options gone, she took a card from the deck.

"Enculer!" she snapped, and dropped the 'Exploding Kitten' and her cards on the discard pile. Ariadne and Nina chuckled with excitement as they, the remaining players, locked eyes.

A flurry of invisible and visible attacks flew between the combatants in the epic battle to avoid the remaining 'Exploding Kitten,' which would have been exciting had the two runner-ups bothered to watch for more than ten seconds. But there was something Shu found a tad more interesting than a game she just lost.

"Astrid, are you French?" she asked.

The dark-haired girl shot her a confused glance. "No. I *am* fluent in French, though. Why?"

"You were using French words during the game," said Shu. "I'm pretty sure *merde* means *crap*. But what about *on-cool-ay?*"

Astrid snickered at the girl's poor French pronunciation. It was only a slight giggle, overshadowed by the realisation that she'd switched languages mid-game. She coughed gauchely and said, "The school I used to be at, a while ago, I'd play this game with a friend all the time. She was French. So, she rubbed off on me, I guess."

"Oh really?" asked Shu, her interest even more piqued. "What school was it?"

Astrid started to panic: *Oh, crap! I didn't think of this. Newton's Apple is all the way up in Queensland! How would I explain meeting Nathan?*

Amazingly, she kept control of her face and managed to fake a vague expression. "Oooh, I can't remember. Besides the games, it was a pretty boring school."

Shu giggled, "You must have a really short-term memory."

Astrid made a silly expression, which only made Shu's laughter more infectious.

"BOOM!" shouted Ariadne, shocking the other girls at

the table. Nina's eyes glazed over with dismay at the card in her hand, a cat snuggled up to a stick of dynamite, glaring back at her.

"And Ariadne is the winner!" exclaimed Shu.

Astrid helped to clear the scattered cards from the table. All the while, she could barely conceal the pensive look on her face. Not long into the post-game conversation, she realised she wasn't listening, and dismissed herself. She made her way back to her dorm room. On her desk lay an unfinished geography assignment. She sat down, and made short work of it. When she was finished, it was close to eleven at night. By then, most boarders were heading to their bedrooms.

Astrid took the two Kakugane from her pocket, and eyed the surface of the more weathered of the pair. She pulled Bravo's metal case from under her bed and stashed the worn-out talisman. Then she fell back onto the bed, and gazed at Kakugane fourty-four – the one that had long been her companion.

"Sorry to make you bunk," she said, as if the talisman could hear her words. She realised she was talking to an inanimate tool, and chuckled. "We've been together so long, but we haven't even talked, have we?" Her mind turned toward the past, which she purposely veiled in shadow. The idea of even reliving those memories scared her, and she turned her mind to her earlier game with the girls. It reminded her of her time as Marie Dubois – an assignment she'd found herself enjoying more than she wanted.

Not much different from this assignment, she thought.

Up at seven-thirty, get dressed, breakfast, and then off to school. Not that she needed school – if she so wanted, she could ace every exam in half the time allotted. But the routine was nice, and it was almost *relieving* to socialise about things that, in the world of monsters, magic, and battle, seemed mediocre at best.

When on the battlefield, facing off against a hungry

beast with triple your strength at least, one has far more things to be concerned with than the contents of the next vampire romance novel or which male pop-star is the most desirable to date.

That she could enjoy these things, despite her witnessing horrors from which these kids would run screaming, gave her the sweetest surprise. As she lay there, gazing at the source of her power, she pondered whether meeting Nathan was the best thing that could have happened to her.

"Were it that I hadn't met you," she murmured to the Kakugane. Her thought train veered into that dark realm again. Before she could wrest it back, a piercing screech hit her ears. She shot up, bewildered at the sensation that sought to weasel its way into her consciousness like a weed. She drew a deep breath, and let it flow out her nose, taking her anxiety with it.

What is this sensation? Isolate it, and find it, she commanded herself.

In the void of her subconscious, she saw the manifold tendrils that lunged from the infinite horizon toward her. She recognised them instantly.

A resonance link!

She opened Bravo's case and pocketed the Kakugane fifty-two. She then flew out of bed and burst into the corridor. The green exit sign at the end of the hall sparsely illuminated the hallway. It made for a foreboding atmosphere. She could still hear the high-pitched whirr permeating the walls of the dormitory.

Doors creaked open, and from the darkness beyond crept pyjama-clad boarders. Astrid backed away as the students edged toward her, as if sleepwalking.

The nearest student – a girl in a nightie and bonnet combo – stepped into the light from Astrid's room. Her mouth was twisted into a complacent grin, above which her up-turned nostrils flared like those of a bull ready to charge. Two white, sunken orbs suddenly fixated upon

Astrid. The girl's jaw dislocated, revealing a black maw that unleashed a terrible roar: "Gimme!"

The girl lunged, knocking Astrid onto her back. Panicked, she threw the girl off her and leapt to her feet. She met a wall of yet more girls dressed for bed, with the most hellish expressions smeared across their faces. In unison, they murmured a word that made Astrid choke: "Kakugane!"

They leapt for her at the same time. She managed to divert a few of the taller ones and push the smaller ones to the ground, but there were too many of them. They piled on top of her, murmuring and wailing, "Gimme Kakugane!"

A resonance link carried on sound waves, she thought amid her mounting panic. She felt a dozen hands worm their way through her clothes, seeking out the two talismans in her pocket.

She felt one of the Kakugane loosen itself from her pocket, and a surge of determination filled her. She found her feet and pushed upwards against the weight of the students, who tumbled off her with disinterested sighs. She bounded over them, both Kakugane in hand, and sprinted down the hall. When she came upon the building atrium, she found yet more students, mostly male, lumbering toward her in a daze. They still murmured the same chant as the girls.

A pair of broad arms grabbed her from behind and their owner gurgled, "Kakugane!" Astrid threw her head back into the zombie's face, loosening his grip. She turned and pushed the boy away, realising she'd just broken Jessie's nose. A twinge of guilt gripped her, and distracted her from the advance of Klein. When she saw his face, the guilt vanished and she kneed him in the stomach.

"Gimme a piggyback!" screeched a small creature behind her. Ariadne leapt onto her shoulders and locked her arms around her neck. Astrid felt pressure against her windpipe as the younger girl tightened her neck choke. She lost her balance as Ariadne thrashed about screeching, "Triddy! Gimme present! Gimme big sister present! Gimme Kakugane! Kakugane mine!"

Astrid hit the floor, and the students piled on top of her. A hand clamped over her nose and mouth, while dozens more clambered across her body. A mixture of violation and dread filled her mind. It pushed her, without her realising it, toward the dark recesses of her memory.

There, in that long dark corridor, silent save for the harrowing dripping of water, the little girl happened upon another classmate. He trembled and panted, with his back turned from her. The green uniform was just as soiled as her own, as far as she could see. She neared his huddled form, and reached out to touch his shoulder.

No! Stay back!

A roar burst from Astrid's mouth, and the students fell from her in a flash of blue light. When the tumult cleared, there she stood, her quartet of blades honed to deadly edge, bloodlust radiating from her sunken eyes. Her ears pricked like a wild hunter, seeking out the source of the maddening sound. When she found it, she bounded over the students toward the boys' side of the dormitory.

As she sprinted toward the source of the noise, her eyes started to water. The noise grew in volume, and she knew she was getting close. The threads of her consciousness weaved past the encroaching tentacles with quickened, frantic pace, until they set upon their source. Her eyes flew open, and she saw a silhouette of a tall man. In his hand, he held a Parisian Foil, which wobbled menacingly to the frequency of the sound. The resonance link faltered as the man realised too late he'd been discovered.

With a screech, Astrid swatted aside his foil and slashed with her blades. The man gasped as the gashes in his body spewed black blood, revealing instantly his identity. Furiously, Astrid pressed her attack, swiping and slashing at the homunculus, who only barely managed to parry her blows. Astrid brought her four blades down, blind with anger and fear. The homunculus blocked the blows, and delivered a kick that sent her flying back down the hall. She recovered, wincing at the pain, and glared back at her retreating enemy.

Bloody coward!

She sprinted after him, her blades pointed forward to split the air before her. The man looked back to see the warrior gaining on him. He turned his gaze ahead, and saw something that made Astrid's heart stop in dread: Paul, emerging from his room, noise-cancelling headphones in hand.

Two large claws gripped his shoulders and the homunculus beared its teeth in anticipation of a much-needed meal.

The memory came to her again.

The little girl in the hall touched the boy, who revealed his face. Blood dripped from incisors that could cleave diamond, crowning a circular maw from which a hundred hungry hands lunged at her.

Astrid lost it. Her mind went blank with rage. Her hind blades launched her forward, while her fore blades embedded themselves in the homunculus' side. Straight through the window they flew, into the nearby greenery beyond.

Astrid tumbled through a criss-cross thicket of branches, scraping her arms and knocking her head, before she finally hit the ground. She gripped a handful of dirt and fallen leaves, as if to find an anchor amid a spinning world. A warm liquid trickled down her face, burning against the stark coldness of the midnight air. She finally opened her eyes and looked in the direction of the moaning mass clinging to a nearby tree for support.

The homunculus tossed his long blonde hair out of his face, revealing a mug of almost canine appearance. His facial muscles tensed and quivered as the two stab wounds in his torso, filled with writhing metallic tentacles, sealed beneath his torn sous-plastron. His slitted nostrils flared as he drew in the scent of her blood, hot in the air between them.

"*Incroyable!*[11]" he exclaimed with a thick French accent. "I long suspected the Regiment payed little concern to the art of *Résonance D'âme.*[12]"

Astrid managed to shoot a fearsome glare at her opponent, despite the blurriness of her vision. She snapped, "*Va te faire foutre!*[13]"

The man chuckled with amazement. "I've not had reason to practice my mother tongue since before my second birth." With a flourish of his foil, he switched to French. "My name is François Desbordes. And I must thank you. Not only did you pirate my resonance link – something of which my peers seemed incapable – but you managed to injure me. You offer true contest, *and* the chance to speak French again. My sincerest gratitude, madamoiselle."

His condescending bow fanned Astrid's fury, and she pushed herself to her feet. She staggered into a battle ready pose, her blades at the ready like a spider's forelimbs ready to strike.

Desbordes cocked his head. "You mean to fight? You're losing blood too fast, and you'll just tense up your meat before you die. Let's just proceed to the part where I eat you and take back Janjira's Kakugane?"

"I should say the same," spat Astrid. "Let's skip to the part where you tell me everything about the L.X.E., then I put my blades through your head!"

She sped forward, her slashes faster than a casual observer would see. The homunculus' ears and hairs tingled with knowledge of her incoming blows, and he diverted them with calmness and expert skill. He sensed her downward blows on his shoulders, and parried them

---

[11]　French: "Incredible!"
[12]　French: "Soul Resonance"
[13]　French: "Kiss my arse!"

with his foil. The blade started to vibrate with the impact, and the sound ripped the focus from Astrid's mind. She beheld the vision of the monster in the school, in ravenous pursuit of the crying little girl.

Get out of my head!

She pulled her mind back to the battle too late to dodge Desbordes' thrusts, striking her shoulders, chest, and stomach. She faltered backwards, her shirt reddening with her blood.

"*Le fou,*[14]" he murmured in French. "Did you forget the effect of my blade's singing?"

Dazed, Astrid eyed the blade glimmering in the starlight. Pain bit at her every nerve and pushed her mind into the realms of panic.

I can't touch that blade, or else it'll initiate the link again, she thought. *What do I do? I'm bleeding, tired, and concussed. I can't think straight, dammit!*

"Hand over the Kakugane, and I'll make it quick," said Desbordes, his voice drawing the bile to Astrid's throat.

Eat me? Then eat the students … Murderer … Cannibal … Beast! Dined on the mother, then chase the chick. Chick … chick … run… No! Fight!

"Fight!" Astrid screamed. Her blades spun an arc about Desbordes' feet, which he jumped to avoid. Astrid planted the blades into the ground and soared after him. She flipped in mid-air, her blood spraying across his eyes and blinding him to the kick she delivered to his face. He flew into the ground, and barely recovered in time to dodge her incoming attack. Panic started to creep up on him as she pressed her assault, aiming for wherever his blade was not, so all he could do was dodge. She brought down all four blades with a ferocious scream, which lacked the beastliness of her earlier assault. Desbordes chuckled as he flipped out of the way and then catapulted himself from a tree, his foil making the nose of a missile aimed at her

---

[14] French: "You fool!"

heart.

The blow did not find its mark. A deft flick of Astrid's finger in the last moment saw it, along with the arm that held it, gripped tightly under her armpit.

"*Renouvellement, connard!*[15]" she growled.

A blade deprived him of his wielding arm, and another blade took out his legs. Desbordes fell to the ground into a puddle of his own black blood. Astrid swivelled and kicked the foil away. It tumbled against a tree and reverted to its Kakugane form. Then Astrid turned to the thing writhing on the ground. With his remaining arm, Desbordes reached for his missing arm and legs, in the hopes of reattaching them. Astrid skewered them on her blades, and dangled them over his head. Tears started to form as he feebly grasped for them.

"Tell me where the L.X.E. is," she growled.

"Or what?" cried Desbordes. "You're an Alchemic Warrior. As if you'd return my limbs and let me run away, lest I attack you again."

"You're right," said Astrid. In the blink of an eye, her fore blades sliced up the arm into a pile of mulch that vanished before the mortified homunculus' eyes. "Every question you don't answer, I demolish another limb, you slime mould."

Desbordes sobbed, "Even if you gave me my legs, if I told you, Doctor Butterfly would kill me anyway. I'm already dead!"

"Right again," said Astrid. The legs promptly liquefied, to the resigned sighs of their former owner. Her blades slashed open his fencing jacket, revealing the helix tattoo in the midpoint of his sternum. The blades zoned in on the weak point.

"Go ahead," snapped Desbordes. "Finish me! I failed my mission, so finish me!"

"Tell me where Doctor Butterfly and Victor are, and

---

[15] French: "Renewal, arsehole!" Renewal is a fencing term for a strike following a parry.

I'll make it quick," Astrid growled in a low voice. Desbordes tightened his lips. Astrid gave an acquiescent hum before thrusting the blades into his stomach, far from the tattoo. The homunculus screeched in agony as Astrid repeated her interrogatory. He gave no reply except cries of pain. So, she went lower, and trisected his groin with both blades. That only made him scream with a higher pitch.

"Stop it!" he wailed over and over. "Stop it, sil vous plait!"

With a blank face, Astrid lifted her blades free of the black puddle between his stump legs, and murmured, "L.X.E. base location ... Now!"

"Just get it over with!" he cried.

Astrid eyed the healing mechanical flesh between his legs, and when the things down there had sufficiently reformed, she stabbed them again. Another moan flew from Desbordes' lips, and he thrashed to relieve the agony. Astrid pinned him down by the shoulders with her other blades, and repeatedly stabbed him in that place where he hurt the most. Soon, she stopped waiting for his response before stabbing him, and not long after that, she didn't even bother asking him. Her sunken eyes were blank with a dark hue, motivated by ongoing reprisals of horrible intrusive memories. Any scraps of logic remaining noted the volume with which her victim cried, and she gagged him with a nearby branch before resuming her torture.

Something appeared outside her vision. The being jammed its hand into Desbordes' chest, mercifully ending him. Astrid flew backwards in a daze, quickly broken by the fake Italian accent that proclaimed, "Now here is a riddle, So guess if you can, Sing the bells of Notre Dame, Who is the monster and who is the man?"

Astrid glared at the creature that interrupted her, and her jaw dropped in amazement of the provocatively clad Japanese man with the butterfly mask.

"Papillon!" she cried, her blades quaking with every

syllable.

"Tsk, tsk, tsk! Pa-pi-yon! And put more love into it!" replied the fiend with a flourish.

"How?" was all Astrid could say. "Nathan killed you."

"Pah! Do not underestimate a *choujin*," exclaimed Papillion jovially. "A little death can be good for the health, especially with an ancestor looking to test a new contraption."

Astrid could hardly think straight amid her rage and terror, and she bellowed, "I'll finish the job then!" She sprinted forward, but tripped on an earth-breaking root and fell flat on her face. Her blood loss and fatigue overwhelmed her. She found herself barely able to stand.

Papillon sauntered around her to the tree nearby, and took Desbordes' Kakugane. He gazed at it, as if admiring his perfect reflection in its metal. He then turned to Astrid and said, "Tell Nathan, I'll see him soon."

"The Hell you will!" she growled, though it came out in a hoarse whimper as she stumbled toward the homunculus. But her blades would not respond to her will and she tripped again. She fumed as Papillon leapt into the air and out of sight.

There she stood, bleeding, her mind empty, and her emotions frazzled. Her subconscious stood with one foot planted firmly in her forbidden zone, and it would not budge, even as she punched the ground and screamed.

Whether it was a minute later, or hours later, the sound of footsteps reached Astrid's barely attentive ears. She looked up from her Kakugane, pressed against her healing wounds, and saw Nathan. His eyes were full of panic. He knelt down before her and looked her over. He said something, but she didn't hear anything. He had a bashful glimmer in his eyes before he threw his jacket over her shoulders and helped her to her feet. He kept on talking, but all she heard were dull, unintelligible murmurs barely making it past the throbbing of her heartbeat.

She gazed to her shoulder, where Nathan gripped it

warmly to support her. It reminded her of the times he'd carried her, thanks to the cursed homunculus embryo the scar of which she still bore. That scar she bore, thanks to the boy that now carried her.

The Commander was right, she realised. *I was too concerned with him, more than the mission. Because I liked him. And because of that, I dragged him into this craziness. And because I like him, and I want was he has, I almost destroyed what he has … What I'd lost.*

With a twitch, Astrid shook herself free of Nathan's embrace. She hardly took note of his concerned stammers as she growled, "I can walk on my own." And she marched through the woods back to the dormitory.

I should thank you, Monsieur Desbordes, she thought as if the man could hear her from the depths of Hell in which he surely sizzled. *I've avoided my past too long. But now that you'd dredged it up, I've remembered why I fight. Merci beaucoup, fils de pute[16]. The Spartan Valkyrie is back. And now …*

Her brow tightened.

I'll exterminate you all. Every last one of you!

---

[16] French: "Thanks a lot, son of a bitch."

9 | Whatever It Takes

Astrid wasn't the only one in a bad mood the morning after the L.X.E. attack on the dormitories. Bravo had had his hands full with passing the event off as a gas leak causing sleepwalking, without any help, it seemed, from his superiors. And, of course, he had to fend off the Warrawul School Headmaster, who questioned his ability to adequately look after the boarders, when he was too busy giving 'special training' to one of the students.

School had been out for the day thanks to the attack. The students hadn't any memory of what had truly occurred the previous night, which did make the bothersome chore less of a headache. But, at the same time, they were mostly too tired to keep focused for class. They spent most of the day dozing, helping their friends tidy up their dishevelled rooms, or tape canvas over the window somebody must have broken the previous night.

Astrid and Nathan were part of that latter group. When they finished the job, it was late afternoon. Police had taken statements and left. The fire crews had searched for the alleged gas leak, to obviously no avail. The building was starting to settle down, and soon the boarders were joking about the great sleepwalking epidemic of Warrawul! Stories and accounts grew more fantastic as the discussion went on, until some were suggesting that the Cardcaptor had cast one of her powerful spells on the building.

"Cardcaptor?" asked Astrid obliviously. Nathan eyed his friend and noted how different she appeared from the previous night. What had been a manic woman with vengeful gleams in her eyes was now chipper, chatting with his sister and friends.

Don't forget the first time she met them, he inwardly chided.

Nina clapped her hands together with a grin. "You don't know about Cardcaptor Sakura?" Astrid shrugged obliviously. Ariadne whipped out her phone, navigated through her YouTube feed, and showed her a video of a Japanese girl, a bit younger than Nathan, waving a pink wand and wielding magical creatures to defeat an evildoer.

"Is this some kind of new show?" asked Astrid, a disbelieving smile on her face.

"This girl and her best friend do these videos all on their own," said Nina. "Even little Kero, Sakura does the voice of! It's amazing!"

"God, I wish I could do those kinds of things," sighed Ariadne.

Astrid suddenly grabbed the phone and looked closer at the Chinese boy on the screen.

"What's the matter?" asked Nathan as he eyed the sword-wielding magician in the video. He let out an impressed whistle as the boy flipped through the air like a deft acrobat, and brought his sword through the bodies of two magical fiends.

"Oh," Astrid stammered. "I ... Umm ... I think I know him ... From a long time ago."

"Ooooh! An old boyfriend, maybe," exclaimed Ariadne and Nina. "Maybe Nathan has a rival."

Nathan scoffed while Astrid pursed her lips, "Don't be silly. He just looks familiar is all."

Both Ariadne and Nina snapped their fingers sassily and bellowed, "Oh, I'm sure!"

The teasing went on a little longer. Astrid continued to put up that gauche grin crowned by red cheeks, behind which she pondered the previous night's events. Her eyes darted around the common room, noting the students she'd fought the previous night. Her gaze fell on Jessie, nursing his bandaged nose. She eyed Klein, who surreptitiously rubbed his stomach where she'd kneed him. She didn't see Paul, who was probably still studying, hopefully having little memory of the incident.

Finally, her gaze fell on Nathan, and beneath her chuckles, she wrestled with herself.

Do I tell him that Papillon is still alive?

The conversation drew to a close as people's favourite evening TV shows started to play. Nina drew Ariadne's attention with a notification of a new video featuring their Japanese magic girl. Jessie and Klein were preoccupied with games. Nathan and Astrid took the chance to sneak away, and when they were out of sight, the girl's mask disappeared.

Eying her fixed stare, Nathan asked, "Is there anything you want to talk about?"

"Just that I'm ready to take out the L.X.E. any time," said Astrid curtly.

Nathan huffed, "After last night, me too."

They got to the manager's office and announced themselves. Heavy bags weighed down Bravo's eyes as he gazed at them. He looked as if he were on the verge of putting a hole in the wall.

"I was just about to make a call to the higher-ups," he droned.

"Should we leave?" asked Astrid.

"No, you can stay," replied the exhausted commander. His subordinates took a seat while he jammed a device into the USB port on his phone, and then punched a number into the keypad.

"Line secured," said the computerised voice at the other end. Then the line clicked and another voice replaced it. "Commander Costable, report."

"General Rodrigo," said Bravo, his voice carrying not a

shred of the fatigue on his face. "Situation handled. A gas leak was blamed, and classes will resume tomorrow. A few injuries, but no fatalities. One enemy neutralised, three remain at large."

"You didn't take care of the three that attacked you?" asked the General.

"Negative. Once I realised the enemy was at the gates, I left them unconscious. I felt it was more important to secure our base of operations first."

"Spartan Valkyrie was left to that charge, was she not?" asked Rodrigo.

Shit! I should have made them wait outside, thought Bravo.

"Yes, sir," he said.

There was silence on the line for a moment.

"Very well," said Rodrigo with a sigh. "We'll expect her written report before the end of the day."

"Understood," said Bravo. "If I may ask, was The Scot forthcoming?"

"More than I expected, but he still refused," replied Rodrigo. "He said he would've let his protégé join with us only for this mission, but he feels she isn't ready for Victor. The Lee Clan also refused, insisting that Victor is *our* problem."

Bravo sighed, partially with frustration but mostly with relief.

"What about our own forces?" he asked.

"Still unavailable," said Rodrigo curtly.

The response made Bravo's muscles knot up, and he almost lost control. "What about Shantanu? Surely that psychotic arsonist can take a break from whatever third-world country he's blowing up to help us here. How about Carson?"

"They're all focused on other assignments," said Rodrigo.

Bravo grasped at his last straw, "Then call up the Reaper!"

Rodrigo chuckled sardonically. "Pfft! You think the

other generals will agree to that?"

"Overrule them then!" snapped Bravo.

"Mind your tongue, Commander Costable," Rodrigo sternly retorted. "I understand you've got a situation, but our organisation is stretched too thin. You've got two powerful warriors by your side. Use them."

Bravo ran his hand down his face and pinched the bridge of his nose as if to squeeze his frustration out like a stubborn pimple. He relaxed his brow and said, "Roger, General."

"Give me a count of any recovered Kakugane," said Rodrigo.

Bravo paused for the briefest moment, eying Janjira's Kakugane on his desk. His thoughts went to Astrid's account, intimated to him in Nathan's absence, in which she said Papillon had stolen Desbordes' Kakugane as well.

I really shouldn't have let these two sit in, he thought. *On the other hand, this'll be a good lesson for both of them.*

"None recovered so far, General Rodrigo," he said. "The three that attacked me and the Starlight Lancer were unarmed. And, according to Warrior Rachelle's verbal report, the one that attacked the dormitories had an ally in wait to recover his talisman. We have yet to collect any from the hostile force."

Rodrigo was silent a moment longer, during which Bravo made every effort to not swallow nervously. Finally, he said, "Understood, Commander. Just remember protocol. Recover any Kakugane, you must immediately contact our couriers. Understood?"

"Yes, General, perfectly understood," Bravo enunciated. He ended the call and let out a long breath. He turned to his subordinates. Nathan was a tad fidgety from boredom, no doubt having paid no attention whatsoever to the conversation. Beside him, Astrid had a very perturbed look.

"Commander, did you just lie to the Alchemic Regiment?" she asked.

Bravo looked as if his mental dam had suddenly cracked. He leaned over his desk, bent doubled, and pushed away his frustration.

"Yes, I did," he said.

Nathan finally caught onto the conversation and asked, "What? How did he lie?"

"He just said we haven't recovered any Kakugane," said Astrid. "We've got Janjira's, which I've been guarding. I've been meaning to ask why we don't follow protocol and call the couriers."

"We need it," said Bravo. "We ain't got any reinforcements. From nowhere. We're on our own. And we need as much power as we can get our hands on. Double Arms Alchemy, double our power. We have to beat these bastards, and I don't care what it takes to win."

A memory of a wretched Year-Twelver, doubled over in pain, flashed into Nathan's mind. At that, all of the fear and anguish he felt for Chouno started to waft from Bravo like a bad odour. It spurred Nathan to his feet, and he said, "That's wrong, Bravo!"

"What is?" returned the commander.

"Ends justifying the means," said Nathan. "Doing anything, even wrong stuff, to get what you want? That's no different from what Chouno did."

Bravo marched across the room toward him, and stood at his greatest height. "Warrior Grant, would you prefer we lose to the L.X.E.?"

Nathan grit his teeth and glared fixedly up at the man. "I'd rather not be a hypocrite!"

"And your sister be eaten?" retorted Bravo, his voice barely above a whisper. "How about Stevens, Cuyper, and Nelson? What about Rachelle? You okay with them being monster-chow so you can keep your lofty morals?"

Nathan's heart seized in his chest and his legs felt weak as images of their deaths blasted through his consciousness. He fell backwards onto his chair and buried his face in his hands to banish the images, but they stuck there.

"Remember what I said last night?" Bravo went on, his voice still low but just as stern. "Fight to keep those images in your imagination. And there will come a point where you have to do bad in order to protect them. When that time comes, you'll have to make a choice: whether to lose sleep over sacrificing your morals, or lose sleep over sacrificing your loved ones. You tell me, what'll cost you a bigger sleep debt, Grant?"

Nathan huffed furiously, unable to deny Bravo's logic despite the fiery war it raged in his head. He growled, "The first one, Bravo."

Astrid was silent throughout the altercation, equally unable to argue against Bravo's point. But it was mostly because she didn't care.

Whatever it takes to end them once and for all, she thought.

Bravo quietly dismissed them. They walked down the hall, Astrid's eyes fixed on Nathan's hunched form.

"It's alright to worry about rules," she said gently. "But you'll learn to put them in perspective at crunch time."

Nathan growled, "It's not that. The last thing Chouno said to me was, 'Don't apologise, hypocrite.'"

"So?" exclaimed Astrid with a bewildered expression. "He's the hypocrite, killing everyone so he doesn't have to die."

"But he's right," replied Nathan. "I mean, I can say all I like that I'd never do what he did if I was dying of AIDS or something. But when push comes to shove, I reckon I'd be tripping over my nut-sack to save Ariadne." He glanced back down the hall to Bravo's office and murmured, "Now the guy who's supposed to be training me to fight guys like Chouno is doing the same thing."

"Hey!" snapped Astrid, gripping him by his chin and forcing him to look at her. "Killing people and lying to a superior officer are on two completely different levels. The worst that happens is he gets a pay cut or a court martial. That's small change to save people from those monsters.

It's selfless. Chouno's a selfish murderer, and people lost family members because of him. There's a complete difference."

Nathan had been looking at her face throughout her lecture, and tried his best to ignore the girl. He soon found himself looking directly at her, and could see in those eyes that same determined madness she'd radiated the previous night – the same she'd radiated the night they met.

This is a girl who saves people, he thought. *She saved me so many times. She saved Ariadne, Klein, Jessie, and Paul. All of them, because she was here. She's only able to do that because she's experienced, and she knows what needs to be done. Bravo too. I should be trying to be like them.*

He knew he should be proud of the idea, and he felt it should fill him with determination. But it didn't. Instead, he just felt drained – physically and mentally. He huffed acquiescently and backed away from the girl.

"You're right," he said, completely unconvinced of the sentiment. He faked a yawn and mumbled, "I should get to bed."

Bravo called out to them with a chipper tone that was so different from his earlier drill sergeant mood, to Nathan it felt like nails on a chalkboard. He swivelled to see the grinning dorm manager approach with a phone, and he mused, *These two must be the best actors on the planet!*

"Phone for you, mate," chirped Bravo. "Said he was a friend."

With raised eyebrows, Nathan answered the phone.

"Oooh, you don't sound good, Grant," said the voice on the other end. The sound waves coming from the earpiece slithered through Nathan's ears like a thousand vipers biting at his nerves.

This voice!

The speaker continued, "In case you're wondering, I'm doing absolutely fine … Fabulous, in fact! Seems strange that I'm doing so well, despite my defeat. Were the laurels of your victory not enough to stop your crying?"

No, this can't be him!

"Who is this?" asked a disbelieving Nathan.

"Oh, you know who I am," returned the voice. "I'd like to meet in the mall, tomorrow, at noon." The voice added a tender, "Don't be late!" before the call ended.

Bravo and Astrid's expressions were as concerned as Nathan's was horrified. The boy turned to them and murmured, "Chouno's alive."

10 | Posing Contest

Bravo brought his car into the parking lot beneath the mall on Crown Street. With a huff, he looked at his subordinates in the back seat. The irate look in Nathan's eyes as he glared at Astrid put him a mood he really didn't like.

"So you knew that Chouno was alive?" Nathan said flatly. "And you were going to tell me when?"

"Eventually," exclaimed Astrid. "Seriously, it was only the night before, and the rest of yesterday was too freaking hectic. I couldn't find time!"

The boy glared at her. She trembled with dread at what dark path this would send her friend down, and it shooed off her drive to fight.

"Fair enough," blurted Nathan in a chipper tone. He then exited the car with a smile.

"Wait, what?" stammered Astrid, while Bravo let out a chuckle. They exited the car, and Astrid ran ahead of her superior to catch up to the boy. "You're suddenly okay with this?"

"Sure!" replied Nathan. "I figured you were stressed out yesterday, and now I know why."

That didn't alleviate Astrid's annoyance, and she growled, "Then why put on such a show just then? I thought you were about to cry!"

Nathan stopped in his tracks and giggled, "Any excuse

to tease you, Warrior Rachelle."

Bravo had to butt in to catch Astrid's fist aimed for Nathan's chest. The girl furiously thrashed in her superior's hold and yelled, "Let me at him! I'm gonna get back that Kakugane by force! I'll rip it out with my bare hands, I will!"

The hated boy swivelled and smiled as he said, "I'll handle Chouno now, and then you can have my heart."

Bravo only released Astrid when he was sure she wouldn't disembowel their trainee, and followed him up the escalator and into the mall. Up a few floors, they emerged onto the open walkway through the shopping district. There, in the middle of the walkway, was a crowd of people huddled around something. By the way the people behaved, Astrid and Bravo just mistook it for another performer having earned the attention of the crowd. Their eyes looked for the signs of homunculi they'd been trained to expect.

Nathan, on the other hand, thought differently.

He promptly crossed the intersection and began pushing his way through the giggling, cheering crowd. Astrid followed, more concerned with what the boy had in mind than whether Bravo was on her heels. She managed to catch up to him at the front of the crowd.

"We don't have time to be looking at street buskers, you moron!" she snapped.

Nathan was wide-eyed, more with amazement and confusion than horror. He pointed at the object of the crowd's amused attention, and Astrid finally looked at the provocatively dressed tall man in the butterfly mask. Her breath caught in her throat as she got a good look at the creature in the light of day. The skin-tight leotard left nothing to the imagination. What made it even more scandalous was the fishnet material connecting the front-split of his garment, which revealed what could only be described as a ten-pack wrapped in skin white as snow. A long braid hung from the being's head, and shimmered in the sunlight.

That alone was enough to scare Astrid and Nathan spitless, but it wasn't all.

The coup de grace of the whole sight was that the man was simply posing, in the most provocative of ways, for the phone-wielding onlookers. Astrid almost fainted with shock when people hopped in to have their photos taken with the lavishly lascivious creature.

One woman chortled unrelentingly as the man offered her a butterfly mask of her own to wear in her photo. As she walked away, the man said, "You simply must come back to my abode, where I shall show you the pleasures of the butterfly!" That made the woman, who seemed much older than the man, shriek with embarrassed delight as she fled red-faced into the crowd.

The sight made Nathan and Astrid's skin crawl. Upon noticing some kids approaching to have their picture taken, Nathan stepped forward and yelled, "Oi! Papillon!"

Papillon gazed over at him, and the crowd fell silent. "Tsk, tsk, tsk … Pa-pi-yon!" Then the crowd joined in with the flourish. "And put more love into it!" The people cheered for the performer, laughing and applauding.

Nathan found the applause a little more infectious than Astrid, who surreptitiously clutched her stomach while her other hand edged toward the Kakugane in her pocket.

"Ooh, behold!" exclaimed Papillon upon noticing Astrid's death glare. He hammed it up, Shakespeare-style, and proclaimed, "My friends, I must confess this woman is my love-rival. She longs for the affections of the boy. Yet, his heart is torn between her femininity, and my gender-transcending beauty. Ah, cruel game that is love!"

The crowd broke into a flurry of hoots to put the Warrawul student body to shame. Astrid's face went red with indignant rage, while Nathan just coughed gauchely.

Papillon continued, "Lo, the jealousy has moved her to murderous intent. Yet I must entreat that we postpone bloody contest, for the sake of my beloved admirers!"

Nathan managed to keep his own anger under control, and replied, "Don't worry, Pa-pi-yon! There won't be any fighting today."

Another voice bellowed from beyond the crowd, with gusto to match the magnificently dressed mannequin. "Be that so, need I make no entrance?"

The crowd parted with excitement to reveal the owner of that voice: another tall man, his face concealed by the standing collar of a silver jacket of the finest lustre. Nathan and Astrid did a face-fault at the sight, while Papillon's grin widened with almost lascivious excitement.

"Another titan come to claim the title of most beloved!" exclaimed the homunculus.

"There is nothing more beloved than Captain Bravo, God of Coolness!" bellowed Bravo. And he struck a pose. Papillon harrumphed, and offered his own to rival the most attractive of contortionists. Bravo flexed his muscles, easily visible beneath his Silver Skin, while Papillon rhythmically popped his glistening pectorals and abs.

The crowd went wild. Nathan and Astrid stood dumbstruck as the battle of poses went on another five minutes, before the combatants shook hands and acknowledged their stalemate. Their audience applauded joyously, and dropped a flood of coins and notes into the box near Papillon's feet.

"Oh, gratitude, my butterflies," exclaimed Papillon, blowing the crowd kisses. "You have my most gratuitous gratitude, my delicious delicates. I feel, though, that I must take a break from bringing joy to your afternoons for but an hour. I must fill my stomach and recover my stamina, such that my beauty may once again make love to your eyes!"

At the mention of 'fill my stomach,' Astrid's hand shot straight into her pocket. Nathan caught it just in time to keep her Kakugane hidden, and he kept her still. That said, he couldn't help but feel the same bite of fear as a little girl threw a dollar coin into the box, earning her a grateful chuck under the chin from the overdressed cannibal. When the crowd had sufficiently dispersed, Papillon picked up his earnings. He glanced between Bravo, Astrid, and Nathan, before he finally said, "We have much to discuss."

Papillon led them through the mall, using his earnings to purchase stacks of food from nearly every shop in the food court. Then he took them, along with his hoard, to the roof of one of the buildings overlooking the mall. Astrid was quite perturbed as Papillon sat down and hoed into his meal.

"Ah, that's the kind of food I've been craving," he exclaimed with a guttural sigh. It made Nathan's skin crawl and elicited memories of Chouno devouring his own brother.

"If I might join in," said Bravo, taking a plastic box full of sushi at Papillon's friendly nod. He removed his hat, folded down his collar, and began to eat. "I haven't had a pose war like that in a long time. It really works up an appetite."

"There will most definitely be a rematch, Captain Bravo," said Papillon.

"Definitely, Koushaku Chouno," replied Bravo.

Papillon pointed his fork fixedly at the man and growled, "No one but Nathan Grant is to refer to me as such. You will call me Papillon."

"My apologies, Papillon," said Bravo.

At that, Astrid finally snapped out of her stupor and yelled, "Screw apologies! What the Hell is all this?"

"Lunch," replied Papillon.

"I think what we should ask is, how are you still alive?" said Nathan, his tone a lot lower though equally angry.

Papillon finished his serving of tabouli and went onto the boxes of pork buns. "It's actually really interesting. After you so hypocritically murdered me, the next thing I remembered was being in a tank. It was some kind of healing apparatus. My great grandfather, Bakushaku

Chouno, was operating it. He told me to call him Doctor Butterfly."

Nathan and Astrid's jaws hung wide open with shock. They glared at Bravo, who merely shrugged, "I didn't know he was related."

Papillon went on, "Dear Grandfather welcomed me to his club, the –"

"League of Extraordinary Elects," interjected Astrid. "We've been hunting them for a while." She brandished her Kakugane. "Tell us where they are, and I'll kill you not too painfully."

Papillon smirked at her, a very intrigued glimmer in his eyes. He swallowed another mouthful of food and said, "When the healing tank finished, I was sedated and taken to a mansion near Appin. Grandfather told me that the house was mine, and I could do with it and its resident staff what I will."

"So you've started murdering and eating people, have you?" snapped Nathan.

"Actually, no," said Papillon. "I suppose eating the Chouno household and bodyguards has sated my hunger for *carne di uomo*[17]. This food," he indicated the feast before him, "I have not been able to enjoy for years. When I became sick, I could keep nothing down. Now –" He suddenly started to convulse. He scrambled for a nearby bin and wretched into it. When he finished, he stood tall once again, wiped the brownish red effluent from his lips, and sighed contently. He sat back down and resumed eating, as if nothing had happened. "The disease is still at my core, but the incomplete homunculus embryo, plus the healing tank, has given me a much greater constitution at the least. I can live my life again."

Nathan and Astrid's blood boiled, leaving them speechless. Bravo inhaled the rest of his sushi and said, "Papillon, I hope you had a reason to call us out, aside

---

[17]   Italian: "Man Meat."

from wanting to brag."

Papillon downed a curry-soaked naan and stated, "I need your help."

"With what?" asked Astrid.

"Taking down the L.X.E.," said Papillon. That gave everyone a shock. Before his subordinates could unleash their own respective tirades, Bravo interjected, "Why don't you start at the beginning? You said you were given a mansion."

"And the promise of power to defeat the warrior who wronged me," said Papillon, his eyes directed at the silent Nathan. "Yet, after months, I was not offered instruction in the Kakugane, nor any facet of Alchemy. Grandfather simply said my only concern is to recuperate. It frustrated me to no end. The mansion in which I lived had nothing related to Alchemy, nor anything to expand my knowledge.

"Grandfather would often question me regarding the man who defeated me. Why that would matter, I had no idea. Plus, I wanted to take Nathan's life myself, so why would I give him up to someone else. They also questioned me on any aftereffects of the healing tank. I started to suspect there was another motive behind Grandfather's taking me in … especially when I noticed the cameras, hidden about my mansion.

"It took quite a while before I found a blind spot in the surveillance, in which I hid away what old computer parts I could find. I assembled a device to hack into the video signal and trace it back to the L.X.E.'s systems. I couldn't work out where they are, but I do know what they're doing with the healing tank."

"They're going to revive Victor Powers," said Bravo. "We've had a run-in with a few of the L.X.E., and they're threatening the return of that monster."

"Monster is putting it lightly," said Papillon, his face darkening at the thought. "When I learned of this creature, I was terrified, more than I had been in either of my two lives. It seems Grandfather has built this healing tank to bring Victor to full strength."

By now Astrid had calmed a little, and processed his words. She murmured, "With the Regiment as it is, there'd be nothing stopping Victor. It would be the greatest massacre since World War II."

"Nobody would be spared," said Papillon. "Neither human, nor homunculus."

Nathan shuddered as even more violent images flashed through his mind. A monster conceived in his nightmares slowly devoured the world from orbit, crunching his sister and friends in its massive jaws. He twitched to banish the thoughts and snapped, "Why don't you just make a move yourself?"

"I said I don't know where they are," said Papillon. "I've only learned a small amount by making tiny hacks at a time. I can't arouse suspicion, Grant."

"Why not just risk it, launch a full-blown hack, find out where they are, and then use that Kakugane you stole to destroy them?" asked Astrid.

Papillon slurped the rest of his wonton noodle soup and mumbled, "I haven't activated it yet, lest I be discovered."

Nathan folded his arms with a stressed harrumph. Bravo swallowed a mouthful of sweet and sour pork and mumbled, "So what do you propose?"

"I will feed you every bit of information on the L.X.E. I can get my hands on," Papillon promised. "I'll find where their base is, and more specifically where the healing tank is. As far as I can see, Grandfather is still making adjustments for the Victor's unique physiology. But it won't be long. When I know for sure where the tank is, I will pass the information on. I will also find time to learn my Arms Alchemy and assist you in the attack."

Astrid's gaze never left the masked monster, and when he promised aid, her eyes narrowed shrewdly.

"I don't believe this," she said. "Why would you be so afraid of Victor? Surely he'd spare the L.X.E., or else

Doctor Butterfly wouldn't help him."

Papillon paused a moment, his jaw jerking to the side as he ruminated. He finally said, "I'd intercepted a conversation between Grandfather and his lieutenants the night before last. I learned of the plan to attack the dormitories to recover Janjira's Kakugane. Hearing that they'd confronted you three without me … That alone was enough to make me realise Grandfather's promise to let me fight Nathan was completely empty. Someone asked if I was to go with Desbordes to the dormitories." Papillon's eyes darkened with the same manic aura Nathan sensed from him when they first met. His voice became a low growl, "Dear Grandfather called me a dead weight, taken on for the sake of his healing tank. He said I'd no more purpose other than to nourish Victor when the time came. No matter that he'd given me a mansion that was little more than a cocoon. I was only useful to him in testing his damn pet project."

Nathan's eyebrows reached for the sky and to Astrid he whispered, "I'm reading a serious double-standard here."

"No shit," replied Astrid, her face equally bemused.

Papillon took no note of them and went on, "I won't be a shut-in anymore. I was a prisoner to my disease. Now I'm a prisoner to my Grandfather, to be prepared as offering for Victor's awakening feast. I won't let that happen."

With a sardonic grin, Nathan blurted, "Oh, so now it's come out. You just don't want to die, do ya, Chouno?"

"Don't you remember what I told you the day we met?" snapped Papillon. "I want to live, and I don't care who I have to kill to do it."

To the side, Bravo continued nonchalantly eating Papillon's food. He swallowed a mouthful of pepperoni pizza and said, "So you'll ally yourself with us against the L.X.E. in exchange for what?"

Papillon turned to Bravo and stated in a business-like manner, "I want protection, and assurance that the

Regiment will not hunt me."

"That ain't happening," snapped Astrid. "You're a homunculus, so you'll inevitably start murdering humans, no matter how sated your hunger is now."

"Perhaps an arrangement could be made?" Papillon suggested. "One involving death row inmates, perchance? Truly you'd have no problem with rapists and murderers getting their just desserts."

Astrid shot to her feet and pulled out her Kakugane. "That's it," she growled. Nathan stifled her before she could activate her weapon.

"Let's leave *that* negotiation 'til later," said Nathan as he struggled with the furious girl. "You say you don't know where they are. How soon will you know?"

"I have no idea, but rest assured I will hurry," said Papillon. "In the meantime, I'll give you more information you'll find useful."

"Out with it then," said Bravo.

"You have a spy at Warrawul," said Papillon.

Bravo's face darkened. "Student or teacher?"

"Student," said Papillon. "I don't know who they are yet, but I know they have been given Kakugane. All three of you need to be ready."

Astrid shook free of Nathan's hold and growled, "Is that all? I've had enough of this scum."

Bravo decided he'd had enough of both food and conversation, and thanked Papillon for both. Nathan kept his eyes fixed on the masked homunculus and asked, "So you're not gonna try and off me?"

"Not yet," said Papillon with a scoff.

"Not ever!" snapped Astrid. Her glare, were it a laser, would have disintegrated the man.

Papillon sauntered toward the highly guarded woman and murmured, "You haven't given me an answer, Rachelle."

"To what?" asked Astrid.

"My riddle: who is the monster and who is the man?"

repeated Papillon. He pushed past her and strutted down the fire escape.

Astrid glared after him, her breathing nearing the point of hyperventilation. Bravo put his hand on her shoulder and said, "Control yourself, Warrior Rachelle. Save that fury for the battlefield."

Nathan sighed away his own irritation and said, "What're we going to do about this spy? Do we take him seriously?"

Bravo pursed his lips and thought a moment. He then said, "Until he gives us a reason not to ... at least, a bigger reason than what we've got now."

"He's a homunculus," exclaimed Astrid. "What more reason could we have?"

Bravo rubbed his chin, and smiled with intrigue. "Don't you remember, Astrid? Homunculi have no taste for anything other than human meat, but he just wolfed down enough food to feed a family of ten. Also, they have dark grey blood, not red."

Both Nathan and Astrid gazed at the door to the fire escape down which Papillon had disappeared. Despite their discomfort in allying with the beast, interest sparked as to the true nature of their new comrade. All three knew there were more pressing matters. But Bravo had an epiphany: *Maybe Papillon has a bargaining chip for his life after all.*

11 | Tao's Smile

The days following the L.X.E. attack and Papillon's meeting saw the former fade into vague memory for most students at Warrawul, and the latter bare little fruit in Bravo's effort to find the enemy stronghold. Considering how much energy Bravo spent on analysing Papillon's limited information, Nathan found it amazing he could still train him every night at the grain terminal.

That said, Nathan felt he'd hit a brick wall. True, he was getting fitter, better in P.E. class, and was able to hold up in a spar against the much stronger Bravo ... for at most three minutes. No matter what he did, Bravo always managed to land a good hard blow that sent Nathan down for the count. A ten-minute break and a banana later, he was back on his feet. But that same vexing, energy-draining voice in his head screamed, "The L.X.E. won't give you a break!"

One night, as Nathan attended a meet for Ariadne's fencing club, the boy buried his face in his palms upon intimating his frustration to Astrid. The girl patted his head with a smirk and said, "It's nothing to be worried about."

"Didn't you hear me? I can't hold up more than three minutes against Bravo," said Nathan, his voice a low whisper to avoid prying ears in the sports hall.

Astrid pursed her lips and glared at him, "Neither can I."

That came as a shock, considering how many times Nathan had seen her hold her ground against creatures several times her height. Her human buzz-saw move came to mind, along with the image of Bravo stopping it with his bare hands.

"The Commander is one of our most elite," said Astrid. "Few homunculi can hold up against him for a minute. And you hold for three. Something tells me you're doing fine."

She offered him a warm smile, the kind that made Nathan want to snog the ever-loving Hell out of her. Astrid had become very good at reading his expressions, and recognised the one he wore there.

"Forget it," she said tersely.

He made a face like he had forgotten, but really he didn't. He let the image of Astrid's face push away the defeatist attitude from his mind, and he indulged in a few fantasies of his amazing friend and fellow warrior. He came back to reality when she slapped his forearm.

"Ariadne's duel is next," she said excitedly. She pointed out his sister, who pulled her fencing mask over her face and picked up her rapier. Her posture leapt out to Nathan, who couldn't help but shiver with elation at how badass his baby sister looked. He hooted excitedly, only to be quickly silenced by Astrid.

"Quiet, you'll distract her," she shushed, though she was clearly just as excited as him.

"But it's my little baby sister!" he exclaimed in a whisper.

"Just watch, you idiot," she chuckled.

Nathan turned wide-eyed toward the fencing track as Ariadne took her position at the unbroken line. She faced what Nathan assumed was some scrawny chick from a school down in Nowra. He grinned excitedly as the combatants raised their weapons and readied to fight.

The referee bellowed, "Play!"

Ariadne lunged forward, her thin rapier invisible from

Nathan's distance as it whipped through the air. It found its place on her opponent's torso, signalling a point for her. They retook their positions, and this time her opponent lunged, swirling her rapier in the air between them, until it contacted with Ariadne's. Then the opponent thrust forward, grazing Ariadne's shoulder. A point between the two of them, they retook their positions a third time, then a fourth, and a fifth. Each time, the combatants moved slightly slower to their en garde positions.

"Ariadne looks like she's tiring out more," Astrid murmured.

"Yeah, I see that," said Nathan nervously.

It came to the ninth bout, a four-all tie, and this was the breaker.

"En garde!" called the referee. The combatants assumed their pose. Time drew out like a blade for Nathan, who held his breath with trepidation. Astrid saw the tiniest hesitation in Ariadne's stance, and pursed her lips with disappointment.

The referee yelled, "Play!"

Ariadne advanced toward her opponent with a swipe that missed. Her opponent leaned back only slightly, before pressing forward with her own blow. Ariadne parried, but swiped her rapier too far. Before she could bring her sword to blow, her opponent flicked her wrist and brought her blade tip right into Ariadne's mask – a clear head strike.

The combatants backed away, saluted each other and the referee, and walked back to their respective teams. Nathan let out a disappointed sigh, but retained his proud smile. He gave Ariadne that same smile when they met up outside the sport hall after the meet finished.

"Yeah, I've only been playing for a few months, so I shouldn't have expected to win," said Ariadne, evidently more disappointed in her loss than Nathan.

"But you'll get them next time," said Nathan

encouragingly. He gave her a stiff pat on the shoulder.

Tao, the fencing team captain, leaned over and said, "You shouldn't be that hard on yourself. Your opponent had been fencing for years, and you held yourself pretty well. Be proud of yourself."

"He's right," interjected Astrid. "You've got a real talent if you're this good after just a few months." She glanced at Nathan, his arm slung around his sister's shoulder, and thought, *Maybe it runs in the family.*

"I should come around and see how you guys train," said Nathan excitedly. "Fencing sounds like a crap-load of strategy goes into it. Also quick thinking."

Ariadne coughed gauchely, "I don't know about that."

"Come on! It'll be cool, showin' off to your big brother," said Nathan.

"Observers are always welcome," said Tao warmly. It earned him a very annoyed look from Ariadne.

"Who knows," said Nathan, a facetious gleam in his eye. "I might even join the club."

Ariadne cringed with embarrassment at the thought.

* * *

To his sister's dismay, Nathan actually did turn up to one of the fencing club's practice sessions. Ariadne did poorly with her crazy big brother looking over her shoulder and cheering her every glancing blow. Adding insult to injury, Nathan had brought Astrid, Klein, Paul, and Jessie along for the ride.

Nathan made like a one-man cheerleading squad, while Astrid did what Ariadne could not and face-palmed at his every stupid antic. Mercifully, Klein watched quietly, Jessie sketched the sparing, and Paul pretended he could analyse the fighting moves.

Eventually, Ariadne's fatigue got the better of her and she took a break. She plonked down on a bench, far away from Nathan and his friends. Nathan infuriatingly didn't get the message and marched over with a dopey expression.

"You're doing freaking amazing, Ari," he exclaimed. "Some day, you'll be fencing in the limpdicks!"

Ariadne shot him a disgusted look. She quickly did a double take and said, "I think you mean Olympics, Nathan."

"Yeah," said her brother obliviously. "What did you think I said?"

Ariadne rolled her eyes and sighed, "Never mind. Plus, I'm not that good yet. And I won't be if you're acting like this is a cricket game."

"What do you mean?" asked Nathan.

"Quit shouting and yelling every time I play, for God's sake," snapped Ariadne. "You're supposed to be quiet for a game, and it's distracting as Hell!"

Nathan flinched at the berating. With a gauche purse of his lips he gazed over at Astrid, who nodded as if to say, "She's dead right."

"Sorry," he mumbled, his eyes directed downward.

Ariadne sighed acquiescently. "Okay, Okay! I know you're just trying to cheer me on."

Suddenly, a stiff yell radiated from across the hall. All eyes turned to one of the fencing tracks near the corner, where one of the combatants dropped his rapier. He removed his mask, revealing a face drenched in sweat and twisted into a frustrated expression.

"Damn it, Tao! For Christ's sake, take it easy!" he snapped.

Tao removed his mask. He hadn't even broken a sweat! And that just made his exhausted opponent even angrier.

"Forgive me," said Tao calmly. "I guess I lose myself in the fight."

"Lose yourself?" snapped the opponent. "You're so good, nobody can even land a hit on you!" He threw his mask on the ground and yelled, "Somebody else spar with this guy. I didn't join this club to get my arse kicked every day."

The club coach sent Tao's opponent to the sidelines to rest and looked around for anyone else to be the boy's sparing partner. It seemed that everyone had lost to Tao in a duel, and nobody wanted to relive the experience. Nathan nudged Ariadne, and when she remained silent, he yelled, "Oi! Ariadne'll beat ya!"

As the girl chided her brother for putting her on the spot, Tao chuckled nervously. "I'm afraid she won't be a worthy opponent. I might hurt her."

Nathan scoffed, "Why? 'Cause she's a girl? You some kind of chauffeur?"

Chauvinist, you moron, thought a cringing Astrid.

"Not at all, but I have been studying swordplay for years, whereas she's only been practicing for a few months," said Tao calmly. He eyed Ariadne, "I look forward to the day when we can spar on equal terms, but that's not today."

Ariadne shook her head, "That's fine, Tao. I'll practice more and get as good as you."

Nathan wouldn't back down. He huffed resolutely and rose to his feet. "Fine then! *I'll* be your opponent!"

Every eyebrow in the hall went sky-high. The club coach was about to refuse, but Tao seemed interested, and invited Nathan to the track. Five minutes later, Nathan wore a spare fencing jacket and breeches – which were clearly a wrong fit for him – and stood before Tao.

Astrid shook her head irately.

Here he is again. Just diving in without considering the consequences. Bloody idiot!

Beside her, Klein grinned.

"Should be interesting," he said. "Considerin' his trainin' for *you know what,* it'll be fun to see how good he really is." Astrid eyed Klein as he activated the camera app on his phone, and he said, "It'll also be fun to bag him out for how stupid he looks gettin' his arse kicked."

Now that made Astrid chuckle. Ariadne, meanwhile, was furious, and vowed never to let Nathan near her club activities again.

Nathan stood on the fencing track, fidgeting in the itchy fencing gear. When he was sufficiently comfortable, he faced Tao and held the rapier in both hands. Ariadne pinched the bridge of her nose with a dismayed, "Good God! It's not a freaking lightsaber!"

Naturally, Tao's first thrust went straight past Nathan's immobile rapier and bent against his chest.

"What the Hell! I couldn't even see that!" exclaimed Nathan.

"You need to have a keen eye for this," said Tao.

His next attack knocked Nathan's blade right out of his hands.

"Screw this! I can't even see my own sword," cried Nathan. "How the Hell does someone even play this game?"

The onlooking fencing club just laughed at the boy's stupidity, and jeered at his lack of understanding or even measurable skill. Tao quickly raised his hand and silenced them.

"Perhaps this kind of weapon isn't suited to you," said Tao. He removed his helmet and jacket. "That's fine. Why don't we try something else?"

He went to his sports bag and procured two curved wooden swords. Nathan whistled as one flew through the air towards him.

"I occasionally practice wushu swordplay here, once everyone has left," said Tao as he took a position on the track. He locked eyes with Nathan, and radiated an aura of determined competitiveness. "No mask or gloves required," he said with a militaristic tone. "First blow to the torso wins."

Everyone in the hall grew very nervous, as Nathan cockily threw off his fencing costume, leaving only his jeans and tee-shirt. He took one of the many stances Bravo had taught him, and locked onto his opponent. Tao did the same, his stance reminiscent of every wuxia film

Nathan had ever seen – though this one seemed a Hell of a lot less pretend than on the big screen. His heart raced with excitement not unlike when he faced that toad homunculus, and he remembered what he felt in that moment.

I'm the lightning, he thought.

The slightest twitch of Tao's right bicep announced his attack. Nathan managed to angle his blade just in time to parry the blow aimed for his shoulder, and still had enough momentum to undulate his blade to his right to deflect Tao's next blow. He took a slight step back to gain some footing, before advancing forward, his sword aimed for Tao's forearm. His next blow, fuelled by Tao's diversion, went for his opponent's flank.

Faces that originally billowed suspicion that Nathan was all talk soon turned to piqued interest at this uninitiated boy holding his ground against their star swordsman. Even Ariadne felt admiration, as if she'd forgotten just how cool her big brother could be. Astrid fought to suppress a proud chuckle at how far her friend had progressed in his training.

Tao ceased his attack and backed away, a nod of respect offered to his opponent as he said, "You know definitely what you're doing, Grant."

"You too," replied Nathan.

Tao grinned excitedly and said, "Well then, I don't need to hold back now."

The boy crouched, his blade's tip directed at Nathan's heart. Nathan's eyes widened at the aura that wafted from his opponent. Suddenly, Tao charged, his roar ripping through the air between them. Nathan deflected the thrust, but couldn't recover in time to mount his own offensive. Tao's blows came at lightning speed, and Nathan could only dodge or deflect.

Tao came about from the right, seemingly his first mistake. Nathan tilted his blade to divert the attack over his head and to the side, and prepared an attack to Tao's right. A strike more savage than anything Nathan had ever felt before impacted his left side and, before he knew it, he'd hurtled through the air onto the adjacent fencing track.

It took him more than a minute for his head to clear, during which someone pressed an icepack against his blackening ribs. When he was finally able to see clearly, he saw Astrid supporting him on the right, Klein on the left, and Ariadne screaming at a very embarrassed and worried Tao.

"You could've killed him, Tao! What is wrong with you?" screamed the tearful girl.

Tao clutched his chest with concern. "I'm so sorry, Nathan! Are you alright?"

His wits returned to him, Nathan raised an arm weakly and said, "Everyone calm down. I'm fine." He gingerly wriggled out of Astrid and Klein's support and hobbled toward Tao. "That's one crazy hook you got there, mate," he said, offering his opponent a handshake.

Tao took it gauchely and, as the mood sobered, his subsiding jitters gave way to curiosity. "You've got a real strong constitution to be able to walk after that."

While Nathan just laughed the complement away, his friends were far from assured. Paul stepped forward, adjusting his glasses, and murmured, "Are you trying to say you've done that to other people here?"

"Oh, I haven't gotten that serious in a *long* time," said Tao. "Last time I used that was back in China, and I almost put someone in hospital." That earned him a few horrified glances from the crowd. "But that's one of the reasons I prefer European fencing, since it forces me to keep in control."

The only one still smiling was Nathan, who bellowed, "Ah! It never hurts to let loose every once in a while."

"Hurts who?" exclaimed the flabbergasted crowd.

Nathan ignored them and slapped Tao on the shoulder. "Thanks for the spar, mate!"

"Any time," said Tao with a smile. "Hey, if you'd like, you can come around and duel with me tomorrow night."

Nathan's mind lit up with excitement at the chance for even more combat training. He grinned enthusiastically, "I'm in!"

After that, the club returned to some semblance of normalcy as the members resumed their sparing and practice. Nathan hobbled off toward the exit with his friends in tow, while Astrid lagged a moment to speak with the coach.

"Thanks for putting up with Nathan's fiasco," she said. "And sorry for the disturbance."

"Ah, not at all," said the coach. "To be honest, seeing someone keep up with Tao is really refreshing." He eyed Tao, who practiced his fencing positions in the corner. "He's sort of hit a brick wall ever since the last coach resigned."

"Really?" asked Astrid, her curiosity piqued. "How long ago was that, if I may ask?"

"A couple of months ago," said the coach. "Just up and left. Might've gotten sick of all the crazy stuff happening around here, what with the weird gas leak at the dorms."

Astrid's body went rigid. "He resigned back then?" The coach nodded. An image of a vibrating foil surged through Astrid's mind, and she mumbled, "What was his name?"

"François Desbordes," said the coach. "Honestly, he was a real nice guy, always shouting drinks for us after practice."

Astrid almost lost control of every muscle in her body. She had to fight against an army of innumerable voices screaming in her head, just to keep from soiling herself. She shook all over as she surveyed the crowd of practicing students, including Ariadne – already the victim of a homunculus attack. To think such a creature had been within a metre of Nathan's sister for so long, under Bravo and her noses.

You have a spy at Warrawul, Papillon had warned.

A student no less, thought Astrid. *And if an L.X.E. agent was heading up this club, what better place to put them.*

At that moment, Astrid recalled something she'd seen when she wasn't even looking: Tao, landing his finishing blow to Nathan's ribs, with the smile one would expect of a sociopath.

12 | The Spy Unmasked

Bravo gazed absentmindedly out the window of his office, his thumbnail sliding between his front teeth. Astrid stood behind him in full military posture as she awaited his response.

Finally, he murmured, "You suspect."

"I know for certain that Desbordes was in charge of Ariadne's club," said Astrid resolutely.

Bravo swivelled and glared fixedly at her. "But you don't know for sure that Tao's the spy!"

Astrid's jaw tightened as her mind's demand for evidence fiercely battled with her conviction of Tao's involvement. Her rational half managed to win with the conclusion: *All I have is a facial expression. That is **not** evidence.*

"No, Commander," she said reluctantly.

A clearly exhausted Bravo sighed and rubbed his face. Without meeting Astrid's gaze, he said, "Even still, it's better than anything Papillon's given me. Good catch, Warrior Rachelle."

"There's more," said Astrid. "If Tao *is* involved, then so is his sister, Shu." She spoke with a twinge of regret.

"I've noticed you getting friendly with her," said Bravo. "I hope you won't let that get in the way."

Astrid forced her concerns out of her mind with a laboured breath and gritted her teeth. "It will not. If they are the enemy, I'll destroy them, cost be damned."

Bravo nodded with a grunt. Then he sat down, visibly more relaxed. "That said, I need evidence. Try to get closer to Tao and Shu, and maybe they'll give something away."

"Nathan's determined to go sparring with Tao tonight," said Astrid. She added with a bemused smirk, "He keeps crashing Ariadne's fencing club. I'll see what I can glean then."

"Have you told Nathan your suspicions?" asked Bravo.

"You think I'm that much of an idiot?" retorted Astrid. "If Nathan knew we suspected anyone, he'd give it away in an instant."

Bravo chuckled, "That's true. I'm not going to tell Papillon this either. We'll keep it between us until there's hard evidence."

"Has that *thing* been even remotely helpful?" asked Astrid, exasperated at the mention of the half-homunculus. When Bravo scoffed, she went on, "How do you know he isn't just feeding you false intel and telling Doctor Butterfly everything?"

"He might be," said Bravo. "But we haven't had an attack like Desbordes for weeks, and so far Papillon's holding up his end of the deal." Astrid growled furiously, unconsciously rubbing her stomach. Her actions didn't go unnoticed, and Bravo approached her. His hands on her shoulders, he said, "Don't worry, Astrid. If he pulls a swifty, I'll hold him, and you stab him."

Now that image made Astrid grin excitedly.

* * *

At the request of both Ariadne and the club coach, Nathan didn't show up to spar with Tao until the end of the club's practice sessions. The reason was obvious: watching those two fight was better than in the movies. The entire club dropped their weapons, withdrew to the sidelines of the hall, and found a comfortable spot to watch these masters at work.

Ariadne, initially uncomfortable with her brother crashing her club activities, now looked forward to watching Nathan fight.

Oh, he is so the Starlight Lancer, she concluded as Nathan dodged and parried Tao's attacks with seemingly expert skill. The thought made her so giddy she cheered in a Nathan-esque manner every time he swiped his practice sword.

For other spectators, it wasn't so much of an exciting romp. It took all of Astrid's mental energy to keep a chirpy demeanour as she analysed Tao's every micro-expression for that same psychotic grin she expected from an L.X.E. spy. Her back was pressed against the wall, a small but noticeable distance from the remainder of the enthralled crowd, and her arms gripped her body tightly.

A voice she'd come to loathe sounded next to her. She turned and saw Klein, his eyes fixed on Nathan's movements. He offered to share a bag of chips, which she declined.

"You're worried the love of your life's gonna get mowed?" he asked.

Astrid mumbled under her breath, "He's not my boyfriend, damn it."

Klein chuckled, "You're really nervous there though."

Astrid eyed Klein and recalled the moments she'd shared with the boy. Though he seemed dim-witted, even perverted, at first glance — more so than Nathan — she couldn't help but see the wheels that turned in his head. And she knew that chief among his concerns was for his friends. She had to admit, Bravo might be right that Klein would be an asset.

Let's test it then, she thought.

"What do you think of Tao?" she asked, trying to keep her question as unloaded as possible.

"He's a weirdo," replied Klein as he licked the flavouring from a large potato chip.

"Why do you think that?" asked Astrid shocked.

"I'm pretty sure his sister's also his girlfriend," said Klein.

At that, Astrid cringed and wondered why in the world she'd even bothered to ask this idiot's opinion. She moaned, "Why would you say something like that? What, you're jealous of Tao's sport skill or something, so you try to drag him down?"

Klein looked at her as if she were a moron and said, "Girl, have you *seen* how he looks at Shu? Have you been around them when they're together?"

Though still annoyed with his twisted views, Astrid realised she'd never really observed the twins together. At the very least, she hadn't paid very much attention at all when she *had* seen them together.

Okay, let's see if he's on to something, she thought.

"What're they like together?" asked Astrid.

"I've noticed them holding hands under the table at the dorms," said Klein. "And I don't buy it that they're just close siblings. There's just something about how it looks … kinda like when you watch a movie the first time, and think the movie is about one thing. Then you watch again, and notice all the stuff you missed and you're like, 'Holy crap! That's what it's about!'"

Astrid grimaced at the analogy. Curiosity spurred her to ask, "So, you think you see things as they really are?"

"I guess," replied Klein with a shrug. "If I'm paying attention, that is. And I've been doing that a lot more since you showed up." He scrunched up and pocketed his empty chip packet and whispered, "So, you think Tao might be one of 'em?"

Astrid harrumphed, "Probably."

"Why don't you check their student records?" he asked, as if it were the most obvious idea on the planet. "I mean, if they're L.X.E., then they'd be homers, right? Who enrolled them at Warrawul then?"

"Homunculi," Astrid corrected. "But you're right. They would have enrolment forms, including the details for the parents who enrolled them."

Klein frowned, "Then quit screwin' around here, ya dumbass!" When Astrid's eyes darted to Nathan, still sparring with Tao, he murmured, "I'll tell him you've got an assignment or something."

Astrid stole one last glance at Nathan before she departed, leaving the crowd to watch in awe at the ongoing spar. Neither opponent looked to be backing down nor vying for a break. Their one rule of first blow to the torso kept them going, despite the developing bruises and scrapes on their faces and hands.

Klein kept an even closer eye on Tao after Astrid's warning, but couldn't see anything out of the ordinary. If Klein had to be honest, the guy didn't look like a homunculus – though all he had for comparison was that weird nudist in a butterfly mask. Tao, on the other hand, just seemed like a really athletic guy, who just happened to be holding his ground with a guy Klein had seen scrunch a stainless steel pipe with his bare hand. And Nathan seemed to be tiring out just slightly faster than Tao.

Then, just as Nathan dropped his guard on his left flank, Tao executed his signature attack that got Nathan every time. With a one-handed slash, Tao blasted Nathan across the floor. The boy careened to a halt, clutching his side. While Ariadne and others raced to Nathan's side with the first aid kit, Klein couldn't take his eyes off Tao, having seen the expression on his face. It was so haunting it sent shivers up Klein's spine.

That signalled the end of the night. Nathan and Tao changed into clothes that weren't drenched in sweat and the club readied to vacate the hall. Klein was barely listening to his friends yammer on as his eyes remained glued on Tao. He noted the same expression, albeit much less intense, as he checked a message on his phone.

Once everyone was out of the hall, Tao turned to Nathan and said, "You've been a really good opponent, Nathan."

"You ain't so bad yourself," said Nathan, patting Tao on the shoulder.

"Listen," said Tao, shuffling like a boy about to ask his crush out on a date. And he pretty much did that. "Can I buy you a drink?" Nathan raised an eyebrow. "Since I've been hitting you so hard the last week, I figure I should do something other than apologise, you know?"

Nathan shrugged, "Sure."

Klein stepped forward, "Hey, mind if I come along?"

"Uh, actually," said Tao. "I was hoping to be able to have a private chat with Nathan, if that's alright."

Nathan pursed his lips gauchely and his eyes darted side to side. Meanwhile, Klein couldn't help but chuckle at what was clearly going on inside his friend's mind. Ariadne, too, was a little nervous about Tao's possible intentions.

"So long as we're not gonna talk about feelings," said Nathan.

Then Tao finally caught on to what they were thinking, and he held his hands up. "I don't have *that* intention," he blurted quickly. "I wanted to discuss combat philosophy."

Klein and Ariadne let out a sigh, while Nathan laughed, "Oh, no problem, mate. Sorry for being weird. But sure, I'll have a drink with you."

Tao grinned, though Klein sensed something very off about the smile. His head simmered with worry.

*What do I do? If he's a homer, then he's probably taking Nathan out to off him. And if he's just a regular kid ... And how would I even stop him? I can't say anything in front of Ariadne either or she'll get suspicious. And if Tao **is** a regular kid, he'd be weirded out by this Alchemy crap. What do I do?*

As Nathan walked down the street, chatting amiably with Tao, Klein eyed Ariadne standing next to him with a slightly upturned smile.

"We better hurry, or we'll miss the bus," she said as she turned toward the bus stop.

Klein looked back down the street where Nathan and

Tao had walked and growled breathily, "Fuck."

* * *

Having been in the brightly lit hall for a while, Astrid was a tad taken aback by the darkness of the night sky. She raced to catch the next shuttle to Warrawul. But every stop the shuttle made was infuriating, and she fumed impatiently. When the bus finally reached her destination, she burst from the door in an agitated state. She power-walked toward the gates of the school, and leaped over them with the ease of an Olympic gymnast.

The grounds were almost pitch black at night, yet Astrid found her way by memory alone. The staffroom was locked, but that was of no concern. Her trusty lock-picker device clicked satisfyingly as the entrance creaked open. She waltzed down the aisle of desks, toward the headmaster's office.

While the headmaster's computer booted up, Astrid procured a small device from her kit and inserted it into the USB slot. The screen flickered, before shooting past the login screen and presenting the desktop. Astrid almost kissed her hacking device for how dependable it was.

A quick search through the system brought her to the student files, and she scrolled down to find the folder entitled, 'Wu, Tao.' She printed everything therein, and did the same for Shu's file. Then she switched off the machine, took her kit, wiped down the keyboard, and headed for the print room.

The large print machine had indeed finished its job, as its loud whirring started to die down. And yet, there was nothing in the print tray.

There was a sudden flash of red light, and Astrid's neck hairs backflipped at the activation of an Arms Alchemy. She swivelled, her scythes materialising just in time to deflect a flurry of energy bolts. Her face was white with shock at Shu's grin, reflected in the glow of an elegant bow composed of red metal.

"Tsk, tsk, tsk, Miss Rachelle, that's naughty!" said the girl. She shredded the wad of papers in her other hand and proclaimed, "Student's records are private."

Astrid grit her teeth, filled with a feeling of betrayal. She glared back at the girl and said, "What're you afraid I'll find, Shu? That you're an L.X.E. shit-weasel?" She raised her blades, her whole body aroused with revving bloodlust. She lunged forward. Shu diverted her blades with her bow, and kicked her into the copy machine, which toppled over.

Astrid looked up from the floor to see Shu, her bow at the ready. She swatted the bow aside and used her blades to propel her out the window. Still airborne, Astrid swivelled as Shu rushed to the broken window and unleashed another barrage. Astrid deflected the arrows with her forward blades while her hind blades braced for landing.

Shu's barrage didn't stop, and Astrid dove for cover behind the corner of the science buildings. A few more energy arrows flew her way, ripping through the brick wall like a hot knife through butter. Astrid retreated further behind the building until the onslaught stopped, and she caught her breath.

These ones are dangerous, she thought as she rubbed the place where Shu's powerful kick connected. *I need to warn Nathan!*

She reached into her pocket, finding her phone in pieces and a rather large hole where one of Shu's arrows had just missed her. She growled irately and threw the broken device to the ground. Then she hesitantly edged her way to the corner of the building and looked around it. Shu was nowhere to be seen.

She must've retreated, Astrid concluded. *I'd bet she'll tell Tao and try to take Nathan out first. I need to get to him.*

Astrid broke into a sprint across the dark campus. She deactivated her Arms Alchemy when she was sure Shu was no longer nearby, jumped the car park fence, and sprinted down the highway toward the dormitories. Just as she reached the building, she growled with desperation at the sight of Bravo's car park empty. She raced inside and found one of the students flipping through the channels on the TV. Unfortunately, he didn't know where the dorm manager had gone.

Just as she started to get really annoyed, Klein appeared behind her. The instant he saw her face, he knew he should have stopped Nathan at the sports hall.

"Come on," he said. He marched down the hall with Astrid in tow, and when they were outside, he whispered, "Tao invited Nathan for a drink. I bet you found something on them?"

"Straight from Shu's mouth before she tried to kill me," replied Astrid. "She broke my phone so I couldn't warn Nathan. Where are they?"

"Gwynneville Pub," Klein replied. He reached into his pocket and handed over a set of keys. "My car's in the parking lot. You know how to drive it?"

"I know how to drive a freaking plane," returned Astrid in a low growl. "When Bravo gets back, tell him everything."

Klein handed over his phone as well, but grabbed Astrid's wrist as she took it, and he looked her squarely in the eye.

"You look after him," he intoned.

Astrid nodded resolutely, before pulling away and racing toward the car park. She messaged Nathan: "Its Astrid Tao Shu R LXE"

The phone buzzed with a reply just as she found the car: "I know."

13 | Donkeys

After Klein and Ariadne left, Nathan and Tao headed down the street toward the Gwynneville shops. It was late, and a weekday, so only two shops were open: the 24-hour service station at the corner, and a tavern a few doors down. Tao led the way toward the bar, and reached the door before the owner could flip the closed sign. He gave the tired lady a pair of googly eyes as he entreated her to let them have one drink, and she couldn't help but let them in.

This guy could probably smooth-talk Astrid if he wanted to, thought Nathan with a grin.

They took a seat at the bar and ordered two schooners of cola. Nathan held his up and said, "Too bad we ain't a few years older. Then we'd be drinking Coronas."

"Well," said Tao, raising his own glass. "Here's to sharing a beer in three years."

"Two for me," said Nathan as he touched his glass to Tao.

Soon their drinks were half empty, and Tao's expression turned pensive.

"Nathan, could I ask something?" he mumbled.

"If it's about Astrid, she's threatened to disembowel me if I talk about private stuff," said Nathan, clearly oblivious to Tao's demeanour.

Tao chuckled, "No, not that. I wanted to ask about

your fighting skills." Nathan tried not to cough nervously as he sipped his drink. He swallowed and nodded for Tao to continue. "You're clearly very skilled, but according to Ariadne, you aren't in any sport clubs."

Nathan cringed as an image of a cricket ball materialised in his mind. "I'm not really that keen on sports these days."

"Then, your skill is natural?" asked Tao, a dash of admiration to his voice.

"Not really," said Nathan, reciting a well-rehearsed alibi. "Since all the crazy stuff started happening ... you know, Ol' Chambo going missing and a bunch of students just vanishing, I wanted to get real strong, ya know? I wanted to be able to fight off anyone who threatened the people I care about. It turned out, Mister Costable was a boxer once, so he's been training me every night for the last few months." He kept his gaze fixed a moment longer on the diminishing fizz upon the surface of his drink. Then he turned to Tao and saw the boy grinning.

"You want to protect your friends?" said the boy, his admiration now blatant on his face.

"Yep," said Nathan confidently. "Klein, Paul, Jessie, Ariadne, you and your sister –"

"Astrid too?" interjected Tao.

Nathan scoffed as he recalled the ease with which the Spartan Valkyrie disposed of the snake, defended him against Burrumering, took the homunculus embryo for him, and kept a straight face after a week in agony. His cheerful voice contaminated with self-blame and guilt, he exclaimed, "That's one girl who can handle herself." His body shook with an uncontrollable chill, which he shrugged off and said, "What about you, Tao? You're really good at fencing, but you're still sparring with me. Sounds like you're training hard for something other than a sports meet."

Now, it was Tao's turn in the spotlight, but he seemed to do much better than Nathan. He only widened his grin and said, "I have a wish I want granted. My sister and I've been alone together for so long. Our parents left us a substantial inheritance, so we were able to live. But the world is still very dangerous. Wars in the Middle-East, that hostage crisis in Sydney a few years back – remember that? Also the attacks in London a few months ago. Then there's every epidemic under the sun. And then the stuff going on closer to home, like you said, with Mister Chamberlain and all those students disappearing." He pursed his lips and started to pale with anxiety. He locked eyes with Nathan. "I just wish my sister and I could live together in peace. But I'm not so naïve as to not realise that peace sometimes means having a bigger stick than the other guy." He finished his drink and sighed, "So I guess it's the same as you, really. I want to defend the one most important to me."

Nathan slapped him on the shoulder, and gripped it tightly. He looked at Tao with a resolute gaze and said, "We'll defend them together, mate."

Tao grinned and gripped Nathan's hand. Before the moment could go on longer, the sleepy bar owner snatched their drinks away and booted them out. Nathan gathered his things and headed for the door. Had he looked over his shoulder, he'd have noticed an intriguing, if not alarming, expression on Tao's face as his eyes bore holes in Nathan's back.

They exited the pub and bade the owner goodnight, before making for the bus stop. Nathan swivelled and said, "Tao! Thanks for the drink, man!"

"No problem, Nathan," said Tao, his hands in his pockets and a smirk on his face. That face suddenly turned to horror as he looked past Nathan to the being behind him. Nathan's cheerful expression melted away as he saw a familiar yet dreaded person behind Tao.

The stout, burly creature bellowed, startling Tao who swivelled to face the creature. The lanky beast behind Nathan cackled vengefully, and suddenly the two boys were back-to-back and filled with panic.

"Majuj and Yajuj!" snapped Nathan.

Both homunculi bore wounds that weren't healing, many of them dangerously close to their vital brands. They both also wore the most furious and mournful expressions.

"Our Shaitan died because of you," cried Yajuj. "And now, we'll have vengeance!"

"We'll take your Kakugane and eat your sister!" snapped Majuj.

The pair lunged, their ugly maws wide open to receive their victims. Time slowed to a crawl as Nathan's hand veered toward his chest and his mind spiralled into a panic.

I can't fight them without an Arms Alchemy! But if I show Tao my real power, he'll get dragged into this mess just like Klein. If I don't kill them now, they'll go after Ariadne! Klein, Jessie, Paul, they'll all be next. And Astrid too.

An ethereal cricket ball flew across his mindscape and struck him. He clutched his chest and opened his mouth to roar the incantation that would surely change Tao's life forever.

A long streak of light suddenly girdled Nathan, and when it cleared, Majuj and Yajuj were a smouldering pile of fillet homunculus. Nathan turned, his body rigid with surprise and overflowing with adrenaline, and saw the faintest glimmer of that light remaining in Tao's hand. That light took the form of a Kakugane.

Tao turned, pale from the sudden attack, though he quickly regained his composure and regarded Nathan with a grin. He cast his sports bag aside, and unbuttoned his shirt to reveal a purple brand on his clavicle: the same Nathan had seen on each and every one of his enemies who served the L.X.E.

"I did like you, Nathan," said Tao, his face unchanged. "You were an especially worthy opponent. But I particularly loved how you always fell for that right-side feint. Every time I struck your left side, I knew."

As Tao's grin widened, it reminded Nathan of Chouno, and the sight gave him chills.

"Knew what?" he rasped.

"That I would defeat you in true combat, with real weapons," replied Tao, stroking his Kakugane. "Then my wish would be granted."

Nathan's breath caught in his throat.

Wish? Didn't you say your wish was to live in peace? How does working with the L.X.E. help with that? How would killing me help with that?

The phone in his pocket buzzed. He eyed Tao, who simply nodded politely. The sight was almost revolting, as if Tao didn't care for the implications of what he was revealing. Nathan checked his phone, and saw a message from Klein: "Its Astrid Tao Shu R LXE." Nathan quickly responded, "I know," and then turned to Tao.

"Astrid's on her way too," he said, fixating his glare on Tao. "I'd prefer if we could wrap this up before she gets here."

"Likewise, I'd rather Shu not see what I'm about to do," said Tao.

Nathan cocked his head in confusion. "She's not a homunculus, is she?"

"Not yet," said Tao.

"So, your wish to live together, you decided on your own, without her?" growled Nathan.

Tao's smile softened, "I'd rather she not dirty her hands."

Nathan's body trembled from sorrow and dismay. Just five minutes ago, he was so happy. Barely an hour ago, he was so enthralled in the fun of their sparring. He cursed himself for not seeing any sign of Tao's true nature sooner.

Bloody idiot, Nathan!

Another voice spoke up in his mind.

Now's not the time. Whatever you felt before, you have to ignore it. Tao's a homunculus. Anything they told you, anything you felt before, it was all bollocks. If you don't stop them, they'll kill

Ariadne, Klein, Paul, Jessie, and everyone else at that school. You did what you had to do with Chouno, and you'll do it now!

His hand to his chest, "Arms Alchemy!" The flash of golden light materialised into his lance and he charged at Tao. "I'll end this now, Tao!" He thrust his lance toward Tao's chest, and struck something hard and metallic. Tao braced himself against the concrete and held his Kakugane in front of him, a shield to block Nathan's blow.

"Your weapon is truly amazing, Starlight Lancer," said Tao. "Behold my weapon." Then he roared, "*Wǔzhuāng liànjīn!*[18]"

Silver light flashed from the Kakugane, and Tao swiped it violently at Nathan. The boy only just managed to block the blows that might've cleaved him in two. Nathan backed away as the light cleared and he saw Tao's weapon: a long curved one-edged sword.

"I always found the Dao far more graceful than the Jian," said Tao, as he gripped the humming blade in his two hands. "With this, I'll carve your body in two, take your Kakugane, and secure mine and my sister's futures!"

Tao lunged, swiping his blade from the right. Nathan deflected the blow and tried to push his own frontal attack, but the force with which Tao pressed was much too strong. Tao drove him across the street with slashes so fast Nathan could barely see them.

He's fast, thought Nathan. With a dash of latent cockiness, he mused, *But Bravo's way faster.*

He found his back against a brick wall, and Tao thrust toward his chest. Nathan deflected it at the last moment, and punched Tao in the face. The boy stumbled backwards, giving Nathan enough time to clear the wall and land in the green of the lawn bowls club on the other side. He sprinted into the field to get some distance between him and Tao. He swivelled and saw the boy coming at him through the air.

---

[18] Mandarin: "Arms Alchemy."

Nathan parried Tao's airborne attack, then locked Tao's blade into the hilt of his spear and pulled it aside. He kneed Tao in the stomach and catapulted him over his shoulder. Tao landed on his back with a surprised shriek, but only regained his senses in time to see Nathan's lance vying for his head.

Tao darted aside at the last moment, and swivelled deftly to kick Nathan in the head. His sword in hand, he pressed a ferocious attack that once again had Nathan on the run. His eyes filled with frustration with every infuriating clang of his blade against Nathan's spear. That frustration turned to rage, and that rage fuelled his muscles with ever increasing strength. He swatted Nathan's spear aside and put his foot into his opponent's stomach.

Nathan tumbled head over heels. Dazed, he saw Tao advancing with the force of an oncoming freight train. His determination grew as he summoned into his mind an image of his every companion who would die if he didn't win. He took that and turned it into power. The red sash of his lance shone brighter than a star, and with the power he'd imbued into the lance, he thrust toward Tao.

Their weapons clashed, and Nathan suddenly felt all his strength drain from him. His sash stopped glowing, and the hull of his lance, once brimming with energy, resealed itself. He looked up and saw Tao grinning with greater cockiness than ever before. His sword glowed with bright light, which concentrated into the point where their blades connected. Then Tao barked, and the energy between them exploded.

Nathan's insides lurched with greater g-force than a pitching fighter jet, as the blast launched him over the bowling club building. When he struck the field beyond, he ripped up earth and grass. His body still had plenty of momentum as it coursed through the trees, across the street, and smashed painfully against the gates of a primary school. Blood flowed like a waterfall down his face, and his every bone ached. It was a miracle he could still walk.

He regained enough sense to see Tao coming at him again, his blade still glowing. Nathan tried to parry the blow, but the sheer force of Tao's attack threw him through the school gates and onto the playground. His blood streaked across the ground. Even more cuts and scrapes from the abrasive concrete marred his body. He could barely stand to face Tao, standing at the school entrance with his blade rested on his shoulder.

This must be the real power of a homunculus, he thought. *I was right, and Astrid was wrong. I'm not ready. Bravo didn't train me enough. I'm not as good as Tao.*

Ariadne's voice burst its way into his consciousness and said, "That's fine, Tao. I'll practice more and get as good as you."

Oh yeah, she said that, didn't she? She's in the fencing club with Tao, where she's been right next to a homunculus this whole time! And if I fail, it won't be a cricket ball!

It was as if a cyclone had formed in his mind to cast away the clouds dulling his senses. His extremities tingled as his wounds healed themselves at the tempo of his metal heart's beating. He started to growl ferociously to rally his every ounce of strength, until he could stand at his full height once again. Then he finally opened his eyes to see Tao, whose expression had grown worried.

"You should be afraid, Tao," snapped Nathan as he cocked his spear. "Whatever wacky powers your Arms Alchemy has, I'll rip them apart and kick your arse!"

He prepared to charge, but the ground around him suddenly exploded in a cloud of dust. When the dust cleared, Nathan saw dozens of holes in the concrete around his feet, and heard the swish of four blades he'd come to know well. He looked over his shoulder with a grin and said, "Took you long enough, Astrid."

Astrid raised her blades and directed her gaze to the top of the school church. There stood Shu, the red bow in her hands and an excited smile on her face.

"I was afraid this fight would end too quickly," she

exclaimed.

*She **is** a homunculus,* thought Nathan, shooting his opponent a glare. *Tao, you lying son of a bitch!*

"Nathan, are you in the game?" asked Astrid. Nathan took one more look at Tao, the memories of their friendly sparring still somewhat present. And yet, his resolve did not waver.

"Weren't you listening before, Astrid?" replied Nathan.

Astrid chuckled excitedly. With her eyes locked on her bow-wielding enemy, she held her clenched fist out to Nathan and said, "You handle Tao. I'll take out Shu."

Without looking, Nathan fist-bumped her and yelled, "Bring it!"

While Nathan charged Tao, Astrid sprinted toward the church. She swatted aside Shu's barrage of energy arrows, and with her blades she scaled the wall of the church like a spider on methamphetamine. A growl took root in her throat, and it grew as she ascended the wall, until it sprouted into a mighty roar as she launched herself over the edge of the roof. She spun in mid-air, her human buzz-saw technique aimed for Shu's throat.

Shu leaned back to dodge most of Astrid's savage assault, and twirled her bow to parry the rest of it. Astrid landed on the roof, and her blades quickly targeted Shu's abdomen and head. Shu blocked a blow for her right and ducked another to her left. Then she rolled mid-air over two other blades determined to make stubs of her ankles. She regained her footing, and fired another energy arrow drawn from her gauntlet. Astrid darted to the side, and continued to flip as Shu streamed arrows at her.

"You're way more athletic than you let on, Shu," muttered Astrid, her breathing slightly laboured.

"And you're way more violent than *you* let on, Astrid," returned Shu. She eyed Astrid's robotic scythes and smirked, "Forget 'Spartan Valkyrie.' The way you use those arms, you should've been named after that legendary Witch, Arachne."

Astrid shrieked with fury. Her hind legs launched her forward and her forelegs made scissoring actions toward Shu. The girl continued to loose arrows at her manic opponent, which deflected harmlessly off the whizzing blades. Astrid got too close, and Shu back-flipped out of the path of her blades. She darted back even further, until she almost stumbled off the edge of the church roof. She tried to parry Astrid's swipes and slashes, but couldn't dodge the swift kick Astrid gave her stomach.

Shu tumbled backwards, and managed to hook her bow onto the cross on the roof's apex. Gravity gave her enough momentum to swing about, back onto the roof, and put her foot into Astrid's face. Astrid stumbled backwards, flailing her mechanical arms blindly, and managed to knick Shu's shoulder. The girl screeched, and loosed another set of arrows.

The Spartan Valkyrie had had enough. She blocked Shu's bow and diverted it into the roof tiles with enough force to lodge it there. Then she backhanded Shu with a fierce cry before bringing her blades toward the girl's chest. Shu leaped over Astrid, and dislodged her bow in time to dodge the double-bladed swipe. She held her bow up to block Astrid's blow targeted for her shoulders, but didn't expect Astrid to suddenly backflip, the girl's feet locking onto the bow and wresting it from her fingers.

Astrid landed and glared at her opponent, murder in her eyes. She thrust forward. She barely glanced Shu's sides as energy arrows extruded from the fingertips of the girl's gauntlet and slashed across her chest. The Spartan Valkyrie tumbled over the apex of the roof and dug her blades into the tiles to keep herself from slipping down the slope. She gripped her bleeding chest. The wounds weren't the deepest she'd incurred, but they still hurt like Hell. She fumed as she pulled herself to her feet, but Shu wasn't on the roof. She heard footsteps from below, and looked down to see her hated, treacherous opponent, her bow in hand, charging toward Nathan and Tao.

* * *

Tao twirled, his blade's tip tracing an arc in the air around him. He diverted Nathan's thrust to his left, and swivelled to bring the blade down on his opponent's neck. Nathan blocked the blow with the shaft of his lance. He quickly delivered kicks to Tao's knee, hip, and then stomach in quick succession. Tao stumbled backward and inhaled sharply as the red sash of Nathan's lance flashed brightly. Nathan thrust toward him with a roar, while Tao merely chuckled cockily. He locked his sword against the tip of Nathan's spear.

Nathan was ready for him this time. The familiar sensation of his power being sapped made him falter slightly, but he quickly regained his focus. He saw Tao concentrating furiously, and saw that ball of energy form at the junction of their blades. He began to focus all his will power onto that point, and the hull of his spear began to pulsate as it pumped more energy into the junction. The ball of energy rippled along the surface of each weapon. A gust of wind blew outwards from the junction, fuelled by the sheer force of Tao and Nathan's wills pushing against each other. As if they were tectonic plates made of energy, space itself seemed to quake at the stress.

Tao's frustration finally forced them to break the deadlock. They both flew backward. Sweat poured down their faces and they panted profusely. They locked eyes, the exchange in some ways more intense than their energetic battle of wills. Tao scoffed irately, and took a stance that sent a familiar chill down Nathan's spine.

This is it, he thought. *Every time he took that stance, I'd know I was about to get mowed. I always fell for that right feint and he went at my ribs from the left. And he's damn good at it. And with that Chinese sword, I'll probably lose all feeling from my gut down before I die. I won't be able to block it … Unless!*

Nathan drew a deep breath and twirled his spear to give him that little extra bit of confidence. Then he faced Tao, and did his absolute best not to falter under the boy's steadfast gaze.

With a loud grunt, Tao moved first. He came with a vertical slash, which Nathan diverted to the right.

So far so good.

Then Nathan advanced with a series of forward thrusts, which Tao diverted as he allowed Nathan a little more ground. Tao deflected the last one over his shoulder and came at Nathan's right.

This is gonna hurt!

Nathan dodged to his left and deflected the right thrust. He diverted the blade over his head and to the left, just like Tao wanted.

Oh crap! This is it! Just fix it in time ... Just in time! Deactivate!

What he felt in that next couple of nanoseconds wasn't remotely like that blunt wooden blade bruising his ribs. It started as a hot sting that quickly supercooled, followed by an unfathomable need to vomit and defecate. He gave a strangled, agonising shriek as Tao's blade bisected his chest. His cries were overshadowed by a clink of metal on metal, which turned Tao's expression of glee into one of amazement.

"Thanks for the idea," Nathan gurgled through mouthfuls of blood.

Tao's mouth hung open, utterly flabbergasted at the disappearance of Nathan's spear and the lingering golden glow on the boy's chest. "How can you still be alive? Even with the Kakugane blocking my blow, the shock alone should have killed you!"

Nathan chuckled, "I'm the Starlight Lancer! This is my power, given to me by Astrid Rachelle, so that I can protect the ones I hold dear." He made a triangle of his hands in front of his chest. "And as long as those people exist, there isn't a sorry shit alive who could possibly beat me! Arms Alchemy!"

His lance erupted in a golden flash from his chest, and shot straight into Tao's stomach. A torrent of crimson burst from his abdomen and he cried out in surprise. He gripped the blade of Nathan's lance, ignoring the sharp edge slitting his palms, and tried to pull. But it was far too deeply lodged in his spine. Not for Nathan, though. He gripped the sash and yanked his weapon from the L.X.E. agent's belly.

Nathan's mind was a daze, clouded by pain and nausea, grief and elation. He hardly noticed Shu scream, but he did see the bright green arrow she fired at Tao's chest. Her bow was cocked, with a blue arrow aimed at Nathan's chest. Astrid suddenly appeared between them and deflected the arrow.

With a tearful growl, Shu fired another blue arrow, which again failed to find its mark. She tried to ready another arrow, but her face crumpled with pain as her stomach started to leak blood. Nathan looked to Tao, whose wounds started to heal.

Tao murmured something in Chinese and yanked the green arrow from his chest. By then, his wounds were much less severe but still present. Similarly, Shu was bloodied and weakened so much she couldn't stand. Tao hobbled past his foes and caught his sister.

Only then did Nathan notice the blood smeared across the concrete and splattered on the walls. Some of it was his. But the rest had to be Tao and Shu's.

Hang on, homunculus blood is supposed to be grey, he thought.

He looked at Tao and Shu, whose wounds were not healing like other homunculi he'd seen.

"Holy shit! They're still human!" he exclaimed.

"I'd suspected as much," said Astrid. "When Shu and I fought at the school earlier, her kick wasn't nearly what I'd expect from a homunculus." She brandished one of her blades, coated in Shu's blood. "Then when I saw her blood, I knew for sure." She sauntered over to the wretched pair and slashed away their shirt collars. There, just above the clavicle, was the brand of the homunculus. "It's just a regular tattoo," said Astrid. "They get it done so that they won't be eaten by accident."

"What are they?" asked Nathan.

"The Regiment calls them Donkeys," spat Astrid. "Homunculus communities use these to help them fit in. Those with nothing are slaves, and those with half a name to them offer resources and money."

"Why call them something like that?" asked Nathan.

Astrid smirked. "You know the old tale? A boy sitting on a donkey strapped to a cart. He holds a stick with a carrot on the end, so that it's dangling right in front of the donkey's nose, so that the dumbass will keep pulling the carriage. That's what the homunculi offer scum like this: if they do the dirty work, eventually they'll be made homunculi … *eventually* being the operative word."

Tao scoffed, "Donkeys? I guess it's befitting." Tears started to dribble down Shu's cheeks.

"What the Hell, Tao?" exclaimed Nathan. "Why're you working for the L.X.E.? Why would you put everyone from your club; why would you put Ariadne in danger?"

Tao held his sister closer. He gazed into her eyes, and only then did Nathan and Astrid see what Klein had noticed long ago. Then Tao turned to their vanquishers and said, "Didn't I tell you before, Nathan? We want to live in peace, but we're not so naïve as to not realise that means having a bigger stick than the other guy. What stick could be bigger than the power and longevity of a homunculus?"

14 | Mercy

With a tear streaking down his cheek, Tao began his story.

"I hardly remember anything before we were taken. I don't remember my parents, or even if our names were Tao and Shu Wu to begin with. My earliest memory was of being offered a bottle of lemonade, by a smiling man.

"We were whisked away and put in a building with other children. I remember Shu crying that her ears hurt so much. We might've been on a plane. Then we met *them*, the smiling man said were our parents. I just accepted it, because I didn't know otherwise. These people didn't look at all like us, but said that they'd take us home and give us cake.

"They did, and it was nice at first. Shu looked so happy. We had a bed to share, and got a TV too. It wasn't very big, but it felt nice. Even when our parents locked the bedroom door at night and made us promise to not go outside. They said that the bogeyman would hit us with his big stick if we broke a promise. They fed us and let us wash, but they never hugged us, or said 'I love you' to us, but I couldn't remember being told that so I didn't know to expect it.

"Mother read a book to us one day, about two people being married and living happily ever after. She explained that when a man and a woman loved each other, they made a pledge to never be apart, no matter what. Shu made me promise to her that we'd never be apart either. That we'd get married.

"Eventually, there were others who came along too. Mother and Father said they were our little sisters. But they were black. We had to share a room with them too. Neither of us liked them.

"Then, one night, Mother unlocked the bedroom, and took the black girls and Shu away. She said she needed them for something. I just went back to sleep. When I woke up, Shu was back in bed with me. The next morning, she and the other girls wouldn't even look at each other.

"It happened again the next night, and the next, and the next. I was curious what was going on, so I snuck into our parents' room while they were asleep. It was the first time I'd seen a computer screen, and on it was my sister, with the other girls ... they were ...

"It's funny, you know? I didn't learn the word for that until about ten years later: *pornography*. You want to know what's even funnier? I felt left out! I actually thought it was a game they were playing without me. So I acted out and yelled, 'Why don't I get to play too?' Our parents laughed so hard, while the girls started to cry. The first, and only time, I yelled at Shu and hit her was when she tried to talk me out of the *game*.

"Of course, *my* first experience with the game made me realise quickly just what I'd done to my sister. The man they brought in to *play* with me looked so ... Ugh ...

"I cried so hard afterwards. My Father patted me on the head and said, 'It's good that you're crying. The video will get us a higher price that way.' My Mother promised me an Xbox for crying harder next time.

"But if I had to say anything remotely good about the event, it was this: I couldn't stop crying that night, and Shu came to me and hugged me. She still had the bruise on her face where I'd hit her. She told me that I was her husband,

and she'd be with me no matter what. Seriously, it's one of my most precious memories.

"After, I told our parents I'd cry as hard as they liked, so long as Shu only did the game with the other girls. They promised me that, but they were bastards.

"It went on for years like that. We got bigger, while our parents got smaller, more callous, and even seemed bored. Our black little sisters were replaced, in time, with younger kids – mostly girls but sometimes boys – while we were kept around. Still, we did the games like they said. But soon the games changed. Shu and I were taken into the room one night, and our Mother said she hadn't told us the rest of the marriage story. She told us the rest and said that, since Shu and I were married, we had to finish it. They made a film of it too, to *commemorate* it. They said it was like a royal wedding, and people would pay to celebrate with us … What arseholes!

"The games stayed like that for a while. It made Shu and I closer. I felt like we were truly bonded, and our vow to never be apart no matter what was even stronger. I guess that's why I did what I did.

"The games changed again, and not like they'd promised. Only Shu was taken one night. I tried to stop them, but they knocked me out. When I came to, I could hear Shu screaming in the game room. I'd never heard that before. I tried to break down the door, but it was locked. I must've broken every bone in my hands trying to escape and save Shu. But I failed.

"Now it was Shu who couldn't stop crying. And there hasn't been a time in my life that I hadn't been so angry. They hurt my wife, and I was gonna make them pay. I searched the house for a wig I could use to make myself look like Shu, and I cut Shu's hair to make her look like me. It really fooled our parents, and they took me the next night, instead of Shu. I was presented to a woman, who looked even more horrible than the first man who'd played with me. But she didn't get far before she realised that I wasn't Shu. I quickly grabbed a screwdriver off the bench and jammed it in the woman's eye. I lost count of how many times I stabbed her before my *father* tried to stop me. I killed him too, and then came after *mother*. I jammed the screwdriver into her knees so she couldn't run, and then I took a stick and beat her to death with it.

"I can still remember the cold air around me afterwards, and the smell of blood, like cold steel. And I realised one thing our parents had told us that was true: you break a promise, you get the bogeyman's cane. And *I* was the bogeyman that night.

"We ran away as fast as we could, as far as we could. But it was winter and we had nothing but the clothes on our backs. Shu started to get sick, and I was afraid. I took my stick and screwdriver, and looked around for someone to rob. Who do I find but Doctor Butterfly? When he wouldn't hand over money, I attacked him just like I did our parents. But the screwdriver couldn't even dent his skin, and he didn't bat an eye when I struck him.

"Instead of eating me, he was so impressed that he took us in. He said he'd train us to fight, so that no one would ever make us suffer again. And he said he'd make us homunculi, so that not even death could part us."

A sharp stillness settled over the playground, punctuated by the combatant's laboured pants. Nathan shuffled uncomfortably as the story settled in. He grimaced at the tragedy of their stories. The two defeated L.X.E. donkeys hung their heads in deep anguish, tears rolling down their cheeks. Shu gripped Tao tightly and sobbed through every word of his account.

Tao sniffed and said, "So, you see why we want to be homunculi? This here is our final test. Killing you and recovering your Kakugane will secure that wish."

"Bored now!" snapped Astrid. She cocked her blades and advanced on the twins. "So you were made sex-slaves. Boo-freaking-hoo! You still work for a society of mass-murdering inhuman scumbags, victimised innocent people in their name, put people who called you 'friends' in danger, and if you got your wish, you'd feast on even more humans. You're no different from Papillon. No, you're worse than him. He at least was dying of an incurable disease. There's nothing threatening you at all! You just want to live in a fantasy and make everyone else pay for it!"

Tao tried to raise his sword, but Astrid just swatted it out of his hand and it clattered away.

"You won't have your fantasy, you mass-murdering shitbags!" she screamed. "Your bonds of matrimony end here!"

Her blades flew toward the cowering donkeys, and hit metal. Astrid's eyes widened to see the blade of Nathan's spear, shielding the twins.

"What're you doing, Nathan?" exclaimed Astrid.

"I should ask the same," gurgled Nathan. "These weapons're for killing homunculi, not humans."

"There's no difference here, Nathan," snapped Astrid. "They've given their souls to the homunculi. There's no middle ground."

"What the Hell is that?" replied Nathan. "Sure, once they've gone homunculi, they can't be helped. But they're still human. Offer them a deal or something."

Astrid palmed her face and yelled, "You are so freaking stupid, Nathan. Get out of my way!" Her blades hooked under his spear and threw him aside. Her eyes locked onto the twins and she charged them. Again, she hit Nathan's spear. He swiped at her to drive her back.

"You're not killing them, Astrid, and that's that," barked the boy.

Astrid's face darkened as she murmured through grit teeth, "You're protecting an enemy, Starlight Lancer. You can say we should take them in, but they're already so far gone that they might as well be homunculi. They'd be a liability."

"No, they're not!" roared Nathan, blood spraying on

his outgoing breath. "They can be helped. They'll tell us everything about the L.X.E. if we do."

Astrid started blankly at him. Her pupils dilated with fury as she growled, "You are naïve, Alchemic Warrior. You protect an enemy, then you make an enemy of me!"

Astrid ignored Nathan's desperate pleas as she charged him. She kneed him in the stomach, punched his face, and slashed at him with her blades. Her murderous visage only broke when she glanced his side, drawing blood. When she heard his anguished cry, her strength left her and she backed away. She growled to fight back tears as he clutched his fresh wounds, and that only made the lump in her throat burn colder.

"Get out of my way!" she cried as she kicked him aside. She then turned to the twins, who watched the action absolutely flabbergasted. With no more interference, she scrambled toward them, her blades trembling. She wordlessly thrust the blades home.

She then roared with frustration at hitting Nathan's spear *again*.

A tiny spectating part of her mind asked, *Jesus Christ, how the Hell does he do that?*

"You are *not* killing them, Astrid!" barked Nathan.

Astrid clenched her fists. She realised she'd have to try better to convince him.

"Nathan, these two are L.X.E.," she began. "Say we took them in, and they just fed us crap. We'd be putting the whole town in danger. Your friends, your sister. What you're doing here might kill them!"

"I don't buy it!" snapped Nathan. "You and Bravo saying I should do what'll give me the least sleep debt. This is it!"

"Sacrifice your friends and family? Really?" asked Astrid. "You'd sacrifice them, sacrifice *me*, for those?"

"They're human beings," cried Nathan.

Astrid lost it. "They're L.X.E.! We have to destroy them! Destroy the homunculus! Destroy my enemy!"

"They're not your enemy," replied Nathan.

"They *are*, mine and yours," barked Astrid. "Between these maggots and your family, who do you really want to protect, Starlight Lancer?"

"BOTH OF THEM!"

His bellow echoed throughout the school and the neighbourhood beyond. Astrid stood dumbstruck by Nathan's scream, and couldn't find a comeback.

"That's the path of a hero, Astrid," Nathan murmured when he found breath to speak. "I thought you were one ... a hero. You sound and act like a hard-ass, and act nice when you need to keep a cover. I thought you were just an amazing actor, and weren't really so callous. You know why? Because you fight homunculi on your own, you save people. You saved me! You gave up one of those precious Kakugane for me. You trained me to protect my friends and family. Then you turn around and try to kill someone else you could help, because ... why? You just don't like them? How do you think that makes me feel, Astrid? To learn that someone so important to me really is just a good actor, and beneath it all is just a callous murderer!"

Astrid's heart sank in her chest at the accusation.

"*They* are the murderers," she stammered, unsure of why tears welled so close to her eyes. "I'm defending your friends. They're the ones who want to hurt people, not me."

"And they're not at all worth saving?" asked Nathan. "Not worth at least *trying?*" Astrid choked at the sentiment. Nathan went on, "That's not what a hero should do. He should try to save everyone he can. *I* want to save everyone! And if we can't save them, we should at least be merciful!"

Merciful!

The word struck Astrid like a boulder. Her blades dropped to the ground with enough force to dent the concrete, and her body started to shake. Her thought train suddenly careened into her dark place, as if the twenty-four-hour guard she'd posted in her mind had fallen asleep. And she saw every last memory that was a denizen of that dark place. Every fang-bearing beast that charged her, every friend lost behind the jaws of a homunculus, every failure, and every bittersweet success. The last memory hit her the hardest: a child, his incisors ready to strike, as he brought his claws across her face.

That strike must've activated some subconscious tape-recorder, which replayed something she'd heard when she was hardly listening: "I hope you will always remember the Lord's teachings: feed the hungry and care for the weakest among you. Treat your fellow human beings with decency, even when they do not do the same for you."

Astrid looked up from the wooden pew, the only one in the church. The priest looked right back at her. His mouth didn't move, but she heard his voice.

"We can learn to forgive those who wrong us, and in so doing, move forward with our lives and leave the bad behind. Because, as Jesus knew, holding onto the bad can make us do bad to others – the source of cruelty isn't Satan, Miss Rachelle. It is our own suffering that we over time take out on others. Mercy not only sets our enemies free, but also ourselves. So as you eagerly reach for your Kakugane, remember the greatest teaching of our Lord: to have mercy and to forgive."

Astrid's legs gave out and she hit the concrete. She tensed every muscle in her body in an effort to hold back her fury.

If only I hadn't met this annoying bastard, she thought. *Since I met him, I've been in agony, annoyed, embarrassed, humiliated, and exhausted. And now I've got to deal with all these repressed memories, and now a damn priest in my head, spewing crap about things he knows nothing about!*

While that part of her mind raged, another part spurred her toward an alien path. Images of Nathan, pulling Ariadne from that snake's belly, led her to think of the idiot's younger sister. The memory of giving Ariadne a piggyback came soon after, and it almost made her chuckle. Watching Bravo trounce people in video games had been a fun sight. Playing card games with the boarders over a slice of the cook's brownie was quite the pleasant getaway from the craziness of her world.

Oh, come off it, you idiot! You still have to deal with Nathan constantly trying either to tease you or hit on you. Not to mention his completely weirdo friends.

Absent any desire, she thought of Klein, who had taken her to help Nathan in the final confrontation with Papillon. He'd paid Paul out of his own pocket to do Nathan's homework and keep their friend from being sanctioned by the school. Jessie had always been the first to pick Nathan up off the floor when Tao beat him.

Each of those people, she'd saved by saving him. By subjecting herself to the utterly humiliating nightmare of dealing with Nathan Grant, she'd created the Starlight Lancer who defends his friends, who in turn support him.

No wonder he worships me, she thought.

A vision of Desbordes, screaming as she repeatedly castrated him, entered her mind. This wasn't the first recollection, but it was the first time she imagined Nathan was watching her. The look she envisaged on his face made her cringe. His imaginary form beheld her with such disgust it terrified her.

Now what am I doing?

A vicious war ripped through her mind, as she savagely fought to retain her bloodlust. But the fight did not go her way.

I can't do it!

With a shriek, her blades dematerialised into a Kakugane in her hand. She looked up at Nathan, her eyes riddled with defeat, and she growled, "Have it your way!"

Nathan smiled weakly, and started to turn. He faced Tao and Shu, and said, "We'll call Bravo over, and we'll explain everything. You guys will be alright, I promise."

Nathan didn't see the oncoming blow before he saw

Tao's face, close to his. Everything below his waist tingled, and then went numb. He looked to Tao's hands, gripping the sword with which the boy had run him through.

"I need no promise!" Tao hissed. He ripped his blade out of his victim and grinned psychotically. "My sister and I will not be put in a room! My wife and I will not be parted!"

Nathan fell backwards in a daze as Astrid sped forward screaming in horror. She broke Tao's nose with a single punch, and then scrambled to Nathan's side. Blood gushed over the concrete, and Astrid's trembling hands were powerless to stop it.

I should've killed them when I had the chance, she chastised herself.

Nathan's shoulder suddenly flashed green. Astrid recognised Shu's green arrow. She looked to the girl, who just stood silently. She didn't ready a blue arrow. Instead, she dropped her bow and held her arms out to accept an impending fate.

"No, Shu! Don't do it!" cried Tao. "Fire a blue arrow. Fire one at me if you have to!"

It looked like invisible ghosts started scuffing Shu's arms, legs, and face with sandpaper and needles. Then her left side slit, her solar plexis burst, and blood gushed from her mouth as she fell to the ground. Astrid watched perplexed as Tao crawled toward her and fumbled to stop her bleeding. He broke down into tears as he screamed for help. He looked right at Astrid and said, "Call an ambulance! Please!"

Astrid just stammered and blabbered as the whole sight drained her of any feeling other than downright shock. She didn't even notice Nathan leap to his feet, snatch her Kakugane out of her hands, and sprint across to them. She watched, as if she were outside her body, as Nathan scooped up Tao and Shu's Kakugane, and placed all three of them across the wounded girl's chest. The whole time, she couldn't take her eyes of Nathan. He just sat beside a boy who had stabbed him through less than a minute earlier, and smiled with relief as the girl in front of him, who had tried to kill them both, stopped bleeding.

To have mercy and forgive, the words echoed in her head once again, but in her own voice. *I don't get it. He was traumatised by almost killing his sister with a ball, and he's able to do it just fine. I've been way more traumatised than him ... so why can't I?*

15 | Impending Battle

It was a week before Bravo was even inclined to tell Nathan and Astrid where the Wu siblings had been taken. Not that he was displeased with how they handled the situation, but Astrid recognised that their interrogation would require delicate handling. It was especially important that their fates be kept secret from any remaining L.X.E. agents hiding in the shadows. So for a time, Astrid and Nathan weren't even told whether the twins were alive, much less still in Wollongong.

The rest of the school was told that the twins had been in a car accident and were being treated at a private hospital. Bravo eventually revealed that it was indeed half-true, and took Nathan and Astrid to see the twins in a small Regiment-owned facility just past Oak Flats.

The exterior of the redbrick building gave off an unassuming aura – the perfect kind for an organisation determined to conceal its existence. Nestled amid a patch of evergreen trees, it seemed more like a senior's home than a regular hospital. The sign nearest the front door even said, 'Alexandria Kalinin Memorial Aged-Care Home.'

Inside were a number of rooms, lavishly furnished, and inhabited by senior citizens. Most of them simply waved or nodded kindly to the visiting group as they passed. They especially gave warm smiles, and even high-fives to Bravo when they saw him. Even Astrid couldn't resist smiling at that.

Then they got to the elevator. Bravo tapped a card against a reader. Despite there being no basement button on the elevator panel, the carriage began to descend. It continued downward, on and on, until it finally stopped, and the doors opened.

The colour scheme of the corridor into which they emerged was no different from the one above ground. It confused Nathan's senses as he followed Astrid and Bravo down toward one of the rooms. Inside were Tao and Shu.

Tao had hardly touched the food on the tray in front of him, his eyes fixated upon his sister. A dozen I-V tubes snaked their way into her arms, and her bedside heart rate monitor beeped at a languid pace. Tao looked up upon hearing the arrival of guests, and shot up erect when he saw Nathan.

"G'day," said Nathan. He offered a smile to the boy who couldn't even look him in the eye. Nathan went on, "How's it going?"

"I've fully recovered," Tao replied. "It still hurts to make certain movements, and I might need some physio." He cleared his throat nervously. "You?"

"I'm fine," said Nathan with a grin. He nudged Astrid and added, "Grumble-guts here is fine too."

Astrid walked up to Tao and looked fixedly at him. She eyed the bruise on his face, remnant of the punch she'd landed.

"Your nose still hurt?" she said curtly.

"Oh, only a little," said Tao.

"Good," blurted Astrid, before she slapped him as hard as she could. "*That* was for stabbing Nathan after he convinced me to spare you," she snapped.

Tao stared back at her speechless. His eyes went to Bravo and to Nathan. Both men looked as if they were about to laugh. Some kind of insanity must have gripped him as he said, "So, Astrid, when's the wedding?"

Bravo quickly dragged the savage Astrid away before she could land any further blows on the invalid boy. The grin on Bravo's face and the chuckles Nathan let out were infectious, and Tao just laughed. That only made Astrid thrash more viciously, though no less futilely.

A soft murmur broke through the tumult, and all eyes turned to Shu lying on the bed nearby. Her pale lips upturned into a weak, but warm smile. Nathan moved to the bedside and sat on the stool there.

"How're you feeling?" he asked.

Shu grimaced silently.

"She's able to talk," said Tao. "But the other wounds are taking time."

Nathan opened his mouth to speak, but surprisingly Astrid beat him to the punch.

"Thank you for saving Nathan," she said, her eyes diverted away from the invalid's face.

"Shu, would you like me to tell them what you told me?" asked Tao, his fingers threaded through his sister's.

"I'll tell them," Shu whispered. "The man who took us … the smiling man. We learned years later that he just sold children to desperate couples. He didn't know our parents were such … *people*. I truly believe that. I once looked up a few children who'd been kidnapped by him. Most of them went to families who loved them and treated them right. When I learned that, I thought, maybe we just didn't deserve such fortune." A tear rolled down her cheek, as she looked straight at Nathan. "But then I saw you defend us, even when we were your enemies. And I realised that it wasn't so much that we didn't deserve kindness; it just got a little delayed, is all. And, if someone like you had known what had happened that first night, you'd have saved us without a second thought."

Nathan grinned, his heart filling with warmth as he patted Shu's hand gently. He felt Astrid's hand grip his shoulder, and knew her face was radiating pride whether she wanted it or not.

Tao wiped away his own tears and proclaimed, "You're the hero, Nathan. I think you should let everyone know that you're the Starlight Lancer."

Nathan scoffed while Bravo quickly interjected, "*That,* I'd have to disagree with. The support is nice and all, but it's imperative that we reduce the information leaks. Isn't that right, Grant?"

"Of course, Bravo," said Nathan. "You think I want to be signing autographs and have girls clamouring over me?"

"Yes!" exclaimed Astrid and Tao in unison.

When the group sobered, Nathan looked to Tao. "So, what's your plan now?"

Tao and Shu exchanged glances, and looked as if they'd made a decision not unlike a suicide pact.

"We've discussed this," Tao began. "We've both agreed to be incarcerated by the Regiment. We've done horrible things on behalf of even worse beings. We deserve punishment."

"Captain Obvious," murmured Astrid. Bravo quickly shushed her.

"But," Tao went on. "We've asked to be separated, indefinitely. I feel that if we stay together, we'll never recover from what was done to us. This way, maybe we'll be able to move forward, and try to start a new life."

Nathan's eyes darted between the pair, who looked as if they were subjecting themselves to voluntary dismemberment.

It would be for them, he concluded.

Tao kept his eyes on Shu as he pulled his hand away from hers and stepped away from her bed. He looked to Bravo and said, "I hope the information we've provided on the L.X.E. will be helpful."

Bravo nodded, and motioned for one of the guards at the entrance to escort Tao away. The boy took one last look over his shoulder, his gaze locked on his sister. Shu grimaced, her tears flowing even faster, as he disappeared down the hallway. Nathan's heart ached and he grabbed her hand.

"It'll be alright," he said, a hint of desperation to his voice.

Astrid quickly pulled him away, murmuring in his ear, "Let her cry."

Nathan tried to linger a little longer, but Bravo firmly muscled him out of the room. The group went up to the roof of the facility. From there, they watched Tao, dressed in inconspicuous clothing, disappear into an unmarked van. The boy shot Nathan a wink, before the van carried him away.

Nathan trembled as the vehicle drove out of sight. He felt Astrid's hand on his shoulder as she asked, "Does this help make up for Papillon at least?"

"He should be so lucky," blurted a man with a fake Italian accent. Nathan and Astrid swivelled to see Papillon. With a flourish, the exuberant creature proclaimed, "And yet, despite his hypocrisy, I'll let him have his happy ending."

"Hardly happy, Chouno," Nathan sighed, the image of Shu's tears fresh in his mind.

Bravo approached the rogue homunculus as if he'd been expected. He procured two phones and handed them over.

"These were the phones they used to contact the L.X.E.," said the commander. "Hopefully you'll have better luck using them to hack the network."

"'Hopefully' is a strong word," said Papillon as he studied the devices.

"What's the matter, Papillon? A little hacking too tough?" taunted Astrid.

"Not at all," replied the homunculus with gusto. "Indeed, 'hopefully' is too strongly pessimistic. It is a certainty that I'll crack them now!"

Nathan and Astrid raised their eyebrows at his exclamation. As the self-proclaimed genius set to work, Nathan leaned toward Bravo and asked, "Hey, does a homunculus embryo really make someone so up themselves?"

Bravo chuckled, "Hardly. To want to become a homunculus, you have to be high on yourself already." The man's grin widened. "But it's really an advantage, since most homunculi are undone by their need to kiss their own bums."

Beside Nathan, Astrid started to giggle in a way he'd never heard from her before. When she met his gaze, she shied away and made every effort to stifle herself. Nathan's jaws dropped in amazement when he realised she wasn't acting. Where his next phrase came from, he didn't know — and probably wouldn't ever know.

"Or sniff their own farts," he added.

That was it. Astrid burst into laughter. She gripped the handrail for support, but it wasn't enough and she crumpled to her knees. Loud, high-pitched cackles erupted from her like a million years of pent-up magma from a volcano. With every hoot and gasp, Nathan's malaise blew away and he joined her on the floor.

Astrid finally found the breath to ask, "Where the Hell was that from?"

"I don't know," chortled Nathan. "I think it was an episode of *The Simpsons*, where everyone goes greenie. But it makes them all so smug that they like sniffing their farts."

With every scene and skit Nathan recounted, Astrid grew redder in the face, until she was nearly out of breath. By the time she managed to quiet herself down, her face was full of blood, so much that Nathan could hardly see the scar on her face. The pair looked up from their place on the ground, and saw Bravo and Papillon's bemused stares.

"Stop staring," cried Astrid between pants. She hid her face behind her hands, but couldn't block her ears when Nathan bellowed, "That's what she said." And the laughter continued with a second wind.

Bravo and Papillon gazed at them as Nathan proceeded to yell, "That's what she said" to every single comeback Astrid's laughter-drunk brain could muster. While Papillon seemed confused by the whole scene, Bravo just smiled. He looked to Papillon and said, "It's probably strange, and even a little sick that I'm saying this, but thank you."

"For what?" asked Papillon.

"If you hadn't experimented with homunculus technology, Astrid wouldn't have come to Wollongong, wouldn't have met Nathan, and she wouldn't be laughing like this now. It's taken a whole lot of unnecessary pain, on the part of a lot of innocent people, but ..." He shook his head in amazement. "To see her like this; it's something I've always wanted for her."

Papillon's gaze shifted as Bravo dished out his begrudging complements. He forced his attention onto the phones, but couldn't help himself. His eyes were inextricably drawn to the chortling couple, and the sight filled him with ire.

Why should he have that? I've suffered more than he ever will, so why don't I have that?

He sensed his heartbeat accelerating, which almost always resulted in a bloody retch. He managed to calm himself in time, such that he only slightly gagged, filling his mouth with the tiniest hint of iron. He swallowed it back and focused on his work.

"It won't last," he replied, half-hoping it would be true.

Bravo surprised him by saying, "Probably not."

It wasn't long before Papillon cracked the phones and had access to the L.X.E.'s network. By then, Nathan and Astrid had calmed themselves and started discussing whether a vacation was in order, once they'd beaten their enemies. Bravo called them over so that they could listen in to any intelligence the phones were about to reveal.

"I've got access to the central database," said Papillon. He checked his own phone's screen, displaying a dizzying array of calculations and readouts. "They haven't detected me yet."

"How can you tell what you're seeing?" asked Astrid.

"Because I'm a genius," replied Papillon. Nathan blew into the back of his hand, the fart sound earning a leftover chuckle from Astrid.

Papillon paid it no mind, his brain working too furiously to care.

"I've got the location of their base," he announced. Bravo, Astrid, and Nathan started to get pumped, just as Papillon's face darkened. "It's not there," he rasped.

"What do you mean?" asked Nathan.

"Doctor Butterfly's healing tank, it's not there," exclaimed Papillon. "It's been moved. They'd only do that if the process was nearing completion. They'll move it to the nearest fresh food source."

None of them needed clarification to know where that was. Bravo bellowed, "We need to move, now!"

Papillon dropped the phones and marched toward the edge of the roof.

"Chouno, you're going to help, right?" asked Nathan.

Papillon grinned maliciously. "Why would I? That school is a prison, bereft of pleasant memories."

"So you're just going to sit there and let all those kids die?" exclaimed Astrid.

"*All those kids* were happy to neglect me as they went about their dates and games," replied Papillon. "I'd not lose a wink of sleep if they all died in a manner more painful than what befell me."

Both Astrid and Nathan fumed, and their hands edged toward their Kakugane.

"On the other hand," blurted Papillon as he reached down the front of his tight pants. "Missing a chance to deprive my Dear Grandfather of his dream, and kill him in the process … Why! I'd never sleep again!" He procured the Kakugane he'd stolen from Desbordes, and with a pirouette he roared, *"Busou renkin!*[19]*"*

Thick blood oozed past his clenched incisors. He gurgled and screeched as black wings burst from his back and carried him into the air. His writhing eventually subsided, leaving him with the most lascivious expression of ecstasy. His grin widened and he bellowed, "You'd best keep up, Starlight Lancer. The final battle is about to begin."

Then he shot through the sky, northwest toward Warrawul.

---

[19] Japanese: "Arms Alchemy."

16 | Moonface

Bravo's car peeled onto the Princes Highway. He mounted the curb at an intersection, and ignored the honks of startled midday drivers. His eyes were manically focused upon the road in front of him, the top-most buildings of Warrawul in his sights.

Nathan and Astrid tumbled about in the back seat as the car swerved. Astrid was as collected as could be, given the circumstances, while Nathan was on the verge of redecorating Bravo's car in bile-green. In between gasps and burps, he managed to find breath to ask, "How're we gonna hide our faces?"

"My Silver Skin'll hide my face," barked Bravo, grunting as the car jumped over a speed bump.

"You should be able to use your lance's red sash like a scarf," said Astrid. "It'll hide your face."

"What about you?" asked a hiccoughing Nathan.

"There's a balaclava in the driver-side pouch," said Bravo.

Sure enough, there it was. But this only made Nathan marvel, "Why is that there? You planning on robbing a bank?"

"Previous owner must've left it there," replied Bravo.

Nathan didn't get a chance to inquire further before action started up ahead. At first, it looked like a small band of Warrawul students had decided to skip school and were running to avoid being caught by the on-duty teachers. Then the gates of the school suddenly crumpled as a car flew through it, crashed across the street, and into a house on the other side. Bystanders shrieked and fled the scene, while cars on the road screeched to a halt at the destruction.

"Shit!" moaned Bravo. He stopped the car short of the school, and procured his Kakugane. At his non-verbal command, it flashed into his silver jacket. "Let's move out, Alchemic Warriors."

The trio exited the car. Astrid pulled the balaclava over her face, and activated her Arms Alchemy. She and Bravo raced toward the school, ignoring the screaming rabble of civilians diving for cover. They got to the gates to see the monster responsible for the destruction. The five-metre tall creature turned to them, as if sensing their Arms Alchemies. Its lidless eyes swivelled in their sockets, before it lifted two parked cars – a startling feat given its emaciated physique. With a nasal cry, it hurled the vehicles at them.

Bravo caught the first one, his feet skidding backwards along the concrete as he accepted the force of the blow, and he diverted it to the side. Astrid blades slashed the second one, and the slices of metal passed by her harmlessly. The pair then launched forward, Astrid targeting the creature's legs. She whipped around them, severing the creature's tendons. It fell to its knees as Bravo leapt into the air.

"Bravo Chop!" he roared, slicing down the creature's midsection. The beast gurgled as it disintegrated into a grey cloud.

Astrid landed next to him and asked, "Please tell me that was Victor and we just won."

"No, this looks like a cheap homunculus clone," replied Bravo.

A teacher nearby looked up from the bushes where she was cowering, and saw her masked saviours. Bravo turned to her and asked, "Are there any more?"

The woman stammered, "I don't know. I just saw one. It ate one of the students!"

Astrid looked around and saw the mounting chaos. Survivors attempting escape pushed against the growing group of curious people who had come to investigate the commotion. One face she didn't see was Nathan's. She hopped up onto one of the brick pylons of the school's fence and scanned the crowd that started to gawk at her.

The L.X.E.'s already here, so no point in trying to keep things hidden now, she thought. *Just gotta find that bloody Nathan.*

There was a sudden flash of golden light in the bushes. It drew the crowd's attention away from the masked Astrid. Then Nathan burst out of the bushes, his lance in hand and his red sash drawn around his neck.

"Oh my God! It's the Starlight Lancer!" cried a voice within the crowd. People hooted and cheered, pushing further into the school to catch a glimpse of the local legend.

"No! Stay back!" roared Bravo, but not even Astrid and Nathan could hear him over the screams of the crowd.

They did, however, hear the howls of L.X.E. agents approaching from the middle of the school. The beings licked their fangs maliciously as they encroached upon the crowd. The three warriors leapt over the people and put themselves between the beasts and their meal. Nathan whipped into action, the sash about his neck flashing gold as he attacked the creatures. He decapitated two of the beasts, while Bravo punched through a few of the larger ones. Astrid's buzz-saw technique made short work of the rest.

The victory was far less enjoyable, as the civilians surrounded the battle like spectators at a sport event. It made Nathan nervous, and infuriated Bravo and Astrid.

"For God's sake, get the Hell out of here!" roared Bravo.

"It's not safe here! Run!" exclaimed Nathan, his hands

held up against the onslaught of smartphone paparazzi.

Astrid wordlessly slashed any phone she saw and screamed at the spectators to flee, but that only made the crowd ramble mindlessly. Those nearest to them tried to inspect their weapons or score selfies with the superheroes. The three backed away, only to lure the crowd into the school further. Bravo stole a glance away from the encroaching mob to see more people filling into the campus from the entrance at the top of the hill. Most of them were students.

Suddenly, a mass of cables and machinery floated out of the sky and settled in the middle of the campus. A small group of homunculi moved to surround it. Prominent amid the glimmering mass was a tank, the contents of which shimmered purple.

Victor is in there, thought Bravo, the idea filling him with dread. But what really made his blood curdle was the figure that hopped off the tank with a click of his heels. A black coat and grey pants of fine quality covered his thin, lanky form, which was hardly worth noting in comparison to his head: a hairless yellow ball. The man's grin widened as his beady eyes zoned on Bravo.

Bravo suddenly punched the ground with a roar, and the asphalt between them and the crowd cracked with a sickening sound. Nathan took note, and focused his energy into his lance, causing it flash vibrantly. The crowd fell silent, withdrawing nervously from the trio.

"You are not safe! Run, or you'll be eaten alive!" bellowed Bravo.

A voice bellowed from the sky like the trumpets of Judgement Day, "I'm afraid it's too late for that!"

Every pair of eyes turned toward to the figure standing atop the school hall. His long hair and puffy moustache gave him the appearance of an English gentleman. It contrasted well with his beige coat tails, yellow cravat, and the purple butterfly pinned to his lapel. His eyes were narrow slits revealing reptilian irises of muddy green.

"Commander, is that him?" asked Astrid in a low whisper.

"Doctor Butterfly," Bravo confirmed.

"I thank you, Warriors of the Alchemic Regiment, for you were wonderful lures," proclaimed Doctor Butterfly with a flourish. Wings of silver smoke sprouted from his back and carried him over the campus. He announced, "Now, we may celebrate the dawning of a new age."

He snapped his fingers, the sound clattering through the campus. Glimmering clouds suddenly burst from beneath the school, gushing from sewer drains and chimneys. The horizon, sky, and sun vanished behind a thick blanket of metallic smog.

Nathan gripped his lance nervously as he looked around. Figures that hadn't been there before were staring at the crowd, who only now realised the situation. Confusion and panic set in quickly as people bumped into each other. That led to pushing and shoving, shrieking and screaming. One homunculus, who wore a punk leather suit, beared his fangs and assaulted a crowd outlier. Before the thing could take a bite, Astrid jammed one of her blades through his throat.

Chaos took the crowd, which scrambled and tumbled back down the hill toward the exit. Bravo's relief was short-lived as homunculi charged after the panicked mob like wolves to a flock of sheep. He called Nathan and Astrid over.

"I'll destroy the tank," he said. "You two need to defend the people. Kill every single homunculus you see. Got it?"

"Got it!" shouted Nathan and Astrid. The former shot northward to defend the frenzied students while the latter went to the aid of the horrified civilians.

Bravo turned to the tank, and the comically dressed creature guarding it. The fiend winked at him, and it made his skin crawl. He breathed deeply, and channelled his disgust into fighting strength. He felt his Silver Skin cement around his body, ready to withstand a hydrogen bomb. Then he marched toward the tank.

A pair of eager underlings beside the yellow-faced man charged Bravo. He blocked the blow to his left and put his fist clean through the homunculus' chest, before backhanding the one to his right so hard her head twisted off. They vanished in a puff of grey dust. The yellow-faced man giggled, "Callous and courageous as ever, perpetually prepared to purge my pets. You remain repetitive, Brigadier Bravo."

"That's *Captain* Bravo, Moon-head," replied Bravo, cracking his knuckles.

In the blink of an eye, the yellow-faced man's smile did a backflip and his brow crinkled. He shrieked, "You cursed codger, constantly confusing my countenance! It's *Moonface!*"

With a grunt from Moonface, the entire horde of homunculi guarding the tank came at Bravo. He caught the first blow aimed for his head, and with his foot dislocated the attacker's hips. He then shoved the first attacker's forearm into the voracious maw of the next attacker and roundhouse-kicked the both of them. He dodged blows from two more behind him, and with a growl sliced through their necks with his hand. Next, he flipped over a dark-skinned homunculus with ripped muscles that tried to tackle him. As he went over the creature's head, he reached back, dug his fingers into the knots of muscle on its chest, and tore the grey flesh clean off the being's bones. The burly homunculus howled in agony as grey blood burst from him like a fountain. Bravo landed behind the creature and saw his first two attackers coming for one last hurrah. He reached back, grabbed the burly homunculus by the neck, and used him as a club to squash the stragglers before they all disintegrated.

Moonface exchanged glances with Doctor Butterfly, before giggling hysterically and applauding the show. Bravo glared at the creature, having not even broken a sweat.

"It's just you and me now, Buttface," he barked. "And this time, you'll stay dead."

Moonface's fangs gleamed as he beamed at the silver-clad man. "My bodacious Bravo, even you cannot kill me."

"I will today," returned Bravo. "You ain't got anyone to help you. You're on your own."

Moonface harrumphed, caressing a moon-shaped broach. Bravo heard the man speak, but his voice came from behind him. He asked, "So I stand solo?" Bravo swivelled and saw another Moonface. He glanced either side, just to confirm the first one hadn't moved. His body trembled slightly.

"Twins?" he asked absentmindedly.

"Foolish fool," said the Moonfaces in unison. The first one caressed his broach, which suddenly flashed. His entire body quivered as his brow knitted with malevolent intent. He suddenly grew a third leg, which stepped away from the rest of his body. His body braced against the pull of the third leg as a second pelvis followed it. Then came another pair of arms, another head, and finally a fourth leg.

The third Moonface breathed deeply, "Moon!"

Bravo's jaw dropped.

"What is this?" he exclaimed.

The second Moonface said, "Watch, you wincing worm." His broach glimmered, and another Moonface grew out from him in seemingly mitotic fashion. Another grew from him. Before Bravo knew it, thirty Moonfaces surrounded him. As he gazed around the circle, his teeth grit nearly to breaking point, he saw the creatures' faces slowly disappear like the phases of the moon. One was even missing a head.

Bravo suddenly palmed his fist, "Oh, I get it! Moon *phase!*" With a chuckle, he shook his head. "No wonder I couldn't kill you. I was only taking out one thirtieth of you. This is an Arms Alchemy!"

The Moonfaces cocked their heads. "Shouldn't you be

shuddering and shivering?"

"Ha! I was more thinking Hugo Weaving should sue somebody!" exclaimed Bravo. "You've been haunting my nightmares for about eleven years. But now that I know how you keep escaping, I can finally kill you!" He took a stance, and the ground beneath him cracked. "There'll be no moon tonight!"

The Moonfaces charged inwards and grabbed his shoulders. With lightning speed, Bravo swiped all of their hands aside and brought his heels across their faces. He bashed the one to his left, chopped the one to his right, then grabbed the head of the one to his left and jammed it down the throat of the right one. A trio of Moonfaces came from behind, and he swiftly blocked and diverted their strikes. Whenever one managed to land a blow, he used the momentum to hit another one even harder.

With a final strike and a glorious roar, Bravo destroyed the New Moon phase, leaving only one remaining.

He took a moment to ponder, *What's this one? Gibbous or crescent?*

"Moon!" droned the lone Moonface.

"Enough with your crazy bullshit!" snapped Bravo. He launched forward, his fist vying for Moonface's broach. He didn't even see the homunculus' arms move to deflect his blow before he found himself flat on his back, a footprint on his stomach. He shot up, his abs slightly cramping, and readied to fight again. Moonface cackled, "You figure your facile physique is the only frame fit to formulate fighting forte?" The homunculus assumed a combat stance, and beckoned Bravo with his fingers. "Human versus homunculus! Who's haughty enough to hook this hellish hurrah?"

Bravo advanced. A pair of hands suddenly gripped him under his arms and wrenched him backwards. He glanced over his shoulder and saw another Moonface. The first one charged and pummelled him in the chest. Bravo fell back, on top of the other Moonface. He used his momentum to roll backward, free of the grip, and kicked the second Moonface into the first.

Both Moonfaces came at him, swiping and punching, blurting "Moon!" with every missed blow. Bravo tried to dispatch them as quickly as possible, but when one went down, another just re-spawned him.

"You met your match, you miserable mug," exclaimed the Moonfaces. "The power of a homunculus against the puniness of a human. Silver Skin or no, it's a slippery slope to saunter when you're against a never-ending stream of foes."

Bravo slipped on the grass and fell to one knee. His pants were audible through his metal jacket, and beads of sweat tickled at his eyes. The last Moonface he'd dispatched re-emerged, good as new, from one of its kindred nearest the purple tank.

The thing in the tank, wreathed in turbulent foam, glowed even brighter. As it did, it made Bravo even more nervous, but those nerves just drained his own energy as he recalled another school from many years ago.

I won't let this happen again!

He clenched his fist and pulled himself up. The Moonfaces were already in action. One landed a blow on his face that threw off his metal hat. Then another punched him in the stomach. Another hit his exposed head. Sixty hands seemed to hit him all at once, and he flew through the doors of the school hall.

Inside were a group of confused students, rounded up like cattle by a horde of L.X.E. troops. They shrieked in horror at the rain of metal, concrete, and glass that flew from the entrance. Before anyone could help Bravo, the homunculi wrested the man to his knees, and held his arms apart. The thirty Moonfaces sauntered into the hall, the same malevolent grin on each of their yellow faces.

"I don't think I'll ever enjoy eating someone as much as you, Bravo," said the multi-headed entity. "In fact, the only time I recall feeling this good is when I ate that comrade of yours. I believe it was four years ago."

Bravo grit his teeth at the visions the fiend revived. But he pushed them down promptly with his mantra: *I cannot stop people from dying. Death comes for us all in the end.*

The Moonfaces continued to speak, but Bravo wasn't listening.

He's stopped using the same letter all the time, he pondered. *Must take up a lot of mental energy.*

He glared at the creatures, trying to show an air of powerlessness to disguise the wheels revving in his head.

All those bodies'd be hard to control for a single mind, especially a moron like him. I can beat him.

"Whatever, Moonface," snapped Bravo. "I stopped caring hours ago."

He straightened out his fingers and summoned all his focus into his hands. The sleeves of his metal jacket disintegrated, and the tiny metal plates shot through the chests of the homunculi restraining him. The students gasped as the beasts melted into a grey mess. Bravo stood amid a cloud of floating metal plates, which he directed at the other homunculi threatening the students.

"Go for it, Mister Costable!" shouted a student who saw his face. The fervour spread through the students like an infectious agent, and soon everybody was cheering.

The peons dispatched, Bravo summoned the plates back to him and they reassembled into his Silver Skin. He glared at the irritated Moonfaces.

"Can you not just die quietly?" exclaimed the entities.

"Not while I've got my students to defend," retorted Bravo.

"Well then, we'll fix that!" snapped Moonface.

Twenty-nine of the Moonfaces leapt into the air, targeting the horrified students. Bravo willed his Silver Skin to disintegrate completely and form a wall over the kids. While the other Moonfaces ran headfirst into the wall, the remaining one came at a now-defenceless Bravo. Blood sprayed from Bravo's mouth as he slumped, held up only by Moonface's fist, embedded in his solar plexus.

"Unlike you, I can do multiple things at once," snapped Moonface. He leaned in and whispered in Bravo's ear. "You're just a lowly human, making like a god using the Kakugane. Victor understood that, which is why the Regiment tried to stop him. It's why you couldn't stop me eleven years ago, and you cannot stop us now!"

"Ha!" gurgled Bravo. "You're not *that* good at multitasking, Moonbutt. What happened to your using the same letter all the time? Can't be easy, can it? Focusing on all those bodies, I mean. You don't even know what's happening to them, do you?"

Moonface looked up, and saw the wall of Bravo's Arms Alchemy, wrapping itself around his other selves. They tried to screech but the wall of living metal gagged them. Moonface backed away nervously.

"That doesn't matter!" the homunculus yelled. "If you kill them, I'll just re-spawn from here!"

Bravo grinned as he wiped the blood from his chin. "Exactly why I'm just wrapping them in my web. All I have to do now is take you out!"

"But you can't harm a homunculus without your Arms Alchemy," exclaimed Moonface.

"Bingo, you butt-faced, brain-dead boob!" barked Bravo. He reached into his pocket and procured another Kakugane. "Bravo! Generously donated by that dip-shit, Janjira."

"MOON!" Moonface shrieked in horror.

"Double Arms Alchemy!" exclaimed Bravo. The Kakugane exploded with bright green luminance that swirled around Bravo's body. When the light cleared, there stood a man clad in silver pants, green overcoat, and a hat crafted in the style of a sea captain. And it shimmered like the ocean.

Bravo radiated energy, the embodiment of his fighting spirit heating the air between him and the mortified Moonface. Before the creature could cry with horror,

Bravo appeared before him and knocked his head off with a swift uppercut. Then he commanded the other Silver Skin to eject another Moonface, which shot toward him with a dismayed wail. He annihilated that one, and the next, and the next, and the next, until there was just one left. The metal wall coalesced around the thrashing creature and carried it toward him.

"Didn't I tell you there'd be no moon tonight?" snapped Bravo. He grabbed the broach and tore it from Moonface's lapel. The homunculus shrieked as the broach transformed into a Kakugane with the serial number thirty. He gazed at it a moment, the serial number eliciting a recall of his history lessons. And he chuckled, "I didn't think you went as far back as Restigouche, Nikolaev."

Moonface growled and opened his mouth for a comeback.

Suddenly, a high-pitched squeal reverberated through the hall. At first, Bravo thought it was a fire alarm. The students growled and cried as they boxed their ears. The only one who wasn't dismayed was Moonface.

"What is this?" snapped Bravo. He grabbed Moonface by his collar, his teeth clattering as he screamed, "Answer me, Nikolaev!"

"It's the rejuvenation tank," murmured Moonface. "He's awakened!"

17 | An Ugly Moth

Chaos raged below.

The anguished and panicked screams of those puny humans were as music to Doctor Butterfly's ears. He waved his hands about as if conducting a hellish orchestra of mayhem. His reptilian eyes narrowed as he watched Moonface duel with the leader of the warriors, and scoffed at the endless race the armoured man ran against his unbeatable second-in-command. He looked south toward the crowd running and screaming to escape the pain, only to dazedly wander back into his buffet. The girl with the mechanical scythes scrambled about to control them, her futile efforts simply comedic to him. He gazed north, and watched with mirth the lance boy struggle against his pawns.

His pupils dilated as he watched the lance boy.

That must be the so-called Starlight Lancer, thought Doctor Butterfly. *The one who defeated Koushaku. I'm not surprised at his lack of skill. That said ...*

The beautifully dressed man's nostrils flared as he detected a scent, carried on the air from that boy's every swipe and blow. He knew that scent well – he almost revered it. Yet, he'd only ever felt it from his friend, convalescing in the tank. He raised an eyebrow, uncertain of what it truly meant. But he had a hunch.

Truly, the world may be stranger than my friend knows, he

concluded.

He directed his gaze down to the tank and noted it's radiant glow.

"Not long now," he murmured.

A flash threw Doctor Butterfly into a daze. He struck the roof of the school hall, leaving a large dent in the iron cladding. He scrambled to his feet, looked up, and almost burst a blood vessel at what he saw.

"Papillon!" he growled at the man in the butterfly mask.

Papillon shimmied his hips, and his black leotard glimmered as his wings settled him down upon the roof. He waved his fingers. "Tsk, tsk. Pa-pi-yon! And put more love into it!"

Doctor Butterfly scanned the black wings and sniffed their odour.

"So it was *you* who killed Desbordes and stole his Kakugane?" he growled.

"In a sense, Dear Grandfather," replied Papillon. "I spared him a torturous death at the hands of one Astrid Rachelle. The Kakugane was remuneration."

"Mean you to go against me, who saved you from certain death?" retorted Doctor Butterfly.

"Pah, I was naught but a guinea pig for your healing tank," exclaimed Papillon, his eyes filling with fury. "You considered me nothing but a dead weight. I almost died twice! And I didn't go through the fires of Hell just to nourish Victor when the foul beast awakes!"

With a manic cry, Papillon pointed his fingers at the tank. A cloud of black soot burst from his wings and sped toward the device. Doctor Butterfly flew downward, put himself between the tank and the projectile, and flicked it back at Papillon. The ball exploded with a flash over Papillon's head.

"You will not forestall my dream," bellowed Doctor Butterfly as he ascended above the tank.

"Reviving someone else?" said Papillon, his hands on

his hips. "You call that a dream, Dear Grandfather? Don't make me laugh." He waved his hands and conjured two handfuls of his black dust and hurled it at Doctor Butterfly. They both exploded before Doctor Butterfly could deflect them, and he flew headfirst into the gravel car park beside the hall. He regained his senses in time to see Papillon ready another barrage.

And he grinned.

Papillon loosed his combustible clouds upon the defenceless tank, but it vanished suddenly. The dust balls diverted and flew away from the ground. They ascended into the sky before shooting straight at Papillon. The butterfly man flew across the corrugated iron roof, his leotard smouldering from the blast. He coughed and spluttered, blood bursting from his throat. His chest burned from lack of oxygen as he looked up and saw Doctor Butterfly emerge from within the cloud.

"You're trying to figure out how I did that," intoned the well-dressed man. He raised his hand. "Well, maybe this will be a suitable hint!"

His hand flashed, and he vanished.

Papillon stood and looked around. He couldn't see anything besides the fog and the school hall's roof below his feet. He cautiously tiptoed to the edge of the roof. There was still chaos below, but he could hardly care if a few snot-nosed kids were eaten.

"It's what they deserve, right?" mumbled a familiar voice. The hairs on Papillon's neck stood on end as he turned and saw a man who looked almost like himself. The last time he'd seen that face was as it disappeared behind his teeth.

"Jiro!" gasped Papillon. "But you're dead!"

"You ate me, I remember," replied Jiro as he drew his hair behind his ear. "But why should death stop me? It's not like I'm you." Papillon's chest tightened and he vomited. "Oooh, look at that," chortled Jiro as he sauntered toward him. "Koushaku's a sickie! A sickie, little bitch! He shouldn't be wearing such an elegant mask."

Jiro snatched the mask off his face, leaving Papillon with an overwhelming feeling of nakedness. He fumbled and flailed to retrieve the mask as Jiro held him at arm's length.

"Excellent, Jiro!" exclaimed another voice, which drained the energy from Papillon's legs as he turned to see his father. "You are now truly the head of the Chouno house!" proclaimed the elderly man. He gripped Papillon's hair and growled, "You are cut off! You worthless weakling!"

Papillon shook free of the man's grip and pushed him away. He took to the skies, his wings barely having enough energy to hover. A pair of metal talons dug through his skin and dragged him down to the ground. He looked up and saw the disgusted face of Burrumering.

"This doesn't even qualify as good tucker!" growled the homunculus as he tossed Papillon's helpless body aside. He rolled into a net of vines that wrested him into the air so that their heavily-tattooed owner could study him. She sneered as if he were a rotting piece of meat, and tossed him aside, only for a mechanical toad and a snake to play hacky-sack with his body.

Papillon finally escaped and crawled away. He gripped the ankles of one of the students standing near the school hall and pleaded for help. The red-haired Asian girl looked down, her hazel gaze dampened by her pale visage and the blood that gushed from her neck. Papillon's eyes darted to the nametag on her tattered uniform: Asuna Yuki.

The girl sobbed, "Why me? I didn't do anything to you. I was just nice and asked you to show me around the school. And you fed me to your pets."

Papillon pushed away from the girl, who advanced upon him.

"I just wanted to live!" he retorted. "I didn't care who I had to kill!"

He backed into another person. He gazed upward and

saw the woman from whom he'd inherited his hair colour and defined jawline.

"Would you have killed *me* to live?" droned the woman. "Would the one to whom I gave life have such disregard for my own? Is that who I raised?"

Papillon boxed his ears.

"Leave me alone!" he cried. "I don't care about other people's suffering! No one cared about mine! That's why they left me to die!"

"You shame me, Koushaku," said his mother, her eyes melting into black streams down her cheeks.

His conscious mind was drenched with adrenaline and swam in a sea of fear. He clenched his head even tighter to block out the din of voices demanding he feel guilt. Yet their voices pervaded his mind and pushed him ever nearer to breaking point.

Still, this isn't guilt, thought the tiniest portion of his mind still behind a firewall. *No, I'd felt guilt plenty of times. Whenever I saw a butterfly strike a spider's nest out of my reach, I felt sad. I know what guilt is like. This isn't it. To be honest, I'm just annoyed. This whole thing is just really, really, **really** annoying.*

Let's be really honest. The dead really don't matter. I never believed in an afterlife, did I? Sure, I talk about Hell, but that's just pain. Death isn't pain; it isn't anything. Go under anaesthetic or non-REM sleep, and you get your death experience right there.

My mother's not watching me from Heaven or Hell, nor my father or my insufferable little brother. That exchange student's not here. Not Burrumering, not Rose, not Paddock, not even Chamberlain. None of these people are really here.

None of this is real. This is an Arms Alchemy. My Dear Grandfather's Arms Alchemy. So is this mist: a mind-control device.

Papillon grinned, and every ghost that haunted him withdrew in alarm.

"Don't call me by that name," he murmured. "Koushaku Chouno is dead. *My* name is …" He struck a provocative pose that always got a reaction from his audience, and he roared, "Papillon!"

The air around him detonated, throwing Doctor Butterfly clear off the roof. The man, so completely bewildered by what happened, couldn't slow himself in time to avoid crashing into the asphalt basketball courts near the car park. Grey blood dribbled from his temples and stained the smashed rock. Dizzy, he looked up to see Papillon, floating above him with the most resplendent wings. Much of his leotard had been burnt off and his pale skin smouldered. Yet he held himself high as glared down at Doctor Butterfly.

"Quite the weapon, Dear Grandfather," Papillon proclaimed. "I believe they call it 'chaff.' Metal particles meant to confuse enemy radar. Except these particles confuse the senses. That doesn't really matter, so long as you let off an explosion powerful enough to disintegrate them."

Doctor Butterfly hobbled to his feet and spat a black mass. With a long sigh, he said, "That's the first time someone has deciphered my Arms Alchemy."

"Don't worry, Dear Grandfather," said Papillon as he set down on the asphalt. "Even *I* underestimate how smart I am."

"I won't make that mistake again!" roared Doctor Butterfly as he lunged forward. The pain in his head and the ringing of his ears hampered his movements, which Papillon easily anticipated and avoided. Papillon deflected his blow and retaliated with his own. Doctor Butterfly stumbled backwards and blindly shot a handful of his silver chaff, which met a cloud of Papillon's black powder and disintegrated in a flash and a bang.

Papillon laughed raucously as he wrestled with his grandfather, toying with him and pushing him around like a schoolyard bully playing with an upset nerd. He giggled as Doctor Butterfly stumbled, scuffing his fine trousers on the asphalt. He chortled as his grandfather landed a blow that didn't even tickle him. He caught the blow and, with a harrumph, he kicked the old man in the stomach. It took no time at all for his jovial mood to vanish when he felt the vice-grip that the old man exerted around his leg.

Doctor Butterfly screamed as he hauled Papillon over his head and smashed him into the ground. He lifted him out of the crater, spun him around, and threw him into the retaining wall at the edge of the court. Papillon stumbled forward, covered in dirt and powdered concrete, wheezing as blood sprayed from his mouth. He could barely make out Doctor Butterfly limping toward him, rage radiating from his reptilian eyes.

"No mere hallucinations this time, Koushaku!" the man growled, summoning a thick cloud of chaff into his hands. "I'll just destroy your mind all in one go!"

The air around them shuddered with a deafening squeal. Doctor Butterfly gasped, and a look of utter glee fell over his face. He barely had the breath to say, "The alarm! He has awakened!"

His chest suddenly felt like a meteorite hit it. He looked down and saw Papillon's arm, having stabbed him clear through the L.X.E. brand on his chest. He looked up into Papillon's rage-filled eyes, and chuckled.

"Well done," he intoned. He offered his descendent a genuine smile. "My dream is complete, nonetheless."

Papillon withdrew his hand, soaked with grey blood, and watched his grandfather collapse in a gasping, wheezing mess.

"Ignoble end for the great Bakushaku Chouno," he said with a sneer. "Your dream was little more than to put a Band-Aid on someone's owwie."

Bakushaku laughed, "Oh, it's far more than that, Papillon. You could not possibly imagine the greatness."

"Some Alchemic Warrior who defected when he realised how much better homunculi are," blurted Papillon with a wave of his hand. He readied a blast to end the wretched man, but a wave of fatigue struck him harder than anything he'd ever felt. He gazed down at the ground, and saw a trail of glowing wisps emerge from his body and snake their way toward the levitating tank. Terror filled him as he realised what was happening.

"Is this a function of your tank?" he exclaimed.

"No, this is *his* function," replied Bakushaku. "Why concern yourself with the hunt when you need only extract your sustenance through a high-powered resonance link? Truly a masterpiece of Alchemy, that man. When I found him, buried in that chamber in the middle of the sea, I knew instantly what he was. I was as terrified as I was moved, and vowed to restore him to his true majesty! And now, that dream is achieved."

Papillon glared at his grandfather, his fury the only thing keeping him conscious amid the draining of his energy. He spat, "That's it? You became a homunculus and established the L.X.E., just for *that*? You're a disgrace!"

"Ha, perhaps you're right," replied Bakushaku. "Rather than Doctor Butterfly, I'm more aptly named 'moth-man.' I could only flit about his light, but never truly approach it. But I was satisfied to merely orbit the sun, rather than touch it."

"What kind of homunculus is he?" growled Papillon.

"He's not even homunculus," said Bakushaku. "He's a higher kind of existence. The pinnacle, reaching beyond Alchemist, Witch, Demon Weapon, Asura … Even the Reaper himself would cower at the thought of him."

"How did he become that way?" asked Papillon.

Bakushaku chuckled, his skin wrinkling and his hair splitting. "The answer to that is so horrible, only someone such as you could appreciate the true irony. And if you would seek it, as a butterfly determined to surpass the sun itself, you'd best keep an eye on that lance-boy."

"Nathan?" Papillon's voice caught in his throat.

"Trust me," Bakushaku whispered as his body slowly dissolved in the wind. "Alchemy … hardly scratches the surface … of the strangeness of this world."

And he was gone, leaving behind a Kakugane. Papillon

reached for it and held it close to his chest. He willed it to heal him as he processed his ancestor's final words. He gazed down at the serial number etched on the talisman's surface: fourty-four.

His tired brain did a double take.

Wasn't that Nathan's Kakugane number?

18 | Who got a new life?

The campus reverberated with the screams of the distraught crowd. The rabble of civilians seemed to heave like boiling water, burning in the wrath of their terror.

Astrid caught one of the lankier homunculi in her sights, and leapt toward it. Her mechanical limbs clinked as she locked them onto the creature encroaching hungrily upon the crowd. She lopped off its arms and sliced through its abdomen. She turned to the whimpering children behind her and bellowed, "Run!" She finished off the monster, and then yanked the kids to their feet and shouted, "Back to the south exit. Go!"

She saw more homunculi wrestle with a few guys in singlets and boardies – clearly among the morons who came to get a selfie with the Starlight Lancer. She flipped through the air, her blades spinning with her to deprive the monsters of their hands. With the blunt sides of her blades, she hurled the men down the path, before bringing the blades back and embedding them in the monsters chests.

No more homunculi fell within her sights, and she took the reprieve to jump onto a brick wall over the crowd and yell, "Get to the southern gate! Get as far away from here as you can!"

A part of her mind turned its attention to the blanket

of fog over the school, and wondered why Doctor Butterfly had created it. She didn't give it much more thought, having more pressing matters to worry about. A group dressed in punk clothes soared through the air to attack the crowd, doing what they could to herd the human livestock northward. Some of them transformed into mechanical scorpions and wolves. That made Astrid smirk nostalgically as she sped through the crowd, back-flipped to decapitate one and landed with her blades engulfed in the biomechanical flesh of another.

Astrid turned and saw a pair of familiar faces. Jessie and Paul stood, pale-faced with terror and bewilderment. She looked around and saw a few more people, who were running about confused and dazed. She grabbed Paul and yelled, "I told you to get to the southern gate!"

"We can't!" replied Paul.

"We tried to go through the gate, but we just ended up in another part of the school," exclaimed Jessie. "We keep getting turned around in that fog!"

Astrid's heart jumped into her chest at the realisation. She gazed to the wall of mist that blocked out the horizon.

No wonder, she thought with disgusted admiration. *He uses the homunculus clone at the front to lure us in, and then we bring in a crowd of people itching for their next online post. The mist keeps us all in for Victor's feast.*

Astrid glared northward to the centre of campus, where the tank's glow intensified. She could only just make out Bravo fighting against a horde of identically dressed homunculi, and wondered whether or not she should assist. Just as she started to edge up the hill, a hand caught hers.

"It's you, isn't it, Astrid?" asked Paul, his eyes sunken with the revival of repressed memories. "The night of the gas leak, you were the one who saved me from that thing, weren't you?"

Astrid's skin broke out in goosebumps, and she pursed her lips with annoyance. She yanked her arm away with a growl of frustration and ran up the hill. She didn't get far before screaming sounds reached her right ear. She looked toward the English classrooms, and saw a rabble of mechanical lizards scratching and clawing at the rooves. She could just make out the kids trapped in there.

Her blades launched her up through the air, and she landed on the roof beside the creatures. The nearest one's metal hide glimmered red as it unleashed its tongue at the unwanted intruder. Astrid spun on the spot, her blades slicing up the tongue. She then charged the creature, hooked one of her blades under its jaw to flip it upside down, and then sliced up its underside. The creature vanished with a gurgle and an explosion of tissue and metal. Astrid made quick work of the others, before swinging off the roof and through the window of the classroom. The group of mostly schoolgirls shrieked at her appearance, but shut up quickly as she thrashed the biomechanical spider that threatened them. She sliced off its mandibles and slashed its eight eyes out, and then drove all four of her blades into its bulbous hind section.

"I hate spiders," she grumbled.

She turned to the girls huddled in the corner, but another mechanical spider burst through the wall of the classroom, showering her in glass and shrapnel. She instinctively held up her blades as a shield, which kept the glass from injuring her, but also gave the spider a chance to pin her robotic limbs down.

"You murdered my husband!" growled the spider, which looked a lot bigger than the other one.

Astrid couldn't move her blades out from under the spider's grip. Her stomach churned at the sight of the creature's mandibles, dripping foul smelling liquid and twitching revoltingly. They drew nearer as Astrid thrashed more, but stopped as something hit the monster's back. It turned to see Jessie and Paul, feebly clattering chairs against its carapace.

Now's my chance, thought Astrid. One of her blades

wriggled free and vivisected the eight-legged beast. The rest of her metal arms broke free and finished the job. Astrid caught her breath, while gazing at Paul and Jessie.

"This makes us even, eh?" asked Paul, equally out of breath.

Annoyed, Astrid hushed the m both before turning to the girls in the corner.

"Are you alright?" she asked. A few managed to silently nod. "Good. Go with these two boys, and find a room in the school to hide," she ordered. She looked at Paul and Jessie. "A place with no windows, and a lock on the door. Find it, and keep quiet. Got it?"

"Got it," said Jessie. Paul started rounding up the reluctant girls and headed out of the classroom.

There was one among the girls who gazed directly at her saviour. Astrid didn't immediately recognise the child amid her panting and sweat drenched balaclava. The girl cornered her at the entrance and whispered, "Astrid, is it you?"

Astrid rolled her eyes irately and wondered whether people had suddenly developed X-ray vision. She looked directly at the girl and recognised her as Ariadne. She very reluctantly rolled up her balaclava to reveal her flushed face. Ariadne stared a moment, before her grin widened and her eyes gleamed.

"Nathan's here too, isn't he?" she asked. "He really *is* the Starlight Lancer."

Astrid had had enough.

"Go, now," she slowly enunciated. She rolled the balaclava down and marched out of the room. She left the kids behind and sprinted through the locker areas. Her mood was downright foul, and at least there were homunculi around to take her anger out on. When there were no more L.X.E. left on the south side, she headed for the centre of the campus.

As she got within sight of Bravo, she heard the clashing of Arms Alchemies, and looked northward. She saw

Nathan, his red sash still around his neck, fighting tooth and nail with a blue-clad homunculus wielding chain-scythes. The fiend had just landed fresh wounds on Nathan's chest and face. Her bad mood gave way to concern as he fell to his knees.

You're more concerned with him than the mission at hand, Bravo's voice replayed in her mind. Then she shook her head, remembering Ariadne, Paul, and Jessie, and all the other people who would suffer if they failed.

We can't lose another warrior, she told herself. *Nathan's the hero defending this town. Keeping him alive* **is** *the mission!*

Astrid's blades pushed her off the ground and she flew toward the creature attacking her friend. She caught him off-guard and sliced his knee open. He fell down and she kicked him with all her strength. He flew backwards and Astrid yanked the chain-scythe out of his hands. It reverted to a Kakugane form and landed near Nathan. Astrid then quickly dispatched the homunculus, only to have another larger one come at her with an Arms Alchemy that could only be described as a rocket-powered hammer. She threw her blades up to shield herself, and it took all of her might just to keep the hammer from crushing her. Her attacker grinned, crinkling his facial tattoos, as he pressed harder against her buckling shield.

"Spartan Valkyrie!" yelled Nathan. He grabbed the Kakugane beside him and tossed it at her.

This is gonna be so freaking awesome, yelled her inner child. The thought, and the smile it put on her face, surprised her as she bellowed, "Double Arms Alchemy!"

When the flash cleared, a metal back-plate had inserted itself into the harness of Astrid's Valkyrie Skirt. It fitted along her spine and sprouted four more articulated metal limbs. The ends of those limbs began to screech with the sounds of chainsaws. Her new arms reached around her shield and promptly hacked her attacker to pieces. She caught the monster's Kakugane and hurried over to Nathan.

His bruises and cuts had started to heal, but his fatigue slowed the process. Astrid handed him the Kakugane and said, "Put this in your pocket. Go and hide somewhere until you heal."

"No, I can still fight," replied Nathan, spurred by the screaming from the classrooms near the north exit. He tried and failed to stand, and Astrid forced him back down.

"*I'll* go and handle them," she said firmly. "You need to heal first."

"I can't believe those sons of bitches got the drop on me," growled Nathan.

"Hey," she said, holding his chin so that he would look at her. "Everyone makes mistakes. Don't worry about it." She smiled at him. "I'll tap you back in when you're ready."

Astrid stood and ran northward to help the trapped students. She looked over her shoulder at her friend, and beamed.

That's right, he's my friend, she thought. *That's why I gave him the Kakugane in the first place. I wanted him to be my friend. And now his friends are mine too. No wonder they recognised me. And you know what, me? I don't care anymore.*

Every blow she landed to an L.X.E. homunculus felt different after that, as if she no longer heard screams of the innocent dead as she wielded her Arms Alchemy. Instead, she saw visions of card games with Ariadne, joking with Nathan, and watching them play video games against Bravo and lose spectacularly. Every blow was now another day in which she could be happy.

*I gave Nathan a new life? Bollocks, I did. He gave **me** a new life.*

* * *

Nathan watched Astrid run off. There were now eight mechanical limbs instead of four, and half of them had chainsaws.

Goddamnit, she's so awesome, he thought.

Her smile must have had some mind-control powers, because it somehow forced him to obey her. He sighed and hobbled toward one of the benches. He held the spare Kakugane close to his chest and focused on sealing his wounds. Of course, the moment he stopped moving, his mind grabbed onto the chance to chastise him.

You stuffed up again! They got the tank ready because they tested it on Chouno. They had Chouno because you were too chicken-shit to kill him properly. You had to kill him because you needed that antidote for Astrid, which she wouldn't have needed if she hadn't taken that homunculus embryo for you, which wouldn't have been coming at you if you'd not raced in and bloody —

The brick-paved ground cracked as Nathan jammed his spear into it. His wounds hurt more and his spear threatened to fall apart. He grit his teeth angrily and fumed.

This is my fault. Tonnes of people are gonna be scarred for life because of me.

A faint voice broke through his despair. He stood up and looked southward from where the voice came. It was Ariadne, racing through the chaos, waving at him ecstatically.

He heard a thud, and then another. Ariadne must've heard it too, because she stopped dead in her tracks and looked toward the art rooms in horror. Another homunculus clone, even bigger than the one that attacked the south gate, lumbered through the buildings, demolishing them. Students and teachers fled from the giant beast, which reached for them, its hungry jaws oozing purple muck.

Nathan whipped into action. He pocketed his spare Kakugane and leapt through the air. He landed on the creature's wrist and jammed his blade into the flesh. His chest muscles clenched, and he cried in agony. He came to his senses in time to jump out of the way of the giant's other hand. He stumbled as he landed on the library roof.

He pushed aside the pain in his chest and looked at the beast. He hadn't even dented the skin and his lance's blade was cracked.

By then the crowd had put enough distance between themselves and the giant, and they watched in awe as the urban legend of the Starlight Lancer came to life before them.

Most were disappointed.

Nathan came at the monster again, swiping and slashing, and yet he barely left a scratch on its skin. The beast swatted him away and he fell to the ground, striking it with enough force to make every spectator wince. The beast's four eyes locked onto the Starlight Lancer, writhing in the pile of broken brick and mortar. It's white irises narrowed as it lunged for him. It suddenly pulled back and turned. Nathan looked over and saw Ariadne, trying to drive a broken steel pipe into the monster's ankle as she screamed, "Leave my brother alone!"

The beast grabbed her ferociously and its maw released a torrent of rancid, sewer-scented air as it opened to chomp her down.

Nathan was immobile as time slowed down. The creature's skin started to turn red and leathery, tight stitches lining its form. Ariadne sat on the concrete, blood oozing from her head.

Your fault!

Nathan suddenly roared, and golden flashes of electricity arced from his body. The hull of his lance flashed and he was instantly in motion. He flew at the creature, cleaved through its wrist, and smashed into the library's outer wall. He couldn't be concerned with pain yet. He saw his sister falling with the creature's disintegrating hand, and flew through the air to catch her. He then sprinted away from the howling creature and finally came to a stop.

He doubled over with pain and exhaustion, falling upon his spear for support. The ringing of his ears subsided enough to hear his sister's voice.

"Get up, Nathan," she yelled. "You've still got to take this thing out."

Nathan sensed the incoming attack before Ariadne screamed, and swivelled to block the giant's punch. He forced every ounce of power remaining in him into his lance, willing it to push against the monster's fist. The giant roared furiously as it pushed harder. Nathan's knees started to buckle.

"Come on! Beat its arse!" roared a voice. He looked over and saw Klein, punching the air above his head. Behind him was a horde of Warrawul students, Astrid at the front. Together they all started to cheer. Behind him, Ariadne led the other students in applause and support. People emerged from the south end of the school, led by Paul and Jessie.

Nathan's ears filled with the sounds of the people roaring, "Get him, Starlight Lancer! Smash that pushover! Go for it!"

His wounds sealed. His sash glowed brighter than ever before. His senses cleared, and the force of the monster pushing against him felt little more than a light breeze. With a flick of his wrist, he diverted the oversized fist into the ground beside him. Then, with a fierce roar, he launched himself forward, and thrust his spear straight through the creature's chest. The thing wailed as it toppled to the ground and melted.

Nathan landed on the roof of the library, in full view of every single witness. He didn't stand up straight, nor did he open his eyes. He just sat there, and listened to the cheers of the crowd.

When he did stand, the crowd was still applauding. He turned and saw Ariadne, her eyes wet with pride as she hooted. Then he looked at Paul and Jessie, who thumped their chests. He saw Klein, who just wore a smile. Then he looked at Astrid. Underneath her balaclava, she mimed, "You're the hero."

The crowd suddenly fell silent, gripping their ears and wailing at the piercing screech that ripped through the area. Nathan looked over and saw the flashing beacon on the tank as it started to ascend. Its purple glow outshone anything else, its intensity matched only by that of the siren that blared from it.

That can't be good, thought Nathan.

He looked down at the crowd and saw them shudder and grip their heads. Tendrils of shimmering energy snaked their way along the ground and gravitated toward the tank. The grass directly beneath the floating apparatus started to wilt and turn brown. That colour radiated outward, until even the trees around the school were dying. People started to collapse. Nathan glanced over Astrid's way. She too had started to falter, but not as fast as those around her, who fainted one by one.

It's sucking their life force, Nathan realised.

Filled with fear and worry, he leapt from the roof, across the campus, toward the tank. His lance flashed gold, and he launched toward the device. Its flimsy hull crumpled under the force of his blast, and the machine disintegrated.

Nathan suddenly found himself halted in mid-air. A pair of deep red eyes glared into his. The owner of those eyes furrowed his luminescent green brow as he wiped his similarly glowing hair aside. Nathan glanced to where his lance's tip had struck the being, and found it hadn't even touched the being's crimson skin before it stopped.

"Good morning," mumbled the being with a thick European accent. "Who are you?"

19 | Revival

With the least perceptible twitch of his palm, Victor shot the boy before him into the ground below, faster than a bullet from a gun. The earth crumpled where he struck, and he spewed blood as he bounced inside the crater. Victor gazed down at the vanquished boy and sneered, "I assume you merely stole a Kakugane. An Alchemic Warrior with such a lack of training would be truly inconceivable."

He smelled another Arms Alchemy, and glanced downward from his airborne perch. He saw a dark-haired girl running toward the boy's body, and hummed with genuine admiration for the truly impressive-looking Arms Alchemy she wore. He glanced over to the entrance of the school hall, and noted the dress of the man who sprinted outward. The metal coat reminded him of paintings of Napoleon. The style really didn't appeal to him.

"This is the world after seventy years?" he mumbled as he gazed around the strange architecture of what he'd been told was a school. He growled, "What other horrors has Alchemy conjured in my absence?"

* * *

Astrid retracted her eight mechanical arms and tried to lift Nathan up. Panic filled her as he gurgled incoherent responses to her inquiries. Bravo appeared, clearly wearing a variant of his Silver Skin, and helped shoulder him away from the beast. Astrid's legs knocked and she stumbled as the energy seemingly vanished from her body.

"This is Victor's real power?" she exclaimed before collapsing.

Bravo looked down in panic and saw the puffs of energy slip away from her body toward the shining green and crimson entity gazing down at him. Debris from the healing tank lay scattered about the dry brown grass below the creature. Bravo clenched his fists at the sight, and knew they'd failed.

"Victor!" he roared.

"Commander," whimpered Astrid. "It's not happening to you. Look!"

Bravo looked around him and saw none of those streams departing his body. He realised he didn't feel tired either. He glanced into the sport hall and saw Moonface, unconscious with the other Silver Skin wrapped around him like a cocoon.

My armour must defend against this drain ability, Bravo concluded. He waved his hand, and the flurry of metal plates left Moonface and coated the kids in the hall. The energy streams flowing from their bodies suddenly stopped.

"He can't drain energy through the Silver Skin," he yelled. "I'll take him out."

By then, Victor had set himself down, his bare feet threading through the brittle blades of grass. Bravo locked his gaze onto the creature and charged. He summoned every ounce of energy into his hand, which he brought down on Victor with a roar: "Bravo Chop!"

He struck the creature's forehead, and his skeleton almost shattered with the vibrations that rippled along it. Victor swatted Bravo's hand aside, and the man flew backward, only barely able to recover. Dread filled him as he comprehended the extent of the being's power.

I need to be stronger!

He willed his body to still itself, and accumulated all his focus. He then sprinted forward, his fists directed at Victor's face and torso. He hit nothing but air as Victor dodged his every blow.

Faster!

His fists sped through the air between them, fuelled by his maximised fighting instincts. Yet they frustratingly missed Victor's crimson hull by fractions of a millimetre. The being kept the most bored look, as if he were more concerned with where the bathroom might be than the strength of the man failing to strike him.

Bravo aimed a strike directly at his heart. Victor caught it in a vice-grip strong enough to crinkle Bravo's impenetrable metal sleeve. The beast twisted Bravo's arm, tearing tendons and ligaments. Bravo didn't get a chance to cry in pain before Victor's knee went into his stomach and blasted all the wind out of him. The beast dug his luminescent nails into Bravo's back, scrunched a handful of the Silver Skin, and threw the man into the wall nearby. Bravo hit the ground and was motionless, the tattered remains of his Arms Alchemy left in Victor's hand.

"Lacking in substance *and* style," snorted the beast as the metal jacket reverted to a Kakugane, which he tossed aside.

Astrid gazed in awe at the motionless body of her seemingly invincible commander. At the very least, the trail of energy that wafted from him proved he still lived. And yet, she couldn't believe the ease with which the undefeated Captain Bravo was bested. She glared at the seemingly monolithic entity, draining everyone's energy. Fatigue started to overcome her, which subsequently filled her with panic.

I have to stop him, or he'll kill everyone!

Her mechanical limbs quivered as she pushed herself up and advanced. She willed any strength she had left into her legs and raced toward the being, which merely raised its eyebrows at her roaring attack. She swiped, slashed, and stabbed at Victor with every blade. And yet, even when she felt them contact with the searing surface of Victor's skin, they didn't even depress it. Frustrated, she brought her chainsaw blades down on Victor's shoulders. He caught them with his bare hands and the motors within them screeched and stalled under the force of his grip. He grunted as he shattered them with a twist of his wrists, and then grabbed the metal stumps of her limbs and swung her around. Next thing she knew, her Valkyrie Skirt lay as a streak of scrap metal leading from Victor to the pancaked car on which she lay, unable to feel a thing except agony.

Victor harrumphed as her weapon dematerialised into another pair of Kakugane. He droned, "Disappointing. I actually thought *your* weapon showed promise."

"Stop this!" screeched a voice. Victor turned to see Nathan hobbling toward him. "Stop sucking everyone's life force!"

Victor raised an eyebrow. "Unfortunately, that's not possible."

"You already revived, so you don't need to feed any more!" cried Nathan. "You're killing my friends! Stop it, please!"

"I cannot stop this any more than I could stop the beating of my heart," replied Victor. He pursed his lips, as if only slightly bothered by the death around him.

His expression made Nathan's blood boil.

"Then have it your way!" the boy shouted. He hefted his lance out of the dirt and charged. He kept his eyes fixed on Victor, who rolled his eyes with a sigh, but made no move to deflect or even block his blow. Nathan roared even louder and thrust his spear home with all his might.

Victor actually stumbled off-balance, his eyes radiating surprise and his brow furrowed with discomfort. Nathan looked at the bright blue blood that gushed from the stab wound.

I actually got him! I beat him!

Astrid's eyes lit up with amazement at the sight as she

hobbled toward the combatants.

"I did not think I would ever feel such a sensation as this again," Victor mumbled. He looked at Nathan quizzically. "Who are you?" Nathan, perplexed by the beast's nonchalance, didn't respond. Victor ripped the lance out of his abdomen, the wound closing instantly. He studied the lance, now drenched in his blood, and hummed with interest as its sharp edge slit the skin on his fingers.

"Your Arms Alchemy does not appear to be terribly unique," said the beast, backing away from the boy. "Nevertheless, you are one too dangerous to fight bare handed. I shall arm myself."

Nathan and Astrid gasped as Victor placed his hand over his heart and bellowed, "*Waffen Alchimie!*[20]" His nails penetrated the skin, flesh, and bone of his torso and wrenched something from within his chest. In his palm, coated in blue and red tissue, was a hexagonal talisman of lustrous black metal.

"A Black Kakugane?" Astrid gasped.

The talisman exploded in a maelstrom of dark purple discharges that condensed into an axe, the blades of which shimmered in the radiance of Nathan's lance. Victor raised his weapon, and his hair glimmered with greater brightness as he raised his fighting instincts to full strength.

Nathan readied his lance, his own spirit soaring with determination as he roared.

"Nathan, stop!" cried Astrid. "We don't know how strong this guy really is! Fall back!"

"And let him suck everyone dry?" bellowed Nathan. "I can wound him, which means I can kill him!" He charged at Victor, a blast of energy spewing out the back of his lance like a rocket nozzle.

A streak of light flew about Victor and bisected the path of Nathan's lance. The lance disintegrated under the

---

[20]   German: "Arms Alchemy."

force of Victor's axe attack. His mind went blank save for the searing, indescribable agony of his chest exploding. The blade, the handle, even the sash of Sunlight's Heart evaporated, as Nathan's body flew backward and rolled away like a rag-doll. His Kakugane clattered to the ground nearby, cracked, cold, and inert.

Astrid felt as if she'd left her body, and she was watching herself scramble across the campus to Nathan's motionless form. She watched herself frantically cradle the boy's head on her lap as she tried to rouse him. She noted the tears tumbling from her eyes down over his face, as she grabbed his Kakugane and tried to push it into the gaping, bloody hole where his heart should have been. Her body finally resumed breathing, inhaling stridently, and dragged her mind back into her head, where she found herself consumed by the unfathomable need to scream.

"Calm yourself, woman," droned Victor. "Alchemic Warriors were far more composed seventy-years ago."

"You killed him!" Astrid wailed.

"And you grieve?" murmured Victor. "You expect to stop people from dying. It is something not possible, especially for Warriors of the Alchemic Regiment. Death comes for us all in the end."

The beast's voice sounded so much like Bravo's as he spoke, it made her sick. She involuntarily blurted, "No! Nathan wasn't like that! He was just a regular kid!"

"Hardly for one with a Kakugane," mumbled Victor.

"*I* did this to him," shouted Astrid. "He dove in just to help me, and I let it happen. I brought him back to life so that he could go back to his friends and family, and continue to have what I couldn't! He didn't deserve to die!"

Victor gazed down at the crying girl, cradling the corpse of her friend. He cocked his head and pondered a moment.

"Neither did I," he intoned. "But life isn't about what you deserve. It's what you receive." He leaned down, grabbed Astrid's head and hefted her into the air. "Allow me to grant you a merciful death, so that you may follow him," he said, his voice faltering slightly.

Astrid made no effort to stop him. Even if Victor hadn't been draining her energy, she wouldn't have found the will to fight back. Her brain swirled with regret and dismay.

For the first time in my life, I fought not for revenge on homunculi, she thought as Victor's blade neared her throat. *I actually had someone I wanted to fight for. Someone I couldn't bare to lose. I told him to use his power to defend those he lived for, but I couldn't defend him.*

Images of his dopey grin crept into her mind and made her smile.

But you know, I think I've had enough. I'll go and have some pancakes with him, and finally take that holiday I'd been looking forward to.

From deep within the bowels of the Earth, a mighty thump resounded. Astrid's eyes flew open to see Victor expressing something other than boredom. His eyes widened with shock, even fear, as his gaze looked through her. He released her and stepped away, allowing her to turn around and see Nathan, on his feet, each breath clawing its way down his windpipe. Her heart filled with searing hot joy at the sight, instantly quenched as he gripped his Kakugane with a loud, animalistic growl. He squeezed the talisman with enough force to grind diamond, and it exploded with an excruciating hiss.

A violent gust picked Astrid up and threw her into a wall. She watched, bewildered at the purple glowing maelstrom swirling about Nathan's revived body. The boy held up his Kakugane, its dull grey hull eroding to reveal shimmering black metal. Astrid jaw dropped in horror as Nathan's skin turned deep crimson and his hair exploded in bright luminescence. The Black Kakugane in his hand formed a dazzling cloud about his body that coalesced into a gold and silver gauntlet on his left arm, and a short, sleek, razor-sharp lance in his right hand. His red eyes bored holes into Victor's.

Astrid's heart fluttered as her stamina left her at double the speed.

The winds continued to gust about the two juggernauts. They suddenly vanished, and the trees on the hill nearby exploded with a deafening crash. Trees turned to sawdust, bedrock to powder, and dirt to mud under the force of their battle. Victor flew out of the cloud of dust and smacked the ground beside Astrid. The man scrambled out of the crater just in time to parry Nathan's frontal attack. The newborn demon's high-pitched yawps fuelled his attack as he pressed against Victor, who seemed only barely able to keep the boy at bay.

Victor grunted with panic and diverted Nathan's blow, swiped his axe to deprive the boy of his right arm, and then kneed him in the stomach. Nathan flew through the air, but his still-intact left arm reached for his lance. The weapon took on a mind of its own, and skewered Victor's shoulder on its way back to its master. Nathan caught his lance in his teeth and Victor's amputated arm with his left. His gauntlet flashed as the foreign flesh liquefied and flowed through his fingertips, while his missing arm regrew like a lizard's tail.

Victor looked up from the ground, his teeth clenched with irritation. He picked up Nathan's dead arm and absorbed it to regrow his own. Then he took his axe. Much to Astrid's surprise, he deactivated it and returned it to his chest.

"This battle has run its course," mumbled Victor. He ascended into the sky, his eyes glued on Nathan.

"Running, are you?" exclaimed Nathan.

"Indeed," replied Victor. He gazed into the now cleared sky and said, "The fog has already cleared, so I must be going. It's been a long time since I saw the outside world. It would interest me to see how it has changed." He glared back down at Nathan. "Congratulations on achieving immortality, as I have. Yet be warned, Boy. You shall suffer at the hands of those you call 'friend,' as *I* did. Be prepared."

The air about Victor's feet flashed white, and he vanished. All that remained was a streak of mist leading clear across the sky. Nathan growled. The tendrils of energy still snaking from the people in the school brightened as Nathan sprinted in the direction of Victor's trail.

"Stay and fight, Victor!" he screamed.

Not even Victor had been able to stop him. And yet, the moment Nathan felt a pair of hands on his chest, he stopped dead in his tracks. He looked down and saw a wheezing Astrid. She was so weak she could barely keep herself standing.

"Nathan, we've won," she whimpered. "You don't need to fight anymore. Just calm down." She pressed her forehead against his red skin, which was freezing to the touch. She willed her wearied muscles to move her head so that she could look straight into his crimson eyes. "I did this to you," she cried. "I swear I'll do everything I can to undo it. But only your body has changed. Only your body has become a monster like him! Don't let your mind go too."

Her lips quivered as tears rolled down her face. Nathan's frigid hands crept up and took hold of hers. From where they connected, the crimson tint of his skin subsided, as if chased away by her touch. The green luminance of his hair died down, revealing the light brown colour of his former self. The gauntlet and spear dematerialised, and their light crawled back into his chest.

Astrid felt her stamina return, and she tightened her grip on his hands as much as her fatigue would allow. His skin felt warm again, and his eyes betrayed the soul of that dopey schoolboy she knew. She smiled, and threw her arms around him.

"I'm back," he whispered to her.

The both of them, completely exhausted, held each other tightly, and let themselves enjoy the moment. If only they could've enjoyed it a little longer.

A flamboyant voice bellowed, "Papillon!"

Nathan flew headfirst into a wall with the imprint of a fist in his cheek. Astrid stumbled to the ground, completely bewildered at Papillon's roughed-up appearance.

"Grant, you goddamn hypocrite," snarled Papillon. "You interfered with my plans, killed my homunculi, lured Jiro in to destroy my embryo, and killed me, all to deny me my cure – my new life! And then what do you do? Turn around and become like Victor!" The homunculus hissed and growled with incredible volume and ferocity. His every blood vessel bulged with his fury, eventuating in an eruption of reddish-brown vomit.

Both Nathan and Astrid stifled a laugh as Papillon collapsed.

"You alright, mate?" asked Nathan. He held up his normal-coloured hand. "Look, Chouno. I'm fine. I'm still human. Astrid was able to stop me from transforming."

"Plus, it's not like he wanted it that way," yawned Astrid.

Papillon glared at her, his hand in motion without a second thought. He brought his palm across her face and roared, "Nobody asked you!"

A gold and silver blade appeared dangerously close to Papillon's jugular, held in place by Nathan. The boy locked eyes with the bastardised homunculus.

"Don't ever touch her again," he growled.

Papillon very quickly calmed upon noting the red tinge that tried to claw its way along Nathan's skin. Nathan started to tremble when he saw it, his mind filling with horror as he felt himself overcome with insatiable hunger. He breathed deeply to push the feeling away, to reclaim some semblance of the peace he found when Astrid touched him.

Astrid scrambled over and gripped his wrists. She locked eyes with him and cooed him into a state of calm. The crimson started to subside, yet his Arms Alchemy didn't deactivate. He gripped his lance tightly, and felt the material of his new gauntlet scrunch in his hand, as he locked onto every harmonic of Astrid's voice.

"I'm calm," he stammered. "I don't feel anyone's life force coming to me." He looked at Astrid. "You alright?"

"I don't feel any more tired," she replied.

The boy sighed, and his Arms Alchemy deactivated once more.

Papillon scoffed, "Still human, my arse! Look at you, Grant. Whether you *wanted* it or not, you're now an interim between Victor and ordinary humans: a larval form. Sure, you may have control over it now, but based on Victor's own words, you might eventually lose that control."

Both Nathan and Astrid gasped as they recalled Victor's parting words: *You shall suffer at the hands of those you call 'friend,' as I did.*

They exchanged nervous glances, broken only by the sounds of groans and shoes scraping against concrete. They looked over and saw Bravo, bruises and grazes carpeted across a face saturated with concern and worry. He looked into the hall, and saw Moonface was gone. He let out a groan of dismay before gazing at Nathan.

"We got a lot of questions to answer," he mumbled.

20 | Revelations

Nathan sat in the airport foyer, hunched over and trembling. His hands were red and sore from his nervous wringing. Absentmindedly, he edged his hand to his sternum to rub an infuriating itch. The band on his wrist beeped softly, and his entire torso lit up with a sharp electric shock.

"Goddammit!" he growled under his breath, not for the first time since he sat down.

Astrid pursed her lips as she watched him fret in the corner of her vision. She flipped to the next page of the magazine she wasn't really reading, and intoned, "Stop scratching, and it won't shock you."

Nathan sighed and leaned over to mumble, "Easy for you to say. When they get here, I won't be able to not scratch." He sat on his hands to keep them away from his chest. "That friggin' Bravo," he grumbled with an irate shake of his head. "I promise that I won't use it, and I got a good reason not to. But he still insists on these bloody shock collars."

"Hey, it's not *his* fault," said Astrid curtly. "*He* trusts you. Believe that. The others don't." She glanced to the arrivals screen, and then to her watch. "Plus, it was the price for being able to leave the compound."

Their eyes, focused on the arrivals screen, drifted to the screen beside it. The news readout displayed the title,

"Warrawul Rebuild Commencing." A stream of subtitles crawled across the screen, recounting for those who couldn't hear the reporter's transmitted voice:

"The Illawarra's Warrawul Boarding School has commenced reconstruction after the devastating gas leak of July Six. An underground gas pipe allegedly ruptured, causing an explosion that damaged large swaths of school property, severely injured hundreds of students, and threw a plume of hazardous smoke over the school. It has taken three weeks to clear all the debris from the incident, after which authorities have confirmed that there was no risk of further explosions.

"As the rebuilding begins, rumours continue to swirl amongst students, and the wider Internet, as to the true nature of the event. Several tweets around the time leading up to the explosion mentioned monsters attacking the school. Adding to the strangeness, the tweets described a group of heroes that saved the school from the monsters. Leading this group, *allegedly*, was the much-speculated Starlight Lancer.

"Several witnesses, most of them Warrawul students, have claimed that the Starlight Lancer is in fact a school attendee. Multiple reports identify Nathan Grant, of Warrawul's Year Eleven. The school has issued a statement denying the allegations, and Mister Grant is expected to make a public statement to such an effect tomorrow.

"It should be stressed that these reports cannot be corroborated. Many of the innocent civilians caught up in the incident were subsequently rushed to hospital with severe fatigue. Many of them now suffer memory loss, and have little recollection of the event.

"Warrawul aims to have its doors reopened within two months. In the meantime, local halls are being considered to allow classes to continue."

Astrid's eyes finally pulled themselves away from the screen, and gazed Nathan's way. The boy hung his head silently. Astrid cringed at the sight, but could not comfort him before an elderly lady approached them.

"You're that boy, aren't you?" asked the woman, a mischievous grin on her face. "The one on the news?"

"Nope," said Nathan. "I wasn't even there to see the thing."

The lady cackled, "Well then, I think I should say that, whoever this person is, he's amazing for saving all those people."

Nathan snorted, "I'm sure he is."

The lady took her leave with a smile. Astrid sighed to calm her nerves.

"Do you want to go over the alibi one more time?" she asked.

"I think I'll be fine," said Nathan. "We were on a date when the whole thing occurred, yada, yada, yada." He shot her an annoyed expression. "Seriously, though, my parents won't really care. All they'll do is bitch, 'You weren't looking after your sister.' And I'll just diligently whip myself with a cat-of-nine-tails[21] and say, 'Yes, Mummy! Yes, Daddy! I am bastardo de la supremacy!'"

"That's not even French, Nathan," retorted Astrid. "You need to make sure you can sell it to them so that they won't suspect anything."

Nathan glanced back at the arrivals screen. The flight he'd waited for just checked in. He stood, adjusted his belt, and said, "Trust me, Valkyrie. You're about to see just how good an actor *I* am."

He walked out of the lounge and took a spot near the customs exit. The glass doors opened to admit a small trickle of extremely well dressed people: the first-class passengers, just arrived from the United States. Two individuals, a man and a woman, emerged. The man straightened out the collar of his suit while the woman

---

[21] A nine-pronged whip commonly used to discipline convicts in the old Australian penal colonies.

adjusted her cardigan, and they both locked eyes on Nathan. His Adam's Apple chugged up and down in his throat as the people approached him with stern expressions.

"Mother, Father," said Nathan with a strangely calm tone. "It's good to see you again." He indicated his friend. "This is my girlfriend, Astrid Rachelle." He turned to Astrid. "Astrid, this is my Mother, Blythe; my Father, Henry."

Astrid smiled and offered a handshake.

"It's lovely to meet you," she said with a chipper tone.

The parents didn't even look at her.

"Take us to our daughter, right now," snapped Blythe.

"At once," said Nathan, indicating the way toward the exit. He took their bags and walked behind them in dead silence. A flabbergasted Astrid shook off her initial shock and followed them. Outside the airport, Nathan skipped ahead of his parents and opened the door to the limousine he'd prepared for them. They hardly looked at him as they entered the vehicle, which bothered Astrid even more. She shot him an amazed glance, to which he responded with a silent hush. She hopped into the limousine, and Nathan soon joined her after stowing their luggage in the boot.

"Royal Prince Alfred, please," Nathan intoned to the driver. The car began to move, but the passengers were silent. Astrid glanced to Nathan, whose eyes were focused downward. She could see his nerves were still quite heightened by the twitching of his thumb. She then glanced to the parents, who gazed out the windows.

They're probably worried about Ariadne, she thought.

That said, they didn't even ask Nathan if he was all right, if he'd been doing well in school, or even about how he and she met.

I'd even practiced our paintball alibi, she thought.

She cleared her throat and said, "I'm really glad I finally got to meet you. I just wish it had been under better circumstances."

No response.

Astrid went on with an increasingly desperate tone. "To be honest, when I met Nathan, I didn't think his friends would take so well to me. People are a little put off by my nose scar, you see. But everyone's been so nice to me. And I *adore* Ariadne. It's almost like I have a little sister."

Blythe finally moved. She turned and glared at Nathan, as if she'd embodied an enraged snarl into her stare.

"And yet you skip school to go on a date, leaving her to get hurt in an explosion," she said.

"Nathan, we'll deal with you later," said Henry monotonously. "Once we're satisfied that she's alright, we'll discuss your delinquency."

Astrid's jaw hung open a little, and she stammered with shock. She glanced Nathan's way, and saw that his expression had hardly changed. With a deep sigh, she leaned back in her seat and kept quiet.

After an extremely uncomfortable half-hour drive, the limousine pulled into the car park of Royal Prince Alfred Hospital. Blythe and Henry promptly exited the car and made haste for the entrance. They didn't wait for Nathan and Astrid to lead them, and instead asked the attending nurse for Ariadne's room number. They found her room, and instantly their demeanours changed. Ariadne's eyes lit up brightly when she saw her parents, who showered her with hugs and cries of joy.

"Oh, our little Ari, we missed you so much," exclaimed Blythe. "Have the doctors here been good for you."

"Yes, Mum," replied Ariadne with a warm smile.

Nathan moved to enter the room, but Henry stopped him.

"We'll talk later," he said sternly, before shutting the door on their faces.

Nathan trudged to the waiting room and plonked down on a chair. His face was blank with fatigue. His body twitched when he unintentionally scratched his chest, and he growled irately. Astrid sat down next to him, her mouth ajar with bewilderment.

"What are those people?" she exclaimed in a hoarse whisper.

"My parents," droned Nathan with a shrug.

"How could they treat you like this?" she asked. "Does it have something to do with the cricket ball?" Nathan shot her a surprised glance. "Klein told me. Yes, it was traumatic for you. Let's move on."

"It's not the cricket ball," said Nathan. "It's always been this way."

"Why?" asked Astrid, her eyes reddening.

Nathan just shrugged.

"Parenting style, I guess," he mumbled. "Maybe they expect me to be friggin' superman or something."

"They almost sound like how you described Papillon's family," said Astrid.

Nathan snorted, "No. If I were actually sick, they'd be concerned. Trust me on that. They were once worried that I had appendicitis – really it was just bad gas. But they freaked." He paused a moment, and sighed away his fatigue. "They *do* care about me … in a way. It just sucks." His eyes started to water.

Astrid cringed. Nathan's reassurances aside, she wished the Regiment hadn't confiscated her Kakugane.

"Hey," Nathan stammered. "I know it'd just be pretend, but … could we, maybe, hold hands?"

Astrid coughed up a chuckle, and threaded her fingers though his.

"Trying to use your abusive parents as pity points, are you?" she half-joked.

"No, it'd just feel nice," mumbled Nathan as he slumped in his chair. "And I'd like to feel a little nicer, all things considered."

Astrid tightened her grip on his hand, and hoped that it really helped. It did a little for her, but her mood was still terrible. It didn't really bother her that Blythe and Henry didn't even acknowledge her existence. However, seeing Nathan, the bravest boy she'd ever met, be treated like a valet by his own parents really upset her. Rather than make her angry, she just wanted to cry.

Just help Nathan get through this, she ordered herself.

When Nathan saw his father emerge half an hour later, he promptly stood and said, "Everything alright?"

"I want to hear it from you," said Henry slowly. His gaze shifted to Astrid, "*Privately.*" Nathan left Astrid and followed his father to an empty room down the hall. He shut the door and moved to look straight up into his son's eyes. "She almost died," he growled softly. "If *you'd* been there, she might not have."

"Yes, Father," droned Nathan.

"She almost died!" roared Henry.

Nathan flinched. "I understand, Father. I was derelict in my duty."

"Where were you?" snapped Henry.

"With Astrid, on a date," said Nathan.

"On a school day?" asked Henry.

"We were bored," replied Nathan. "But I should have anticipated the possibility of a gas leak and made sure that Ariadne was safe. I should also not have skipped school for any reason."

"You're damn right!" snapped Henry. He shifted on his feet, running his hand down the front of his face. "You are the responsible one, Nathan. *You're* the elder. When we're not here, our daughter should be your *first* concern. Your studies, second concern. And yet you squander all that so you can go on dates with some bimbo and –" His eyes looked over Nathan's form and found the black armbands Bravo had strapped on his wrists. "What the Hell are these?"

"Fitbits, Father," Nathan lied.

"Why do you have two of them?"

Nathan merely shrugged and monotonously replied, "I bought one, but hadn't told Astrid before she decided to buy me one as a six month anniversary present."

Henry threw the boy's wrists down with dismay.

"Anniversaries, girlfriends, skipping school," growled the man, pinching his nose. "And yet your grades are just fine. It must be that friend of yours, Cuyper. And don't give me that surprised look. You think I'm stupid? Your teachers notice you're sleeping in class all the time, and yet you do fine. You're clearly bribing someone to do your work for you. And the reason is obviously this Astrid girl." He suddenly yelled, "Where is she even from?"

"France," mumbled Nathan absentmindedly, having completely numbed himself.

"Well, we're going to have to move you and Ariadne to a different school," Henry said. "You have too many distractions at Warrawul, and I can't have that. And that *girl*, you are *never* to see again. Understood?"

"Yes, Father," said Nathan, though he inwardly chuckled at the irony. Normally, he'd be terrified. But, as the metallic thumping in his chest had told him every day for the last year, there are far greater forces at work than the combined temper of Henry and Blythe Grant.

The Regiment's not letting me out of their sight, he thought. *And I'm not letting Astrid out of my sight, either.*

Whether Henry saw his thoughts betrayed on his face, he didn't know. The man just sighed and waved him to leave. Nathan exited the room, and marched down the corridor toward Astrid. She'd clearly heard everything, judging by the sad look on her face. He threw his arms around her and hugged her tightly.

"I'm going to head back to the dorms and grab a few things," he said as he veered toward the elevator.

Astrid nodded. "I'll say goodbye to Ariadne."

She moved to the hospital room and raised a hand to knock. Henry grabbed her wrist.

"You're not welcome," he spat.

"I'm going to wish Ariadne well," said Astrid curtly.

"Leave," snapped Henry.

Astrid looked fixedly at him, gauging the man's strength as well as his grip. It gave her a little pleasure to know that she could dismember him, but also knew it wouldn't be worth it. Yet, she felt glad that she didn't have to pretend any longer.

"Does it make you feel big to stomp on your much taller son? Or do you just play favourites with your daughter?" she asked. Henry didn't respond, no doubt filled with anger. "You don't need to be so hard on Nathan," she continued, unfazed by his reddening face. "He is an amazing man, the most wonderful I've ever met."

"I'm sure you decided that when you saw his trust fund," retorted Henry. "I'm tough on him so that our wealth doesn't make him a monster, or a *target*."

"He could be poor and still be worth a million people like you," growled Astrid. "If he could see the future and predict a random gas explosion, he'd take the whole explosion on himself and save everyone, not just Ariadne. If a suicide bomber were threatening Ariadne, he'd try to save both his sister *and* the psycho terrorist! You'd know if you bothered to stick around and actually talk to him. Now, remove your hand, or I'll remove your head."

With that, she effortlessly moved her arm toward the door and knocked.

"Hey, Ariadne," she called out in a sweet tone. "Nathan and I were going to head off. Just wanted to say 'bye.'"

"Sure, come on in," said Ariadne.

Astrid edged past Henry and pushed the door open. Ariadne beamed when she saw her. Blythe even regarded her with a dulcet smile that was clearly masking her contempt. Astrid paid it no mind and veered around the bed. She gave Ariadne a quick hug, but the patient caught her sleeve and said, "Wait a minute, I wanted to have a quick chat." She turned to her parents and asked for the room. Blythe and Henry gave a momentary glance of reluctance before leaving, closing the door behind them.

Ariadne sighed as she regarded Astrid.

"Don't let them get to you," she said, her lips pursed. "I really wish they weren't so hard on Nathan."

"You know about that?" asked Astrid.

"I'm not as much of an idiot as my creepy brother," replied Ariadne. "He's always so sad when they're around." She grabbed Astrid's sleeve and implored, "Don't let them push you away. You and Nathan work so well together." She grinned, as if she had just figured out Santa wasn't real. "You gave him those powers, didn't you?" she whispered excitedly. "It was because of you that he saved me when that snake ate me."

Astrid's jaw dropped. "You remember?"

"It took me a while," said Ariadne. "I'd had nightmares for a while, but when I saw that news article about that Japanese house, and the Starlight Lancer, I remembered everything about that night, but I was happy. And when I saw you two and Mister Costable fighting, I was overjoyed." She took Astrid's hand and gripped it tightly. "I know that as long as you two are together, you'll protect me, and everyone else. You two are everyone's heroes."

Astrid beamed without any permission from her brain. Her entire mind lit up brightly, casting out any shadowy areas of her memory. The source of that light was a new collection of memories, with Nathan and Ariadne smack-dab in the middle of it.

"You know," she said. "Your parents don't deserve you two."

"Who cares?" replied Ariadne.

Astrid threw her arms around her adopted little sister, and held her tightly. She pulled away and kissed her forehead – something she'd never done before.

"You should do that for Nathan too," said Ariadne as she wiped her forehead clean.

Astrid snorted, "One step at a time."

She waved Ariadne goodbye, and maintained her polite

demeanour to the Grants as she left with Nathan. Her mind swirled with emotions as they rode in the limousine. The busy streets of Sydney blurred past them, filled with people going about their daily lives. Normally, she'd have less regard for them than she would a rabble of seagulls. Her world had been monsters and battle. But now, with Ariadne's words fresh in her mind, she felt part of them. She turned to Nathan, who had dozed off, and part of her wondered whether it wouldn't be so bad if they really were a couple.

He's still a complete moron, and a bit of a perve sometimes, she concluded, recalling all the times he'd tried to kiss her without permission. *But it's really worth being his friend. Fist bumps are more fun, I think.*

The thought of a fist bump reminded her of their first victory meal. Excitedly, she roused him and said, "I'm hungry. Want some pancakes?"

Nathan grinned.

* * *

Nathan sat in his dorm room. A suitcase, packed with his stuff, sat at the foot of the bed. A sealed envelope sat in his hand, absorbing moisture from his palms as he twirled it. A knock at the door startled him.

"Sorry," said Klein. "You packed?"

"Yeah," said Nathan. "My parents are expecting me back at the hospital after the press conference. They think I'm going with them to the U.S."

"But really you and Astrid're gonna run off together," Klein jibed.

"Yep, run off straight into a Regiment facility," said Nathan sardonically. "And I'll be a prisoner there until they can undo this freaking Black Kakugane thing."

Klein huffed, and leaned against the wardrobe. His eyes darted side to side as he tried to come up with something profound to say. His gaze eventually fell on Nathan's bed, where Astrid once lay infected with a robotic demon baby.

"When I found out about this whole thing, I thought 'How the Hell could something like this be real?'" he said. "I wondered how something like Arms Alchemy could be a secret. But when I saw that big red guy, Victor, I realised it was a secret for a *really* good reason." He sat down next to Nathan and said, "But now, as far as *you're* concerned, that reason is crap."

Nathan rolled his eyes. "I can't tell anyone."

"I think you should at least tell your parents," Klein insisted. "Astrid told me what they did. I told her that her experience was a cakewalk compared to what I've seen. Tell them, and they might lay off a bit."

"Klein, it's a miracle that people barely remember the attack," said Nathan. "It's still a good reason to keep it secret. If people knew someone like Victor was around, it'd be like friggin' Armageddon. People'd freak and go crazy. Then what? How'd Bravo and Astrid and the Regiment stop him then?"

Klein fumed, his knuckles white with frustration. He stood up and marched to the door. He stopped and blurted, "Forget the whole 'People deserve to know,' nine-eleven-truther-movement, coof-coof conspiracy, stupid anonymous hacktivist bullcrap! People don't deserve to know anything, because they're morons." He pointed at Nathan. "But *you* deserve to be seen for what you are: the greatest guy there is."

Nathan chuckled at the sentiment, but recalled Victor's words. He stood and faced Klein. "Life isn't about what you deserve. It's about what you receive." He handed over the envelope. "Give this to Ariadne, after I've disappeared."

Nathan grabbed his suitcase and left his friend alone. Klein looked down at the envelope in his trembling hands, and thought of the pain his friend must have suffered.

"Fuck," he growled.

* * *

A huge crowd of reporters and cameramen gathered outside the remains of the Warrawul staff building. Near the front of the crowd, Nathan tried to focus on the speech notes Bravo had given him, but his gaze kept drifting to the drains overhead. It was those drains that Ol' Chambo had made him clean in what seemed like another life.

"You ready?" asked Bravo. "Just read the cards, get this over with, and then we'll head back to the compound."

Nathan sighed and nodded. He glanced over to Astrid, who shuffled nervously at the sight of the press. She smiled at him, and motioned for him to give his speech.

The school headmaster stepped up to the podium in front of the whole crowd, which simmered with the sounds of clicking shutters. He promptly introduced Nathan, who walked over. His body quaked as if he were running through a blizzard in the nude. Every single pair of eyes felt like lasers pounding on him. He coughed gauchely and started reading the cards.

"Good morning, ladies and gentlemen," he began. "I have been implicated in a supposed attack that occurred during the gas explosion that damaged Warrawul Boarding School three weeks ago. I can honestly say I was not involved in an attack, nor was I even present during the incident."

One of the reporters, who looked like he was determined to get a scoop at any cost, interjected, "Excuse me, Mister Grant. You say you weren't around or that you have nothing to do with the rumoured Starlight Lancer. But what do you have to say about reports linking you to the damage caused at Gwynneville Primary School, or links to the disappearance of Tao and Shu Wu?"

Nathan stammered, his body trembling. Bravo quickly stood up and said, "Excuse me, this is not an interview. No questions, please."

He had to repeat himself for the first reporter, who zealously pushed his luck. When the press crowd backed down, Nathan returned his gaze to the notes now crumpled in his sweaty hands. He glanced over at Astrid, who smiled and made a motion for him to breathe slowly.

The girl who saved my life, he thought. *Here she is. I wouldn't be here, if it weren't for her. She gave me the power to save people, become someone who fights the bad guys, and was there to stop me becoming a monster. And I can't tell anyone that.*

Nathan turned to the crowd, and noted the cameras. He was certain Papillon, Tao, Shu, and Ariadne were watching him. Then, he saw Klein, Jessie, and Paul standing at the back. His friend's words echoed in his head: *You deserve to be seen for what you are.*

Nathan huffed, and his trembling stopped. He tore the cards up and threw them aside. He locked his fingers through the shock bracelets and tore them off. When the gasps of the crowd subsided, he looked straight outward. He didn't dare look at Bravo or Astrid.

He placed his hand to his chest, and relished the startled shrieks of the crowd as his chest exploded in a golden cyclone. He pushed past the encroaching, ravenous hunger that the Black Kakugane instilled in him, and willed himself to stay human.

He held his lance above his head, much to the horror and amazement of the crowd, and proclaimed, "I am the Starlight Lancer."

Epilogue

"I am the Starlight Lancer," bellowed the recording. The video playback froze. Eight pairs of eyes stared at the paused image of the seventeen-year-old Australian boy, holding an Arms Alchemy over his head for all the world to see. The owners of those eyes radiated expressions, ranging from partly amused to extremely terrified.

General Rodrigo sat nearest the wall-mounted television. He tossed the remote control onto the table, and faced the seven other individuals with whom he conferenced. Each of them wore the garb of a Regiment General, the 'A's on their lapels glimmering in time with their trembling.

"Well," he huffed. "*That* happened."

A British woman to his left exclaimed, "Is that all you have to say? Someone under *your* command has exposed our entire organisation."

The American man seated opposite her growled, "How do you plan to handle this leak, General?"

"I don't sink zat es possible now," said the Frenchman beside the American.

An African eyed the Frenchman across the table and said, "I concur. The hundreds of recordings of Nathan Grant went viral within ten minutes."

"Faster than Kinomoto's freak show," mumbled the

Chinese woman beside him. "These children have already gone too far out of control. Why didn't we stop them when we had the chance?"

"The House of Lamperouge was entrusted to keep things quiet, but we should have known better than to trust The Scot," replied the British woman.

"No, we cannot take responsibility for Kinomoto," said the African. "The Lee Clan kept asserting jurisdiction, and responsibility rests with them only." He paused to dry his palms on his shirt. He pointed at the cursed boy on the screen. "But *this* is completely on us."

"I repeat: *why* didn't we take action before this happened?" exclaimed the Chinese woman.

"Because we had no more warriors," blurted Rodrigo. "Every time I raised the issue, you six were fixated on other agendas." He eyed the American and African. "*Some* of you weren't even convinced that the L.X.E. really were a threat, or that Victor was going to return. If you'd issued more Kakugane to warriors readily available in Australia, we wouldn't have needed to keep Nathan Grant in play."

A chuckle broke through the increasingly heated discussion. All eyes turned to the man of Hindu descent who had theretofore kept quiet. His laughter grew in intensity when they fell silent. As he wiped away a tear, he said, "If one can't laugh at this, one can't laugh."

"It's no laughing matter, General Vasuman," snapped the American.

"Apologies, since you clearly think it's a blaming and finger-pointing matter," replied Vasuman.

"Do you have anything to actually say, Shantanu?" asked Rodrigo.

"Plenty," said Vasuman. "Did no one really think a leak of this magnitude was inevitable? These days, most people don't even use the bathroom without tweeting about it. If someone with a smartphone were attacked by a homunculus or – God Forbid – an Asura Egg, they'd try to post a selfie on Minds before they even considered running. DWMA can't control information flow, so how can we be expected to, ya? All things considered, we cannot ask for a better outcome. Nathan Grant is under our control. He's in a Regiment facility, right where he should be. Think about that: a larval Victor that we can study in the hopes of defeating the original one. Not once has anyone here addressed what to do about Victor. I suggest we focus on that."

Rodrigo slapped the table top with an excited hum. "I agree. Anyone else?" Nobody replied, though the mood around the table was tense. Rodrigo switched off the television so no one would be distracted by the irksome boy's picture, and then clasped his hands together on the table.

"Vasuman is right," he said. "We need to focus on defeating Victor. To that end, I would like to open the discussion up to our guest." He looked straight down the table to the figure seated at the other end. The boy looked so sickly pale, as if he were at death's door. His yellow irises fixated upon Rodrigo. His eyebrows twitched, so much that it disturbed the three white lines that stained half of his head of jet-black hair.

"I must say, I did not expect to ever be in the presence of the presiding Generals of the Alchemic Regiment," he said eloquently, as he unthreaded his fingers and stroked the cartoonish skull hanging from his neck. "Yet, before discussing Victor or DWMA's involvement in an alliance toward his capture, I wish to voice my own thoughts about a far more pressing matter."

"By all means," said Rodrigo.

The boy huffed slowly and said, "My father can forgive the negligence of the Alchemic Regiment concerning Victor Powers, the foolishness of researching the Black Kakugane, the hypocrisy that went into its fabrication, and the incompetence with which the Nathan Grant situation is being handled. My father wishes that to be clear."

"We appreciate that," said Rodrigo, despite the

grumbles and exasperated huffs from the other Generals.

The boy's hands suddenly hit the table as he stood. He hunched over, as if about to keel over in agony.

"But there is one thing that *I* simply cannot, and *will* not, forgive!" he growled. He looked up at Rodrigo, his yellow eyes bloodshot from a sudden and catastrophic rise in blood pressure. He roared, "Will you fix your goddamn crooked tie?"

About the Author

Craig Stephen Cooper grew up in Wollongong, New South Wales, Australia. At a young age, he quickly developed a flare for the dramatic, an obsession with various video games, and an aptitude for expressiveness.

In response to his desire to develop video games, his parents allowed him to study software engineering under a tutor while still in primary school. At the same time, he took dance lessons after school. He later decided drama was a path better suited to his love of storytelling, and studied speech and drama during high school.

While completing a Bachelor of Computer Engineering, he underwent practical and theory examinations for an Associate Diploma of Performance Art. During his Doctor of Philosophy in Telecommunications, he taught speech and drama to primary school children. As a member of the Fellowship of Australian Writers, he has presented workshops on storytelling and poetry, drawing on his speech and drama studies.

Cooper conceived of *The AXOM Saga* while on a train from Fukuoka to Nagasaki in Japan. Under encouragement from his friends, he wrote the stories with a passion to equal his first novel, *Final Flight of the Ranegr*.

He also dabbles in video game and mobile app development.

About the Illustrator

Tessa Eden grew up upon the shores of Australia's sunny beaches, frolicking in the sand and exploring the beautiful underwater world. Her father being a software engineer, and mother an illustrator, it was natural that she would grow to combine the two, becoming a digital artist. She now spends her days painting digitally, and creating 3D animations and CGI for animation studios in Sydney.